Dreaming in Subtitles

Winter Krane

Published by Paper Krane House.

www.WINTERKRANE.com

ISBN: 978-1-957595-01-6

Cover design and chapter art by Winter Krane

Contents

This book is dedicated to people no longer here.
Their lives still matter.
Each of them.

Chapter One

THE DAY I DIED

"What a trooper," one nurse kept saying. "She sure is holding on, isn't she?"

"Not going to be here much longer," the other nurse murmured, her voice a breath so my family wouldn't hear. "Just too stubborn to die." She must've seen a million tragedies to make apathy into a shield. I should've felt sorry for her, but I couldn't. I'd become the tragedy.

I clawed to the minutes—hoarding time, captive in a vacant black. This agony didn't hurt like pain should. It was an edgeless cavern between soul and skin, pushing pressure, trying to force me free. My eyes betrayed me, refusing to open. My heart rattled the cage of my ribs. Every beat, every breath, a cadence:

Inhale. *Please Loralay.* Exhale. *It's time to die.*

Behind my eyelids, memories danced like music notes in a motif, keeping time with the heart monitor's tempo, playing along with the song of hospice—the song of goodbye.

But I wasn't docile, and I wasn't done. I was angry.

Was that it? One chance living? What's the point of life when you're born naive? I used the time I'd stolen to fantasize another try, calculating changes I'd make if I could adjust the past. What if I'd convinced Dad not to leave? Recognized the signs before our neighbor killed his family? Maybe prevent my father-in-law's suicide or go back to the moment my fingers flicked the turn signal, sliding into the lane in front of that old beater truck. A driver on the hunt for insurance fraud, pressing his foot to the gas when I was half in, so it'd look like I'd swerved.

The split second that stole everything.

"Are you still in there?" my husband Drew asked. He and my daughter stayed with me, stroking my arm, holding my hand. I tried to squeeze back. Willing my mind to move with such tenacity that, if by any chance I was the hero in a comic book, my dormant telekinesis would awaken in me.

But it was a stupid idea. I never moved.

Drew brushed back the hair on my forehead. He hated my bangs —worst surprise haircut ever. I thought I was keeping things fresh, but when I came home, he'd smiled through a grimace, asking how long until they'd grow out. I'd only maimed my hair four days before the accident, so he shouldn't have trouble finding a good photo for the funeral bulletin.

No. I will not die. But time was scratching at the cracks of my fingers to escape, my body crying out to me.

Please Loralay. Exhale. *Please die.*

My nine-year-old daughter leaned in, whispering promises like secrets. If I came home, she'd be a better daughter. She was sorry for the water stains. Why was that the last thing? I'd even yelled. Like leaving a wet towel on the piano bench was an unfathomable tragedy. Horrible last words were a cliché I never thought I'd be on the other side of, but I'd left her with guilt.

The curtain opened again.

"Bye, Mama," Makenzie said.

"We'll be right back," Drew said, but I didn't know if he was talking to me or our Makenzie. "Just gonna get some dinner."

"I don't want to eat," Makenzie said. "It doesn't feel right. I wanna stay with Mom."

There was a shuffle—the sound of coats rubbing together in a hug, Makenzie starting to cry. They didn't walk away, standing there, as if I'd get up to say goodbye.

I would have. I wanted to.

My daughter's sobs echoed in the hall. It's stupid that hospitals aren't soundproof, forcing everyone to share misery. I wanted to nuzzle her, shelter her. Be Mom.

If only I could make it right.

But once they left, there was no sound. Not even when Death pulled back the curtain.

No bony fingers laced around a scythe—no halo, harp, or cloak. He didn't fit any mold for anyone. He was the everyman.

You can tell a lot about a person from the way they dress. The style of their shoes, the cut of their hair, but Death wouldn't allow that. He kept changing. One moment he wore a purple blazer, then a mustard-yellow flannel, shimmering shades of honey that wouldn't settle. And if a frame, race, or age hinted information, those kept changing too. First plump, then well defined, hair slicked back, then wavy blond. No, it was short and black. No, he was bald with a goatee. An abyss of identities, transforming like an oil spill in the sun.

He was emotionless, like the face in a coffin. Disorienting, like the emptiness when life is gone. He came abruptly the way all death comes. If nothing else told me who he was, I'd still know because I could see him, all versions of him, when I couldn't even open my eyes to look at my Makenzie.

"Good morning, Loralay," Death said through ever-changing lips. His voice was a thousand things at once. Masculine, but quiet, milky, and deep. I hated the way it called and calmed, compelling me to move in closer so I could hear.

I sat up. It should've been impossible. All those medical devices and monitors strapped to me, not to mention I'd been paralyzed, but now I came up as easily as water finds its level. I zipped around, expecting to see my body left behind like a double-exposure spirit in a B-flick film, but I was tethered to myself. No corpse, just freedom. Cords and bandages slipping out of existence.

I checked my hands first, worried I'd never again play piano. Next, I patted through my hair. No matted blood—no section of skull cut away because of brain swelling—just messy curls of brown hair tangled down my back like I'd been sleeping.

Only, this wake-up was intended to be my last.

I looked around the room for the first time. It was cramped. Ugly mauve-pink walls, a window overlooking a parking lot, an array of medical equipment on wheels. Impermanent objects ready for rolling away when my impermanent life was gone.

Death stood over my bed. He was eyeing some unfinished Jell-O on a tray, probably brought in for my daughter. *Flick*. He was a ruddy tween in blue jeans. *Flick*. He was a middle-aged woman with an underbite.

And he was closer.

"It's not fair!" I said. The words had been sealed inside me for so long they were buoyant, floating to the top of my throat. "I'm not ready!" I grabbed the bed's assist rails as if they'd save me.

"I can see that. Didn't even finish breakfast." He didn't smile—not one of him.

"That's not mine. I . . . " This wasn't what I needed to argue. I had to stop whatever was coming. Maybe I should've been in awe. He was an angel, right? A majestic creature, force of nature, my personal appointment with the rider of the pale horse? Or maybe I should've questioned my sanity, but anger isn't questions. It's action.

"So," Death said, taking off his gloves. Unlike the rest of him, they were unchanging—worn leather, sometimes the same color of his skin. His gloves hit the bed in a vacuum of sound.

Pat. Pat. Then nothing. A new reality where only he and I existed. The room was still there but faded and bleak.

"That's why I'm here," he said. "You should've come to me. You've been holding on too long."

"It can't be time yet. It's not enough."

"That's not how this works," Death said, morphing from a little boy into a dreadlocked man in a basketball jersey. The changes made me dizzy, but I wouldn't ask about them. A new fear was rising in me. A fear that his quiet voice could distract even the world from existing, making life fade.

"It's not? Then why am I still here?"

"Because you have more choice than you think you do."

I looked Death in the eye, right at the center of his pupil. I didn't understand how, but they were the only part of him that stayed anchored. Those pupils were bottomless. Not empty, but a black spot of ocean, teeming with things unnamed and unseen, things bigger than me. I looked away, shaking my head.

"Choice?" I asked, resentment as my only weapon. "Then why aren't I home with my family? Where's my happy ending?"

"They're not far off, but where would that take you?"

Death's many hands gestured beyond the hospital curtain. My head jerked up. My daughter and husband must've been just down the hall, probably still close. My legs fell over the side of the bed like the first few drips of a waterfall. *Plip, plop*, then all of me.

I took one glance at Death, now a biker with a Santa beard, then bolted past the curtain, leaving my room. Bare feet slapping on tile.

A few doctors in the hall looking at a chart paused like department store mannequins. Stripes of light came from a large window, slashing the ground in orange. Leaving Death's side, everything turned that color. Icy-orange. The color of Creamsicles or an overexposed photo. From the doctors to the mass-produced art on the walls, all of it coated in an odd, dreamy way, growing darker at the edges of my vision.

Death didn't stop me, letting me run along the timeless hall, searching until I could see them. Hold them. Become the superhero and squeeze back.

There was my Drew. His arm around our girl, frozen midstep, reaching to push open a swinging door. The last time I'd seen him, I was brushing my teeth as he dressed for work. He'd reached past me to grab his razor, kissing my cheek mid-sway, surrounding me in the scent of lemon pomade.

Now Drew was disheveled, hair cascading over tired eyes. When did mid-thirties start looking so old? Maybe I hadn't noticed it because no one looks their age when they're smiling, and Drew always managed to smile—even a sad little grin when he stubbed his toe, committed to not burdening anyone.

My last failure would be taking that smile from him.

I slid my arm around them both. Their clothes moved, but I was holding immobile hands. In this place, this prison, they were supple statues, suspended in a moment.

"I'm here," I whispered in Makenzie's ear. Her fingertips were cold. "I love you," I said. I was crying. Mostly because I wanted something else to say, something bigger. But love was the only word English gave me.

Death was there—a teenager, then a thin man with a broken nose, appearing ahead even though he hadn't followed me out of the room.

"Get away from us!" I screamed. My voice didn't echo like it should. This was the soundproof room I'd wanted for my daughter, only too late. Everything was too late, an entire life of too late. I couldn't stop him. Being powerless made me savage. "You won't touch us! Nothing will make me leave. You can put me six feet down, but I'll claw back. In all this miserable life, everything's been taken from him, from me, but not this time! I won't die!"

Flick, flick, flick. Faces moving ever closer. The deep of his eyes growing, burying us. I threw myself in front of them, blocking Death's path.

Flick, flick, fli—

I slapped Death. Hard. Hard enough that his head jerked to the side. But my hand hadn't hit anything like skin. He was smooth, cold. Stone.

The walls melted, all orange, bunching up thick, an overflow of lava. I screamed, reaching back for my family, but I was falling through the floor, spinning.

And then I was back in my hospital bed like I'd never left.

No more orange filter.

I'd won.

Jacob wrestles the angel and gets a new name; I slap Death and get a second life.

Then I saw his gloves at the foot of my bed.

"You don't understand," he said. Death was beside me, looking out the window to the parking lot. "Me, coming here, dressed in reflections, it's no small thing. You've been gifted."

"Gifted? Oh, *thanks* for taking me when the last thing I did was yell at my daughter!" I tried to kick his stupid gloves off the bed.

My foot slammed into something like a brick wall. The gloves hadn't moved. I sat up, looking at them.

"Stubbornness is a gift," Death went on. "It's often thought of as a trait to overcome, but stubbornness for the right reasons is integrity. It could've been your strength, but you spent this life

8

pretending you weren't enough. Stubbornness to belittle your own value. That's a gift misused."

I wasn't listening anymore. Those gloves—they were powerful. Maybe I could overcome him with his own weapon, but even as I slid my hand between the sheets underneath them, I might as well have tried lifting a semitruck.

"Are you even listening?" Death asked. There was the tiniest bit of amusement to his voice, the first sign of personality. It halted me, making me look back into those pupils.

"I've been told to take you," Death said. "But only if you refuse the deal."

"Deal?"

"You should know. You brought me here. If you agree to the conditions, your experiences will be prolonged with a new life. I don't understand why. You've suffered enough. But it's not for me to decide."

I opened my mouth, but no sound came out. A deal with Death seemed like a bad idea, the kind smarter people warn you about.

"You think your life would have been better if you'd known more, acted sooner. Wished for foresight before your time. A story where you're the hero."

"No," I said. "There's more to it." But he was right. Those were my deepest desires. I just didn't like them lumped in sentences short enough to fit on a postcard. It made me feel as insignificant as I was. "What would be the point of living again? Another chance to watch everything fall apart? I was a stupid kid that didn't know better. If I go back, I'd still end up here, wouldn't I?" Death didn't answer. Coward. "All the good intentions in the world don't matter when it all goes wrong. Oh, but good thing I was *stubborn*. Look at what a fantastic hero I am."

I cried harder now, silently, and this time for myself.

"Lying in bed, thinking of your failures," Death said. "You're not alone in that. Sometimes that's when people call to me, asking for it all to end. Well, you are different. I haven't been slapped before. That was new."

"You deserve it," I said.

"You misunderstand your choice. You can come with me and leave the suffering, or you can try again. This time burdened with the memories you've been bitter over all these years."

I sat up straighter. Death seemed to expect me to speak, but I wasn't about to interrupt, not when things might move in my favor.

"This life would be over. No coming back to this point."

"You mean I won't end like this?" I looked around the room, a place I never wanted to see again.

"Not if you change the variables."

"What's the catch?"

Death sighed. "That is the catch. All of it."

My skin crawled, but maybe there were second chances. "Everything's up in the air? Maybe I'll step on a beetle, and my daughter never existed. That's ludicrous. I'd never risk her."

"It doesn't work like that. Your daughter will exist. You can't unknit a person."

"It's all fate then? What's the point in trying if I can't change anything?"

"It doesn't work like that either."

"Then what does it work like?"

"You die tonight, and you come with me, or you die tonight, and you start over again."

My fingers tightened on the bedsheets. "So, I die and get nothing, or I live and make a difference?" I laughed, right in the face of Death. Another cliché I never thought I'd be on the other end of. I liked this one better.

"You already made a diff—"

"Deal," I said.

His words halted. Sound, then silence, like a recording cutting out. His face was still shifting, but this time through an index of people I knew. My mother, my father, childhood friends. My husband, my daughter.

And then myself.

I was looking into my grey eyes, my parted lips, and then there was nothing.

I was nothing.

I was starting over.

Chapter Two

THE DAY DAD LEFT

I woke up in the dark of the mobile home I grew up in.

I was on my parent's couch. The smell of those fibers alone was nostalgia incarnate, but my brain accepted Death's visit more than this moment. This was impossible. Our house was just like I remembered. Popcorn ceiling, dark wood paneling, ugly dried flowers nailed to the wall in an attempt at decoration. I ran my hand across the armrest I'd been sleeping on, my fingers getting caught in a doily. They'd had this couch since before I was born—a wooden monstrosity, complete with orange flower print. My mother's crochet cover sat on the back along with an itchy Native American–print blanket that I was under, tassels tickling my chin.

I kicked it off, sitting up, looking around in the glow of our boxy faux-wood television. A blue-green light was flashing, the credits of a Disney movie. Popcorn littered like chicken feed across our brown, speckled carpet.

I looked down at myself in the TV light—me. But I couldn't remember it as me. Tiny fingers, soft skin tipped in pink. Seven-year-old me, two years younger than Makenzie, creating a strange maternal instinct for this body I was now attached to. I wrapped myself in a hug, feeling the boundaries of my skin. Small hands reaching out to rub purple pajama shorts, touching toes covered in messy glitter polish, and then sliding back up to my hair. Thin brown curls held in place by two infinity knot hair ties. I'd forgotten about those—the ones with jumbo beads on each end. Sometimes when I'd put my hair up, the tie would snap, shooting the plastic ball right into my thumbnail. But the sound they made, *click-clacking* together, was something magical. It was childhood.

My mom was there—asleep on her chair, hand holding up her head, bunching her neck up in rings.

My breath caught.

I knew where I was, *when* I was, and I was terrified.

A door shut softly down the hall, followed by a jingle of keys quickly muffled by a palm. My dad coughed again, reminding me it was the first cough that had woken me up. The sound was as light as he could make it, but years of smoking penetrated every hack.

"Dad?" I asked before I'd thought about it. My mind shifted from dead adult to living child all too quickly. It was like a photographer had switched the lens in front of my eyes.

Adulthood's filter sharpened my focus, blurring the background into obscurity. But at this tender age, all of life was thrust together at once, so keen and vast I could hardly make out the contrast.

Mom hadn't moved, lost in a deep sleep. It was the same every time they argued. She'd close her eyes, pretend everything was fine. But this time, Grandma cut us off the bank account.

This was the beginning of the end.

I got up. My feet falling over the edge of the couch, *plip*, *plop*, then all of me, forming a flashback in my mind of running through the hospital. I tried to steady myself on the coffee table, but my hand knocked into the popcorn bowl, sending it rolling off the edge, clattering into the table leg.

My father's footsteps stopped. He was probably holding his breath. Did I knock over the popcorn last time? I couldn't remember. That hadn't been important to me. When I was a kid, I'd missed so many details because I'd only cared about myself.

Panic set in. This was it. The night that tainted the edges of my childhood.

Dad was moving again, shuffling sounds as he tried to sneak out through the hall. Leaving me, leaving us.

I was out of time, but I didn't know what to do, where to go, what to say. Mind thick as mortar, legs turned brick. I looked at the doorway, then Mom, stuck in a never-ending swivel between the two as panic closed my chest.

Mom stirred, turning to face me. It wasn't her face anymore.

She was older me—Dead me.

I fell backward as Death got up from Mom's chair, the room turning orange just like before. He didn't seem to notice, busy using my old nose to smell the eucalyptus branches on the wall.

"Never understood this stuff," he said. He may have been using my mouth, but the voice was still his—a forceful hush, the predator enticing me in. "Smells like every old lady's house. Believe me, I know old ladies' houses. Waiting for them to settle down and die. I once waited on 736 stitches for a woman to finish her great-grandchild's baby blanket. Nice sentiment, but she wasn't fast, kept sleeping between purls. You're not much of a knitter, are you? *Professional* pianist." He looked down at his hands—my dead hands—studying them as I had when I'd woken up.

I stayed on the ground, jaw slack, too many things I wanted to say, until anger revved my words.

"That was it? I say *deal,* and you drop me here?" I kicked at him, but he dissolved before my foot found his ankle. *This is a hallucination,* I told myself. *All of it. Neurons firing off in my last moments.* But it was too real. "I didn't want this!" I said—a lie. This was exactly what I wanted. It just scared me.

"Don't want to hear the rules then?" Death said, emerging behind me.

"You can't add rules now!" I stamped my foot, an act that lost any power since I was still sitting on the ground. Why did I do that? I mean, I knew I didn't like the way he made this sound like a game, but my body was out of control.

"I'm not adding them," Death said. "They were already there. You agreed before I explained. You start on the day your father left."

I crushed a popcorn kernel with my thumb. "Obviously," I muttered.

"You won't redo anything from here on out. This life is the definitive version, unalterable like your previous life should've been. That life is with me now." He waved a glove, displaying my old face.

"Wait," I said, holding up a small hand that still didn't feel like my own. "Why aren't you changing faces anymore? Something isn't right."

"I don't wear faces. They come to me."

I snorted. "Then take mine off because I didn't come to you." I touched my fingers to my mouth. This wasn't how I talked as a child. Childish me was shy, simpleminded, but my nerve hadn't died in that hospital bed. What kind of hybrid had I become?

"You brought me this face when you made the deal," Death said. Did he sound tired? There was a clip to the lilt in his voice. "That deal is final."

"So, you have my face because I'm dead."

My old head nodded back at me.

"You wear the faces of the people you kill?" I tried to sound horrified by the prospect, but childish me reveled in the novelty.

Death shrugged.

"You see it that way—putting on faces like they're masks. Portraits of those who come through me. I don't have a physical form, not the way your kind assumes I would."

I stood to get a better look at my old face. My new body lurching upward, slightly unbalanced. Death seemed to understand what I was doing. He knelt to my height, meeting me face-to-face. It was unnerving—me, not straight on like in a mirror, but from any angle. There were wrinkles around my eyes. Dead me

16

should've worn more sunscreen. I leaned in to get a good look at the gap between my front teeth.

Death leaned in too.

I lurched backward, tripping on the popcorn bowl. Death stood up. Unemotional, unconcerned. No matter how relatable this creature in front of me seemed, he was the enemy. I needed to remember that.

"You're lying," I said, standing on the coffee table to make us level. It didn't help. Death's dry eyes still belittled me.

"I don't lie," he said.

"But if you were every person who died around the whole world, you'd be hundreds of people every minute. You've got a lot of faces, but not nearly enough. Besides, you're just me now. You expect me to believe everyone else is taking a break on dying? You're just trying to scare me."

Death glowered back, cheekily disagreeing, or at least as much as he could without an expression.

"Humans. You live inside time, so you think everyone runs down that path. It's narcissistic, really. Took you all a while to accept the sun doesn't revolve around you either. I marvel at it sometimes, longing to look under the seals of your covenant."

He wasn't making sense anymore and my belly was fluttering like it was full of moths. I realized my hands were swaying, playing with the hem of my shirt. I forced them still, but my knees took their place, knocking together, undermining the authoritative look I was going for.

"You're drunk on childhood," Death said, nodding toward my legs. "Hormones, impulses, attention span, all of it reverted. But for this to work, you've been allowed to retain your rationale. So, if you try, you'll sober up. Now, be still."

At his words, my body stopped. Motionless, bordering on lifeless, like the statue version of Drew. I fought, but there weren't any bonds to break. No arms to push. No breath to hold. This was the hollow cavern between soul and skin I'd feared.

I felt eternity.

It was heavy, torturing me with a million moments collapsed into one.

Death was becoming paper-thin—my old body over his, a veil slipping. Iridescent light of the creature he was, peered through the silhouette.

I'd never tasted fear this deep.

"Listen," Death said. "You won't keep all your knowledge. There will be things to relearn—no awareness of current events. You'll only have mindfulness of that which pertains to your regrets. You are free to live this life how you choose. But your condition is outside of humanity. That condemns you to an experience that no one shares."

"Is this purgatory?" I blurted out, surprised I was back in the helm of my mouth.

"No."

"Or hell, or whatever?"

"No. When you cross the carpet, time will resume. You'll need to prepare. Collect yourself before you move on. There's no turning back."

"I'll wake up, then? All of this a dream? I hate movies like that. It's a cop-out."

"If only it was."

He sat back down in Mom's chair, and the room switched to orange. A color so thick I almost drowned in it. I started to ask him what was going on, but he wasn't there. My mom was, sleeping in his place.

I looked around, alone in orange, standing on the coffee table like an idiot. There was a crack in the wall near the door, fingerprints on the light switch plates, things that I hadn't locked into my memories as nostalgia, making these moments more than a re-creation of the past.

This was now.

I sat on the table cross-legged, closing my eyes, surrounded by the regrets I'd carried with me. Every thought made my chest burn. Death must've wanted me afraid, telling me to stay and overthink. There wasn't a point in waiting, not when I could fix one choice at a time.

I left the living room carpet at a run.

Chapter Three

DAD

As soon as I was in our checkered kitchen, the orange filter flicked off, along with my adult mind.

I was still at a run, feet pounding over linoleum that crinkled where the glue had given out. Dad was at the back door, the quickest way to his car. One hand on the lock, the other holding his sneakers, a large duffle bag over his shoulder. I'd remembered that part the most—an old gym bag, striped neon green, with a ripped side pocket.

"Where're you going?" I called, just like I had all those years ago.

Dad turned—sturdy brown stubble on a handsome chin. He was a short, broad man, but to me, he was a tower. I'd never known he was a shaky tower, ready to fall.

"Loralay? I didn't see you there." Dad smiled. Oh, his smiles! The way they made the room slip out of focus, made you proud you existed.

He fumbled to get his sneakers on before leaving, toes stuck between the tongue and laces. I moved in as close as I could, wanting to be near him, hoping he'd pick me up. "Is your movie over?" he asked. "You can put a new one in. You don't even need to rewind the one you finished—any movie you want. I was heading out to the store, and . . ." he swore, his smile glitching out of existence because he couldn't get his foot to slide in. He put his duffle bag on the ground, bending over to try again. "I didn't want to wake you, that's all." He ripped out the inserts and threw them on the table too hard, making a loud slap. He quickly glanced at the living room where Mom was sleeping, waiting, seeing if he'd gone too far. Not realizing he was so far over the line, he couldn't see it anymore.

"Never get cheap shoe inserts," he said, voice low. "They're worthless. Everything good takes money." He wasn't smiling when he got to the word money, but he laughed a little. Not his real laugh, just close enough to it most people wouldn't notice. His feet went in this time. After a double knot, he stood, lifting the duffle bag, flashing that smile. "Go on." He prodded me toward the living room, his hand naked without his wedding ring.

"You're going shopping in the middle of the night?" I asked. Then I frowned, realizing I'd said that before too—the next thing I said needed to be different.

"Yeah," Dad said. "I'll bring you back something. Want some ice cream? I'll get those bars you like, the Creamsicle ones with the vanilla inside. How's that sound, lady-girl?"

One of my feet twisted away, but the other stayed firm. Out of the childish intoxication, I could hear my own voice telling me to stop. Last time I'd run to watch a movie, then another, anticipating him coming home with a loaded shopping bag. I'd stayed up the rest of the night, my first time seeing the sunrise. Alone until my mother woke up.

From then on, it was us alone, together.

"No, you won't," I said, older me slipping through. "You're leaving us."

Dad's smile faltered. "What? Hey, there," he chuckled. "Where'd you pick that up from? What kind of movies is your mother letting you watch?" His laugh turned sour, but he kept it playful, flicking my nose too hard. I blinked past the pain. "Come on now," he said, holding my gaze until his face turned jittery. "That's not . . . hey, I think we already have some ice cream in the freezer. Hang tight."

He set his duffle bag down on the table, digging around the freezer until he pulled out a dented box of Rocky Road. "Here. You can have as much as you want. Just sit your butt down." He popped the top and stuck a salad fork in it. "Dig in!"

My body tightened. I knew I hadn't said enough for him to stay, but it was ugly, watching this play out. Probably because I couldn't imagine doing it to Makenzie. Ice cream and run, the equivalent of yelling fetch before abandoning Fido in a field.

My dad took my wide-eyed expression as excitement, putting his hands under my armpits to hoist me onto a wobbly wooden chair. I should've been mad. I was, but embarrassment eclipsed it, even though I didn't know why.

The ice cream had crusted over in a solid layer of ice. The fork already frosting at the prongs. This *was* reality, wasn't it? Not the daydream where I only had to let Dad know he couldn't disappear unnoticed. But I knew my lines, even though I'd never said them to him. I'd said them to myself a thousand times.

"You don't have to leave, Dad. Whatever's out there that you want, you could have it all and still keep us. We'd stick with you."

His smile tensed. "What did you say?"

"We love you. If you leave, Mom'll have a breakdown. You can't imagine how bad it'll be. She'll get a job cleaning rental houses, but it won't be enough." I was losing him, so I sped up. "I won't be allowed to answer the phone anymore because it might be collections calling. We won't buy new light bulbs because we need to eat. And then they'll turn the power off, and she'll be different." I'd started crying. I forced myself louder. "We'll pack and go. Live in the van, just me and Mom." Why couldn't I hold myself together? My sobs were screwing it up. "She'll unravel. You don't know how scary it'll be at night. Sleeping in a parking lot, hoping no one taps on the window. Hoping no one tries to hurt us."

"Hey!" Dad shoved me. His temper, one thing I'd chosen not to remember, was now on display. I was botching it. Death was right. I should've thought this through but being wrong only made me angrier. I pushed the ice cream, knocking the carton over, fork clattering to the floor.

He grabbed my shoulders, so large and strong that I was as powerless as when Death had me.

"Stop it, okay?" Dad leaned in. His voice was white noise blasting in my ears. "Your mother's sticking things in your head.

You think I want this? Call me a walkout failure when she's the one ripping down your old man?"

"I didn't say—" I started, but his hands tightened, Dad growing blurry through my tears. "You're hurting me!" I wailed.

He let go, bending down even lower, so we were eye to eye. "Hey, quiet down! Just shut up, okay, Lady-girl?"

"Jay?" My mother's voice from the living room, waking up, confused.

Dad cursed again, sliding in front of the bag. I watched him hold that pose before she came in. He was ashamed. He should be, but why did it make me feel worse?

Mom was in the door frame, fluffing her closely cropped perm—mousy brown hair clouding up around her head like a dirty halo. Her puffy eyes went from Dad to me, then the fork on the floor and the sideways ice cream.

"What's going on? It's two in the morning."

"Loralay's hungry," Dad said. "She needs more than popcorn, Sandy. She's a growing girl." He rubbed my head, his eyes asking if I was his Lady-girl or a snitch. I looked at the floor.

Mom fluffed her hair again, opening the kitchen drawer, rummaging for the cigarette pack they kept there.

"That's odd. . . . You got the smokes?" She dug through utensils.

Dad hesitated.

"Uh yeah," he muttered, turning stiffly to pull them from the ripped side pocket of his duffle bag.

Mom's eyes went wide, seeing the bag for the first time, but she didn't mention it when he handed her the pack. She must've noticed his missing wedding ring too, but she pulled a cigarette, tossing the rest of them on the counter, holding a smile as fake as her curls.

"Everything's better after a smoke, right?" she asked Dad. When he didn't answer, she took the lighter out of the drawer and lit the end. "You still mad, Jay? I'll call my mother again. She probably didn't mean it. She's always helped us out." Puff, puff, a billow of smoke coming faster with her breathing. "It surprised her you took so much this time, that's all. We could give it back."

"Can't. Don't have it," Dad said from the side of his mouth. His eyes flicked to me, seeming to wonder if I should hear this. I busied myself, picking up the ice cream so he'd think I was distracted.

Mom took another drag, her hand shaking. "Well, we'll just give back what we have. How much of the four thousand's left?"

Dad reached behind his back, clutching the bag's strap. "None."

The only sound was me jabbing at the ice cream block to break a bite free. I didn't dare look up, but I watched my Dad's fingers clenched white around that strap.

"I'll get a job." Mom said. "Roger's Rentals is hiring housekeepers."

Dad's jaw clenched to break bone. I didn't know why he seemed bothered by the idea.

"It's okay, Jay. We're past that. I won't cause any problems."

"Doesn't matter," Dad muttered. "Like *you*'d make good money."

My head jerked up in time to see Mom's lips close. If arguments were war, this was the minefield. When we were on our own, she'd made me promise I'd go to college. Do more than she did for us.

Dad looked down, unwilling to watch the pain he caused, but I saw her.

"Fair enough," she said.

"Don't put this on me," Dad said. "You were telling Loralay that, weren't yeah? Stickin' things in her head so I'm the bad guy. You'd get a job and something about not buying light bulbs."

"What?" Mom asked.

"Don't *what* me! You're scaring her. She's just a child! I try to provide, and this is what I get. My own daughter calling me a failure."

"I didn't say that, Dad. I said you don't have to be!"

"Shut up, Loralay! Eat your ice cream. Might as well, seeing that's the last time we'll afford it. Gah! Sandy! See what you're doing to us? You should be on my side!"

Mom sucked in three little breaths, sobs starting to escape. "Oh, Jay!" she said, smashing out her cigarette in the sink, so she could hold her arms out. "I didn't!"

Dad snorted in response, head jerking around like an angry gorilla.

"Jay?"

"No. You did your part with all your pushing. I wouldn't've taken that much from your mother if you weren't so demanding."

Mom's arms stayed open, but my father left them empty. She took the steps he wouldn't, coming up to wrap herself around him, nestled under limp limbs. Dad's fingers clung to his duffle bag. Holding his way out before he'd hold his wife.

"You're a good man, Jay, I know it. Jay? Jay?" She kept saying his name like she was trying to remind him who he was. "You're right. I pushed too hard. I'm sorry." Her voice muffled through his shirt as she rubbed her face in his chest. "I know I won't make much, but I'll work. You'll figure something out. You always do. Don't go."

Dad let go of the bag, putting an arm around Mom's head, flattening her circle of hair.

"You're talking like I'd leave, worrying Loralay. It's not right." He glared at the refrigerator. "I don't deserve it. After all I've done."

"And I don't deserve you, Jay," Mom said. "But I'm the one you chose. Okay?"

"You got me wrong." He pointed to the duffle bag. "I was putting all this junk in the car to drop off at the thrift store. Thought you'd like it if I cleaned up around here." He laughed, a little manically, head still bobbing around. "Can't do anything without someone thinking the worst of me."

I didn't need an adult's mentality to know no one packed cigarettes in a donation. Mom had to know too, but she didn't show it, giggling with him.

"All of this is just a big misunderstanding!" She laughed out tears. Fat ones rolling down her chin now that they were masked by a smile. "Oh Jay, I'm an idiot, aren't I? Forgive me?"

When they left the kitchen, the duffle bag stayed on the table. I stared at it like an animal on the road, not sure if it was dead or alive, not sure if this was over.

Mom called me to help pick up popcorn. The bag hadn't moved, so I decided it was dead.

Or maybe I didn't want to believe anything else.

When I said goodnight, I didn't think I'd sleep, looking up at glow-in-the-dark stars. But children can sleep anywhere, and this narcoleptic body dragged me with it.

When I woke up, I was still there—same house, same weak arms that wobbled when I poured orange juice in a cup. I couldn't remember my times tables or who the president was. I knew seven-year-old things, like my favorite color or that my front tooth was wiggling. But I also knew dead things, like a forest on a warm summer night; blood running cold on a quilt. Things my mind couldn't process.

So, I pretended the old me didn't exist.

Ages seven to ten

We went trick-or-treating, and I got caramel stuck on my princess dress. Mom bought me fingernail polish on my birthday, and I gave Dad a manicure. I got a used bike on Christmas, and Dad taught me to ride it in the driveway, Mom's crochet scarf trailing behind us. It didn't have training wheels, but it was so cold I'd grown numb and didn't care how many times we crashed.

I had three years to adjust, to forget Dad's anger episodes as he smothered Mom and I with sweet nothings. Forget the neon bag hidden in the closet. So much to relearn, taste, touch, and see that I could almost forget. Drunk on childhood, a narcotic that was mine alone. It would have been perfect if there wasn't an itch. It picked at my belly and drove my feet to the hall closet, breathing in mothballs. I was looking at the striped bag, but I saw a time that wasn't—when Dad was made of glass. Mom and I picked up his leftover shards like souvenirs. She wove her pieces into a nest, crawling inside to bleed. I'd kept mine close, slivers festering under my skin.

If I stared too long, it might be real, so I'd slam the door and run back to my room. Dad would laugh, asking if I saw a monster. I was too ashamed to tell him I had.

But the itch had a voice. It drank air from my lungs, lived deep inside me, waiting.

I was homeless, it said with my heartbeat. *I was you.*

Chapter Four

THE DAY GRANDMA DIED

"I can't watch Lady-girl tonight," Dad said as Mom put on her coat.

"But Jay, it's Saturday. I got work. Right now."

"Don't tell me what day of the week it is," Dad said.

Ten-year-old me was practicing Pogs on the kitchen table. I tossed my slammer down on the tower of cardboard milk caps in front of me, most of my tower fell, but only three pogs flipped over all the way so I could take them. Not the best turn if I'd been playing with someone else, especially if we'd been playing for keeps.

"We agreed," Mom said softly, trying not to prod Dad too hard. "It's your responsibility to watch her on weekends."

Sensing the oncoming fight, I started stuffing them in my windbreaker. I wasn't about to get sent out of the room without my slammer—the one with the holographic butterfly at its center. That thing was as good as gold.

"What's she going to do if she comes with me?" Mom added.

I laughed. Loud.

My parents looked at me.

If I could've, I'd be looking at me too, because it was the dead me that laughed through my mouth.

"What?" Dad asked, defensive like I'd mocked him.

"Nothing," I said, flipping the last pog with my slammer as if it was what I'd found amusing.

"Jay, what'll she do if she comes?" Mom asked again.

I shut my eyes, trying to stop the memories.

Go away, I told older me. I used to think we could exist together, ignore what didn't happen, play along, but she didn't want to be a child. She was made of regrets, not whimsy. The older I got, the more she raged. *"What would I do?"* she said in my mind. *"Mom used to take me straight from school to clean rentals. I scrubbed frozen fish blood out of the cabin freezer, threw our personal laundry in with the rental bedding. I'd get a kitchen done before she managed to make a bed. Then I'd make oatmeal. Oatmeal breakfast, lunch, and dinner. Oatmeal even when I couldn't without gagging because that was all I knew. She should've worried about me then, not now."*

I squeezed the pogs, bending the stack of cardboard in my hand. *But that doesn't exist.* I whined inwardly, closing my eyes tighter, but my unresolved past was still with me.

We had each other now, and they were wasting it.

"If you'd told me last night, I could've planned," Mom was saying. "I've got the Lakeside cabin today. *Lakeside!*"

Dad grunted, making a show of looking through the refrigerator instead of at Mom. She stood there, waiting. Dad refused to look up, reaching around as if he'd discover uncharted worlds just beyond the mustard and the half gallon of milk.

"Any other day and—"

"It's okay," I cut in, not just over Mom but over the other me. "I'll come."

"You sure? Honey, there's not anything to do there," she said, but I was already through the kitchen door to the garage, Mom following me with her jacket half on. I had something to prove.

Mom unlocked the Lakeside cabin, a dim, cutesy shack covered in forest green wallpaper.

"Ugh. I can smell it already," Mom said, ditching her shoes in the entry. "Fishermen's retreat. Can't they rent this place to water ski or something?"

As soon as I stepped inside, any mushy feelings I had for the past hauled off and died in a ditch.

Mom watched my expression. "Plug your nose. It helps."

I didn't. It wasn't so bad. Old fish was nothing compared to the carrion festering in my mind—her mind, the older, jaded me.

"You sure you wanna help?"

I nodded back, set to get this over with. The living room was a disaster. A family must've stayed last, sand in the carpets, cheerios crumbled on the couch.

"I guess you'll take out the trash . . . no, there's a system. If you use the wrong liners, Rosie'll flip. You can't make beds unless I show you how she likes them, but you could strip the beds? Bedroom's that way."

Mom nodded toward the hall. It was plastered with mismatched frames, each with mawkish phrases like Cave Sweet Cave or Bearly Sleeping. Bear decor was everywhere. Even the overhead fixtures had stained glass bears that muddied the light.

I held my hand on the wall to get past a thigh-high statue of yet another bear, this one a chainsaw-carved stump with the sign Welcome, Come in Bear-Foot strategically jammed into the narrowest space to endanger guests' toes when they searched for a bathroom in the dark.

"Take *all* the pillows out of their covers to wash," Mom called after me. "Oh, and count the throw pillows. There should be twenty-three on that bed. If someone stole one, we report it, or we're paying for it. She checks every time. And don't make the bed on your own, there's—"

"A system," I said, gritting my teeth. "I get it."

Old me had taken over, vengeful over the first time I'd done this on my own—Mom sitting in the van, vacantly staring at the lake, refusing to go inside. She had nearly been fired the following day. "The whole place was nasty!" her boss yelled. "Did you even check the cleaning manual? That's the—" He paused, looking down at me, a stupid little girl wearing the same clothes as yesterday. I could feel his pity. I hated it. He'd sighed then, digging through his desk for a new manual. "Last chance," he'd said. When he'd held it out, I'd been the one who had stepped up and taken it.

That was when I became the parent.

"How's it going?" Mom called.

"Fine!" I lied, accidentally banging my chin into the headboard when I pulled off the comforter.

"What?" Mom said, but I didn't answer, too busy trying to skin a king-sized pillow from its cover. It bumped into the nightstand, knocking over a knickknack statue of two baby bears kissing.

"Are you sure—"

"I'm fine, Mom!" I called, looking over the collection of pillows. Most of them were ditched on the floor so the guests could sleep. The one I held had rough burlap edges and the words Bear with Me cross-stitched on the front. If someone stole one of these things, it'd have been as a gag.

I yanked the king-sized pillow out by sheer force. A couple stitches ripped. I pulled the thread off to hide the damage. As soon as I collected the rest of the bedding, I stumbled to the living room with my armful.

Mom shut off the vacuum when she saw me. "Done? You can put those by the door. Wanna dig through the couch? Never know what you'll find there."

I tossed the bedding down, looked around. And there it was—the reason I came, waiting for me. "You did all this already?" I asked still, taking it in.

"Just got the easy stuff cleared away." Mom laughed, then she immediately frowned. "Oh, it's because you want to go. You're sick of it already. I knew it. Look, Baby, I hate this place too. I can't even smoke inside, but we—"

I wasn't listening, too busy smiling at her, at me, at what I'd done for us. What other signs did I need? Mom was nothing like before. Older me could go away; our lives were better.

"Are you wearing your shoes?" Mom asked pointlessly as she stared at them. "I told you this house is shoe-free when we came in. Rosie hates that!"

I didn't remember her saying it, but I remembered Rosie. Shoe hater, bear decorator, and owner of the lakeside cabin. Roger's Rentals handled the cleaning, maintenance, and scheduling, but all the homes were personally owned with their own rules in the manual. Rosie was the most meticulous, most likely to complain, and most likely to dock pay. I'd never seen her, but there were always sticky notes in the cleaning closet, yellow squares covered in pink ink. *Dustpan wasn't hung up, found cigarette butt on lawn,* and *pepper shaker left out on table.* Of all the houses we'd sneak into for a place to sleep in the last life, this was the one we never tried because Rosie would know. But dear old Rosie never caught me wearing shoes.

"I'm not going barefoot," I said. "This place is a toe-stubbing death trap! Besides, if we vacuum backward . . . " I turned the vacuum on. "No footprints."

"Loralay," Mom whined at me.

The phone rang. I flicked the vacuum off. We both looked at it, nestled between two gaudy lamps with shiny brass fish at the base. Rosie hardly ever called, but when she did, she wasn't happy.

Mom took a twitchy breath before picking up the receiver, tugging the coiled cord.

"Roger's Rentals, Housekeeping speaking, how can I help you?" She paused, listening. I stayed close. "Jay, that you? We're not supposed to make personal calls. How'd you even get this number? No, I didn't mean it like that. You're right . . . sorry. Good news? What good news?"

Dad calling was odd, but it was better than Rosie. I started lifting off the couch cushions when Mom's voice changed pitch.

"Wait, what did you say?" She slumped into a nearby recliner, eyes searching the floor. "But . . . "

I moved to sit in the seat opposite, listening to the tinny phone copy of Dad's voice.

" . . . didn't leave a will, but it goes to the closest kin, so it's ours! Thank God you're an only child. Can you believe it, Sandy? Sandy, you still there?"

I sat up, reaching my arm out to Mom's chair. She didn't see me.

"I, um . . . I'm still here," Mom said.

It takes a special kind of idiot to be blindsided by what they know. If only I really were two people, then I could've punched myself.

"Come on, aren't you excited?" Dad practically yelled.

"Yes," She lied, not even trying to sound happy.

"Yes? That's all you're going to say?"

Mom cleared her throat. "It's a lot to take in."

"It is, it's a whole lot! And it's all ours!"

They didn't talk much after that. Dad got off the phone to call a friend with the news. Mom hung up. Her body limp, empty hands resting open in her lap.

"Grandma's dead," I said plainly.

"Oh good, you heard," Mom said to her hands. "I didn't know how to tell you." She added as if I'd be hurt by the news. I'd never met the woman.

The phone rang again. Mom answered it, dropping the company greeting. "Hello?"

"Rosie?" Dad asked.

Mom's eyes lit moist, bleeding depression. "Jay, it's me."

"Oh!" Dad said. He paused for a moment. "You sound different." Apparently, he was aiming for an achievement award in understatement. "Thought it was Rosie when you only said hello."

Mom shook her head no as if he could see her doing it.

"Cleaning her cabin, huh?" Dad asked. It was a stupid question, but mom only nodded. There was a pause. "Sandy, I forgot to ask, how many rooms did the house you grew up in have?"

"I don't know, Jay," she mumbled.

"What was that? Four?"

Mom kept shaking her head, staring off. She held the receiver to her chest, muzzling his voice. Then she hung up.

Dad didn't call back.

We sat there, Mom frowning at a teddy bear next to the hearth.

"I'm going to smoke," she said.

"No, Mom, don't . . . "

She ignored me, holding the furniture to steady herself.

In our last life, the cost of smoking forced her to quit. Now we had Dad, a home, and she'd kept the habit too.

But who was I to bother her about smoking today? I was a traitor. I knew this was coming. Some future bits were hazy, but Grandma dying was a big deal. A new beginning, one that got us a home. Why hadn't I thought to warn her? Would it really have been so hard for me to encourage a phone call before Grandma was gone?

I followed her outside, Mom balancing barefoot on the gravel, digging through the glove compartment. Both of my lives crisscrossing in consistency—Mom and I at the van, the depression smothering her again. So much for proving anything.

Mom took a drag. I looked away, watching the water, so I didn't have to watch her fill her lungs with tar. We were parked next to the muddy fishing lake, blue buoys bobbing on the water, a rope line in front of Rosie's house designating the water to be her own front lawn like she feared the space would be taken if she didn't claim it.

I squinted across the lake; someone was fishing on the other side. How weird life was, this unknown. A person so close, but with no idea who we were or the dark news that'd fallen on our family. And not just us—he could've been fishing out here to hide from his own troubles. But watching him steadily cast his line, that seemed impossible. Why was it that strangers always seem so put together? As if their boulevard wasn't full of potholes.

"Want one?" Mom asked. I turned, shocked to see her holding out a cigarette. She laughed it off, a smoker's laugh. Last time all she had were empty eyes. More proof living with Dad had been better for her. "You're a good girl, Loralay."

I looked back at the water, not sure where this was going.

"I wasn't a good girl when I was your age. Grandma would've loved you. I wish you could've been her daughter. Then maybe I could've been yours."

My gut twisted. Those words had a bottomless sting. She *had* been like a daughter. Even now, I was chasing after her, trying to lick her wounds. But that was a guilty thought. She was the hurt one.

"I'm sorry, Mom."

She didn't answer, finishing her cigarette. When she was done, she tossed it toward the water, something Rosie was sure to take note of. Then she walked straight to the van and got in the driver's seat, door slamming behind her.

"We're leaving?" I asked, grabbing her shoes from the entry and locking the front door. Adult things she'd missed. She was slipping fast.

Mom made a face through the glass to show she hadn't heard what I'd said, shoulder pivoting as she rolled down the window.

"Where're we going?" I asked.

"Taking the day off. Get in."

"What about Rosie?" I moved the box of cleaning supplies out of my seat. Three different sizes of lavender-scented trash bags so Rosie's cans stayed classy.

"She can write me a Post-it." Mom slipped her shoes back on.

We didn't drive straight home. We just drove. Windows down, my curly brown hair a tangled whirlwind, mom's circle perm flattened in a sideways poof.

"My hair used to be curly like yours," Mom yelled over wind and motor. Her cigarette trail flushed out by the flood of air.

"Then I took birth control, and it lost all its pep. Enjoy it while you have it. Boys love curly hair. It's got personality."

I frowned at the passenger side mirror. My hair was always curly, even more so when I was pregnant with Makenzie. Mom took her eyes off the road for a moment to check my expression. "Can't talk about boys with your mother yet? Too embarrassing?"

"It's fine, Mom, I just think getting a perm seems like a lot of work for boys to like you." *Like stupid bangs that don't make anyone happy.*

She tapped her skull to show she thought I was smart, but I wasn't sure if she'd even heard what I'd said, her face melting back into sadness.

I leaned back, watching the curving lines on the road. She couldn't have known how nostalgic it made me feel, going nowhere together like when we'd look for a place to sleep.

When we'd pulled up to the house, she adjusted the rearview mirror to see herself, putting a smile on before she went inside, the way some people put on lipstick.

Dad was standing by the door, beaming. "What happened to you?" he asked, but he didn't wait for an answer. "We lost connection. I didn't hear. How many rooms was it?"

"Five," Mom said, squeezing him tight to keep him there.

"Did you hear?" Dad asked. "Four bedrooms!"

I nodded to show I was his Lady-girl.

"Five," Mom corrected.

He looked down at her like he'd forgotten she was there. "Five? Five!" he laughed the word out as I headed for my room.

I stopped short. The thin wooden door seemed different, the knob stained a brassy orange. I rubbed at it to see if the color would come off, but it stayed. I shook my head, then opened the door, walking into Death's filter.

Everything was orange—my room, my metal bed we'd found at a garage sale for fifteen bucks, the single-pane window with residue from old birthday stickers. But Death wasn't there yet. I sucked in a breath when I saw my diary sitting on my pillow, open to a doodle of a heart and Drew's initials, DN, a boy I'd never met. I scooped it up and stuck it back under the blankets. The orange filter turned off.

Death was in my room again.

"Good evening, Loralay." He was a little old lady sitting on the bed beside me. Snowy white hair, dark brown skin, moles sprinkled under her eyes. But it was Death, still wearing the warm leather gloves. I flattened the pillow over my diary, feeling stupid.

"You!" I said. "Where have you been?"

"Here. Everywhere. Roaming the earth, and under a seal."

I blinked at him. I needed to be calm, find a way to keep him here, answer all the things I should've asked before.

"Are you better off?" he asked before I could collect myself.

"What?"

"With the deal. Are you better off now?"

"Yes!" I said, still a little girl standing on a coffee table. "I'm not stupid. I know holding on to Dad was dangerous. I didn't have a choice. You didn't offer me better parents, and it's not like I could change their personalities. You gave me the same

41

ingredients and left me to make something new. I made do. But look at them! It's working!"

"Who are things better for?"

"Everyone!" I grit my teeth. Here he was trying to make me think I was selfish. "Have you seen my mom? She needed this! And don't make it sound small. This is more than a childhood or my parent's marriage. People died! I'm going to save actual lives!"

"People always die, Loralay. You're delaying the inevitable. How many things need changing before it was fair?"

As I fumbled for an answer, Death's gaze fell to his lap. His hands were fliting together, orange wool swiveling through his gloves. He was knitting? How did I miss those bone-white needles clacking next to me? He held up his work. An orange baby blanket unfolding out of nowhere, a cabled tree stitched in its center. He slipped the needles out of the top, open loops exposed. "how long until you beg to be undone?" he asked, and it was unraveling, stitches disappearing, one after the other.

"No!" I grabbed the string before the row could vanish, but just as I'd touched it, he and the blanket were gone.

"Loralay?" Dad opened the door to my room.

I looked at him, my eyes split wide like he'd caught me sneaking out. Had he seen Death? And if he didn't, I'd yelled. Did he hear me?

"What're you doing in here? We've got planning to do!" he said.

I let out a shaky breath. "Planning?" I managed to ask.

"Of course, Lady-girl! Planning how we're gonna spend all the money when I sell that house!"

42

"Sell Grandma's house?" The house we'd moved to? The house in the town I'd met Drew?

"Is there an echo in here?" Dad laughed. His real laugh, a breathy *key-key-key* sound, punctuated by a smoker's rasp. "Get out here and celebrate my new realtor job!"

"Since when are you a realtor?" I asked.

Dad shrugged, words rolling off his back.

"Well, not yet, but I know people. You don't even need a college degree. Just take classes. Everyone needs houses, you provide. Easy money."

"Easy money?"

"Man, that echo!" He cupped his hands, pretending to shout in the distance. "Loralay's a doofus!" He dropped his hands. "Goanna copy that one?" He kept his tone light, but he wasn't smiling. I'd offended him.

"Couldn't we just live in that house?" I asked. "It's bigger than ours, we own it. Why not move in? Plus, the local schools are better."

"Local schools?" he echoed me now. "What are you? Forty? What kinda kid talks like that? Somebody call the nursing home! Senile grandmother escapes and poses as child. Unsuspecting couple assumes age spots are just unsightly acne."

"I don't have any ac—" I started defending myself, but I realized he'd changed the subject. "Why don't you want to move?"

"I do! Las Vegas! Hawaii, but don't worry, we're not going to your mom's old hick town."

"Oak Ridge isn't a hick town!" I was nearly yelling. I had to act less invested, but I thought I might hyperventilate. I started grasping for straws. "I mean, there're a few farming fields and

43

all, but the local school has college accredited programs and an amazing football team!"

"Why are you telling me this? Is that what took you both so long to get here? Your mother twisting your ear?" If emotional warmth had been a physical thing, he'd have drop-kicked it before it had a chance of survival. "Testing me, eh? Mad I called her the wrong name, so she's got you bombarding your old man. Little witch doesn't trust me. Sandy!" he called down the hall. "Sandy! What's this all about?"

"What? No!" I yelled after him. "No, it was just me. I was excited!"

"Don't push me on this one, Lady-girl. If I crack, it'll be your fault."

"I'm sorry?"

He nodded at me, accepting the apology he thought I'd made, then ticked out a smile and a wink.

"No harm done. I just don't like her doubting me. I know I made a promise. We've got big things on our minds, is all. You forget about it, I'll forget.

He was way too happy, way too fast. I knew I'd missed something, a part of the conversation going over my head, a subject that hadn't been spoken.

My mother came into view beside the door frame. "You called?"

"Only if you're the one answering!" Dad said, swooping her into an elaborate dip and kiss. She mumbled something back that got him laughing. *Key-key-key*, the sound that meant things were right in the world.

Chapter Five

THE DAY WE SHOULD'VE MOVED

"It's the fastest thing around," Dad said, smacking the top of the computer he'd set up on the kitchen table. There was a desk in my parents' bedroom, but it was too small a surface for this bloated monument to technology.

"I bet Grandma's house has a desk big enough," I said, struggling for subtlety. "We could go there, take what we want." *Like the piano*, I thought. But I shouldn't have known about that. "Maybe camp out for a bit. Check out the neighborhood."

Dad ignored me, hitting the power button. The screen popped with light. Mom jerked back as if they were defusing a bomb.

There was a novelty to it. We'd never owned a computer, and this was top of the line. But even with gaps in my mental history for things like technology, something felt dated about all of this.

Dad turned to me. "Time to celebrate. Get the cards."

I sighed, heading to the living room to grab his poker stuff. Last life, Dad hadn't stuck around long enough for me to know he was infatuated with poker. Apparently, he'd played professionally. Funny how I used to wonder why he'd taken such a chunk of cash from Grandma.

I came back in as the kitchen filled with loading music. Mom held a hand to her mouth in glee. "You could learn to type, Loralay! That's good on a job application."

Like a secretary? I wanted to say *she* could learn to type for her own application, but that would've hurt her. Besides, Mom didn't know I'd already had a promising career in music. As soon as we got to Grandma's piano and I relearned how to play, that was.

"Sit down and shuffle," Dad said as the desktop loaded.

I pushed the keyboard out of my way so I could deal his game. Dad didn't notice, busy pulling out the paperback book he'd been carrying under his arm all week. The cover had an overconfident man with a creamy business suit and a cop's mustache. The image faded to black to make way for bold, yellow text: *Rags to Riches, Realtor! Kiss Nine-to-Five Goodbye!*

He thumbed through to chapter 10, "Ahead of the Game! Online!" The same over-punctuated chapter that spurred his drive to the strip mall computer store, spending a chunk of the inheritance from Grandma. "Just gotta dig one of those free AOL CDs out of the trash, and I'll start making connections." He overestimated how far he needed to move the cursor and clicked a file fifteen times. The window opened, then continued to open, boxes appearing on top of one another. The mouse turned into a progress timer. Dad cursed, smacking the monitor like the hood of a jalopy.

I started dealing cards.

"No, sail 'em!" Dad said, turning his aggression on me. "Come on! Mechanic's grip! Ring finger and pinkie on the edge, push the cards out with your thumb." He flicked his wrist to toss an imaginary card.

"Dad, there's no room."

He mimicked my voice, chipmunk style, but didn't push it, seeing that I was right. He turned back to the computer. "It's got a CD drive," he was saying to anyone who would listen, selecting eject from the menu bar, even though the computer was still trying to load. An error pop-up appeared. "Stupid thing. I should have a look inside, make sure they didn't sell me a dud."

Mom rubbed his shoulders like a boxer's trainer.

"That's my Jay! Smart and handsome."

Dad shrugged her off.

"I always liked tapes better than CDs," Mom added, attempting to placate his annoyance.

It only made him roll his eyes. "Computers don't use tapes, Sandy. They take floppy disks."

"I-I know. I was just being stupid."

"Yes, you were. CDs are better. No more rewind, fast-forward, flipping side A to B. Plus, they're indestructible."

"Oh, I don't know about that, Jay."

My hand halted mid deal. "You don't like CDs?" I asked her. "Why?"

"Didn't I ever tell you?" Mom smiled—a real one. "I wouldn't've been born if it wasn't for cassette tapes. Back when they were new, they were sold to businessmen. Important guys in suits, recording themselves talking out letters so the secretary department could type 'em out, yeah know? Your grandma, before she married, she was one of those ladies. Every day she'd get envelopes just full of cassettes. Your grandpa handled big sales, all handshakes and honor, so when someone undercut his price behind his back, he got real mad. You'd better believe he dictated a letter about it. Well, your grandma got that cassette. She flat out refused to write it."

"Why?"

Mom shrugged. "Don't know. She'd never tell. Only said it wasn't a becoming letter for a gentleman. People were proper like that. Girls wore dresses, children seen but not heard. Anyway, all's I know is she sent it back to him with what he should've said instead. He took her out to lunch as thanks, then one year later, I was born."

"One year?"

"They eloped within the week. Your grandpa said it was fate. His letter could've gone to anyone, but it went to the one woman spitfire enough to save his career."

I sat up straighter, not sure how I felt about fate.

"Well, that, and he'd always add he wanted to marry her up before she realized she was getting a raw deal. He died when I was a teenager." Mom's voice went thick, lost in the past. "But your grandma held her own. When the neighbors came around, dropping off casseroles, it'd be her consoling them."

The things Mom didn't say were loudest, comparing herself to Grandma. I looked down at the cards, picking up the piles now that I'd lost count.

"You come from a long line of strong women, Loralay. Don't forget that."

Dad snorted. I knew it bothered him, her speaking so highly of the woman who'd cut us off.

But Mom took it differently, biting her lip. "Well, your grandma was strong," she finished.

The only sounds were the computer's internal fan and dad's endless mouse clicking. I wanted to comfort her, but I'd seen what she'd become without Dad, and strong was the antonym. Besides, it was time to fix other people's lives—like my own. I cleared my throat.

"So, Dad? Can I surf the web when you're done?" Drew probably wouldn't have internet yet, but there wasn't a reason not to try.

Mom beamed. *"Surfing*! Look at her, Jay! Talking the lingo. She'll have herself in college in no time."

Dad eyed me, jaw sliding back and forth as he thought. "Isn't ten young to be a teenager?"

Mom frowned, thin eyebrows twisted by a question she didn't ask. Instead, she went to the smokes drawer, pulling out a cigarette. They both looked at me. Dad's jaw waggling, Mom puffing.

"What?" I asked.

"Nothing," Mom said. "It's just he's right. You don't act ten."

I held my face stiff, re-dealing the cards even though Dad didn't seem interested in playing anymore.

49

"It's your fault," he said to her. "Taking her to work, always talking about college."

Mom was thinking, puffing on that cigarette. I wanted to rip it out of her hands, flush the whole pack down the toilet. Maybe I should've, just to act my age.

It seemed fitting that Death didn't tell me the risk, trading Dad for Mom smoking and me meeting Drew. A storybook lesson to accept the lemons you're given. But I wouldn't let Death win. I needed to be in that town, and I wasn't going to die empty-handed or lemon-handed if that was the idea.

"Did you act like Loralay when you were a kid, Jay?"

"Nope," Dad said. "But I was special. Can't use my life to measure hers."

Mom looked up to check if he was joking.

"Lady-girl, your mother wants to see you acting like a kid. We're mandating some childish behavior tonight." When Mom saw he was grinning, she threw a dishtowel at him. "Watch it, the computer!" he yelled, even though she hadn't come close.

"Oh, sorry." Mom bent over to pick up the towel. Dad lunged, grabbing her middle, pulling Mom down to wrestle. *Key-key-key*, the happy laugh. He reached out for me too, but I jumped up from the table, sidestepping him.

"Come on!" he said. "You both against me. I'll keep an arm behind my back, just like the old days."

"Jay, warn me next time, so I can put my cigarette out!" Mom laughed, reaching up to toss it in the sink. I watched it, floating in a watery bowl of cheerios, surrounded by its tar-filled brethren. I slapped a hand down on the liquid-soap dispenser, trying to hit it, but I missed, squirting a golden soap snake across the bowl.

"That's wasteful, Loralay," Mom said, but Dad tickled her side, causing her to curl up in a ball of giggles, forgetting about me.

"Probably shouldn't sell a house you've never seen," I said.

Mom shot me a glance, begging me to quit, but she was easy to overlook.

"And why all this realtor stuff? Couldn't you just sell as the owner?"

Dad quit playing, leaning on his elbow. "And let someone buy low, then sell high? Not a chance, Lady-girl. Business is all about perception. Look nice, smell nice, sell yourself for the best price."

Smell nice, that explained the new cologne on the bathroom counter. It was like tree sap and musk. I didn't like it, but at least he didn't put too much on. That was one thing about my Dad, he knew how to clean himself up. Maybe real estate was good for him.

It just wasn't good for me.

"But you've never been there—"

Dad cursed, slapping a hand on the floor. He didn't seem mad really, just childish, like me at seven.

"What's your deal, kid? I'll see that house as a professional—first impressions matter, Lady-girl. I won't risk meeting a potential buyer until I get my business cards in the mail. And did you know your face looks like a shrew when you talk like that?" He mimicked me. I didn't play into it. Maybe I should've. He only got madder when I didn't respond. "Maybe she's not acting kiddish because she needs a kid's bedtime—brush your teeth. No surfing tonight—the web that is, not the beach," he added as if he'd made a clever pun.

"Bed? It's not even six!" I needed the internet. If we weren't moving, it might be my only way to connect with Drew.

Dad leaned back, watching me squirm. He could see how mad I was getting, biding his time. "You must really like my computer, eh? Try to act tough, but your ol' dad's got your number."

My jaw went Judas, betraying me by falling open when I needed it firm. He'd turned it into a test. *How much do you care, Lady-girl?* His eyes asked. It shouldn't have been a big deal, but how could I sit out of his game when every choice worked into a circle of manipulation?

"Maybe you can use the computer tomorrow," he said. "If you're *good.*" He laughed. *Key-key-key.* To think, I used to miss that sound when we lived in the van. Dad snatched at my pant leg, trying to tickle me again, but I yanked it away. "You should play poker more. It's all about being patient, then aggressive. You're an aggressive little snot, but you gotta work on patience."

"But—"

"Bed!"

I left, feeling his smile behind my back. I carefully closed the door to my room. I wanted to slam it, but I wouldn't give him more reasons to toy with me. Instead, I took my aggression out on my dresser drawers, yanking them open to find pajamas. The Walkman on top of my dresser slid sideways, headphones dangling down the edge of the dresser. It was last year's birthday present, something we'd never afforded, past life. I grabbed it, wanting to chuck the whole thing at my wall, but my finger squeezed down on the eject button.

The cassette popped out. Classical music. Mom got it for me because she'd heard it made you smarter. I put my Walkman back on the dresser, but I kept the cassette in my hands. I'd listened to it so many times, fingers tapping knees as if I could still play. Hazy images of recording studios and crowded concert halls. That other life was a part of me, like waking up and holding onto a dream. I hadn't had fame; no one bought an album with my picture or recognized me, but I'd been doing something I loved—until Death.

Grandma dying meant us inheriting the house with the piano. Otherwise, I wouldn't learn to play.

Fate.

Without a cassette, my mother wouldn't have been born. No me, no marrying Drew, no piano, no Makenzie.

Fate.

Death said you couldn't unknit a person, so Makenzie would be born. I just had to wait it out. I'd get where I needed to be.

But I didn't want fate, just the best parts.

I put the tape back in the Walkman, tossing it all on my bed, and pulled my diary out from under my pillow. *Regrets,* I wrote at the top of a new page. *Step one: I need to move.* I underlined that, pen digging a rut in the page. *Two, I'll find Sal. Three . . .*

I couldn't write three. The truth was, I wanted nothing to do with Sal. I was overwhelmed dealing with Dad. Sal had only been an acquaintance, and her short life was wrought with things that undermined my own.

"What am I supposed to do?" I asked aloud, hating the whiny sound of my voice. I was crying. I leaned into my pillow, trying to hide the sound from Dad so he wouldn't get the satisfaction.

I cried until I fell asleep, waking up dazed and in a darker room that matched my misery. I rubbed my puffy face, looking down at my pillow. It had a face of its own, wet marks from my eyes, nose, and mouth, looking back at me.

A face where it didn't belong made me think of Death.

I sat up.

"Death? Where are you?" He must still be here, watching. Just like Dad, lording over me in victory. I punched the pillow, expecting the room to turn orange, but it stayed an empty blue. "No!" I said, too loudly, but I didn't care who heard me anymore. "I wouldn't have kept him if I knew he'd be such a pain!" *You're lying,* I thought. I knew Dad was broken glass, but I wanted his shards, just like Mom.

My legs flailed, kicking the Walkman off my bed. "But I didn't have time to think about it!" Even saying it out loud, I knew it wasn't true. I had time. "What kind of question was that? Live or die, Dad or homeless. You're stacking the cards against me! That's cheating."

I paused, waiting for him to appear, but in the silence, I noticed noises coming from the other side of the house.

There was a clamoring, loud like construction. I slid off the side of my bed, stuffing my Walkman and diary back under the soggy pillow, wiping my face on my bedsheets before cracking open the door to—*hammering?*

I came out, tiptoeing.

"Isn't there someone you can call?" Mom said, standing in the doorframe to the kitchen. I slowed down, one step at a time. It could've been the breathy quality of Mom's voice or the way she wouldn't go into the room, but I knew something was wrong. Wrong in a way that wouldn't fix—an undoable thing.

"The guy that sold it to me wanted to charge me for a warranty." Dad's voice was muffled from behind the wall. "Must've pegged me for a rich idiot. Only half right there. Don't worry though, I told him where he could stick that. I know what I'm doing."

I came through, walking into a horror scene.

Dad's rusty toolbox was open on the linoleum. Tools littered the ground, abandoned among strange bits of plastic and cord. I looked up at him, hovering over the kitchen table, flathead screwdriver in hand. He'd transformed the new computer into a Picasso. Misshapen casing split down the center as Dad pried it back further.

My brain was still processing when I realized something among the debris was sticking to my sock. A strip of red tape folded over itself. I bent down and picked it off, unrolling and reading the blocky text printed there: *Warranty voided if sticker remov* —the second part of the sicker with just an *ed* was still stuck to my foot.

"What did you do?" I whispered, still hunched over, rubbing my thumb across the sticker's back—thick adhesive paste, all balled-up in wads of gummy glue. Removing this wasn't any small feat. Dad probably still had bits of it under his fingernails. "What about Drew?" I asked, just as quietly.

"What?" Dad said without looking up. "They wired it wrong. The CD drive doesn't open when I press it. I popped open the *tower*, but it was just a bunch of cords in there, so there must be a release switch in the *monitor*. That's where you hit the *eject button,* anyway." He said it smugly, embellishing *tower, monitor,* and *eject,* as if they were intellectual buzzwords that would endow us with confidence. "Didn't I tell you to go to bed?"

"You," I said, watching him dig through the computer's corpse. "Stupid!"

"Loralay!" Mom said my name like it was a curse word, but I didn't turn around, my mental filter just as busted as the new computer.

"You're an idiot! You had a real chance this time, and you messed it up? Like when you stole Grandma's money? You're an absolute failure!"

Dad's irises swam in a wide circle of white. I'd said the word that had the most power over him. I picked up the detached mouse and chucked it at him, hard. It hit the wall behind his back.

He came at me, screwdriver in hand. I tried to run, but he knocked me to the ground, a knee in my stomach.

"Jay!" Mom screeched, but she was just sound.

"Never!" Dad's sweaty mouth said. The screwdriver hit the ground next to my ear, rolling under the cupboards. He let go of me, reaching for something on the counter. I clawed to get away, but his knee pegged me to the floor until he was back, holding a bar of soap. "Ever!" he added, and the soap smashed into my lips. I clenched, refusing to let him feed it to me, but he jammed it past my pucker, rubbing some of it on my teeth before he gave up. He reached for the counter again.

"No!" I wailed, tasting bitter saliva, waxy suds dissolving in my mouth. "You can't take this from me! I made you stay! I won!" My words didn't matter. He was holding the liquid soap dispenser. "I was homeless! *Homeless*!" I screamed. "I made it better!"

He pushed the pump into my mouth. I jerked away, and the nozzle scratched my nose. Dad grabbed my hands in one of his, holding them above my head, sliding the pump into the corner of my mouth, and squeezing soap between my cheek with one hand. I jerked my head from side to side, but he pushed it into me, keeping my face still, as soap mashed through the gap between my teeth. I sputtered, ooze slipping down my throat, gagging up bubbles and spittle over my shoulder.

56

I thought he would hit me, face so tight that his features were a series of mashed lines.

"Never ever disrespect me."

I was gagging again, his knee on my chest now, making it hard to breathe, the soap burning further down my throat when I tried to suck in the air my lungs needed.

His knee let up. I didn't know if he was letting me go or reaching for the dish detergent. Then I saw my mother's arms, flailing, battling for me.

"Stop it!" she screamed. "That's ugly, Jay! That's wicked!" Dad leaned back, looking at Mom like she was a mythical creature. I sat up slowly, soap somehow getting into one of my eyes, making them both water. "Get up!" Mom yelled. She had to slap my shoulder before I realized she was talking to me. "Apologize to your father!"

I shook my head, coughing, soap coming up through my nose.

She hoisted me up, not strong enough to do it on her own, but I caught the counter, and she managed to right me. "Say it!"

"Sorry," I said like a puppet, too overwhelmed to do anything else. I sputtered again as a bubble gathered at my nostril. I tried rubbing my face across my elbow, but the lather was so thick it only smeared over my skin. The cut on my nose seared with heat, my throat and eye burning the same.

"I told you!" He jerked his finger in my face. "I told you not to push me, told you I'd crack. You don't know what kind of game you're playing! I'm doing this all for *you*!"

Dad stormed off, heading through the back door for a smoke-n-sulk in the car.

"What were you thinking?" Mom hissed.

I smiled, everything too bizarre to accept she was blaming me. I was wrong for losing it, but I wasn't this wrong.

"What was I thinking when he tried to kill me? 'Oh shit,' mostly."

"Loralay! Where'd you learn to talk like that?"

Mom put a hand to her mouth as if my vocabulary was the most shocking thing she'd seen today.

"You have got to be kidding. Did you see what happened?" I asked her, trying not to smile, but the strangeness of it all wriggled inside me. "I thought you were there, but apparently you missed it?"

"I'm not talking about him," Mom said. "We're talking about youall wound up, bothering him about everything." She leaned in close. I could see the regrowth on her thinly plucked eyebrows. "What has you so set about moving?"

"What has me . . . " I couldn't even get the words out. She'd knocked the smile right off my face. How were we still talking about me? "What are you even—he's ruining everything! He doesn't care that we want to move, Mom. He only cares about himself."

"We?" Mom's eyebrows disappeared under her puffy hair. "I don't have any desire to go back to that house. Not now, not never." She dug in the drawer for a cigarette, hands rattling. "I was never good enough for that woman. 'Stand straighter, you look chubby,' wouldn't let me pierce my ears because earrings attract boys. Didn't let me leave that house until she'd packed me off to a college she picked. And when I was pregnant before first term started, you know what she did?" *Flick-flick-flick* until the lighter made Mom's cupped hands glow. "Told me never come home. Gave us money just to keep us away." Mom threw the lighter back, shutting the drawer with her hip. "Your dad stuck with me when everything went wrong. Your father handling that house is a kindness. He's a good man, Loralay." Smoke puffed out of her nostrils, an angry dragon awake. "Even if good men aren't always good."

I blinked, then rubbed at my burning eye, only making it worse. We'd both had daughters during college? That was a strange similarity. Only I hadn't dropped out—Drew had. Staying with Makenzie to let me finish. Was that why she'd given us the house as a wedding gift? Still, she'd never told me that. Or maybe I didn't remember because I didn't have regrets about her past.

"But we're supposed to live there," I said, more to myself than her.

"You keep saying the oddest things, child. What was all of that about you being homeless?"

"I was just saying stuff . . . " I lied. It was obvious I wanted her to rip the truth out of me. It burned, and I didn't want to hold it. She didn't even have to believe—but she looked at the ground instead of pressing me. My holographic butterfly slammer was there, next to Dad's toolbox. It must have slipped out of my pocket during the scuffle. I picked it up, glaring at her. "I wish he'd hit me. Then I could've called DHS."

Her eyes met mine, cold.

"I don't know about you, Loralay. You bring no friends home from school. Whenever I talk to you, you're dazed or ready to bust. And then there're the things you say. How do you even know what DHS is?"

DHS? She was right. I didn't have any reason to know that in this life. Death hadn't taken that memory from me though, it was attached to my biggest regret—because of Sal.

59

I squinted at Mom, eye still stinging, trying to figure out what to say. She was never meant to have me like this. I was supposed to be a dull-minded child.

"Things haven't been easy," she muttered. "You're tired. Go wash up. You'll feel better in the morning."

The magic words to her domestic recipe. Sleep. Forget. If she said anything else, I didn't hear. I didn't even realize I'd walked to the bathroom until I was there, big bubbles cascading off my skin, sticking to the side of the sink, refusing to go down the drain.

I didn't really wish he'd hit me. I just wanted to hurt her for blaming me.

I reached for a towel, but it smelled like Dad's cologne, so I washed off with my mother's robe. Fluffy pink fabric, warm and gentle, the way I'd wished she'd been.

I looked at myself in the mirror. One eye so puffy and bloodshot it'd hardly open, sudsy hair sticking to my cheek, nasty red stripe across my nose. Some part of me was still searching for my adult face.

"Death?" I said to my reflection. "Where are you?"

Even though he didn't come, I knew another part of me had died. Childhood wouldn't work, not when I needed to be the hero. "I'm the adult now," I said. "I guess some things never change."

Unless you make them.

Chapter Six

THE DAY BEFORE I MET DREW

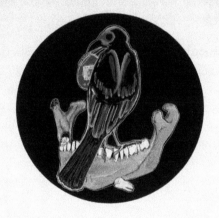

I stood at the school's curb with my fifth-grade teacher, Mrs. Banks. Pulling at my backpack straps, watching for mom's van.

"At least it's not raining," Mrs. Banks said, pushing for small talk. She was a nice teacher, the kind that made up reasons for classroom holidays, wore rainbow toe socks, liked our desks in a circle rather than rows. But I wasn't supposed to have met her.

I restlessly dug my feet in the river rocks that lined the school patio, covering my shoes in stones. Some painted like ladybugs, an art project about the life cycle of beetles. One ladybug was mine, buried, lost in the many. It'd been three months since the soaping. Everything was different now, the direction all wrong. Not that anyone else could see it. If I didn't meet Drew, Makenzie could be my ladybug, a possibility lost in the many.

The *Nevermore.*

I'd found the word printed in my English textbook, a poem called "The Raven," with cartoon bats on the boarders in a Halloween theme. I didn't have a memory of reading it before. It didn't even make sense until Mrs. Banks broke down the lines, but then I wondered if Death sometimes wore a raven instead of a thousand faces.

Nevermore, yesterdays that didn't exist. That was what the child inside me became—nothing more than a place called Nevermore.

"You all right, Loralay?" Mrs. Banks asked. I nodded, watching the wind slap her jean skirt into those rainbow ankles. "You're quiet, aren't you? That's all right. I like quiet too."

I readjusted my backpack instead of answering. It'd been pinching my shoulders all day, a bag's best revenge for overfilling. Favorite clothes, comb, flashlight, all that rolled up easy enough. The zipper started puckering after I'd added a Snapple from the fridge. Even my pencil compartment bulged, although that held cash. I was ready for anything, and money was easy to find this time around. Lost between couch cushions, abandoned next to the bowl where Dad kept his keys. Grandma's wealth put Dad into molting season, shedding dollars like dead skin.

My stomach ached with excitement. Tomorrow was the day we'd met. I didn't want to make drastic changes, but with how off course we were, this body's childish impulses and my adult intuition were on the same page. I needed to make this memory.

And then, of all days, Mom was late. The time 3:40 p.m. glowed on my wrist. *It's okay, I still have time*, I told my pounding heart. Another car passed. Volleyball practice was out. Three girls laughing together in the backseat. Kids I hardly knew, but I still felt left behind.

"You okay?" Mrs. Banks asked for the third time. "I'm not upset. It's not your fault we're waiting." Her eyes were encouraging. Younger me could've used someone like her in my life. "So! What're you going to be for Halloween?"

"A dead lady," I smiled weakly at my joke.

"Zombies? Interesting. Oh, I forgot." She was digging in her tie-dye book bag, stuffed full of ungraded papers and a Tamagotchi on the strap. She pulled out a plastic bag with paper strips and a few poorly folded origami lucky stars. The bag I'd intently left because the paper was, unfortunately, orange. "You left this behind. We could make them together, just like the girl in the story. Make a hundred and you get a wish."

"Get in," Dad yelled out the passenger window of his new car. My gut twisted. I hadn't seen him pull up, so busy looking for Mom.

"Oh, good!" Mrs. Banks said.

Dad reached across the seat to pop open the passenger door, putting himself on display. Slacks, button-down shirt, leather shoes. Dressed to impress—another sign of his money-molting. The only thing he hadn't improved was his expression.

Mrs. Banks put her hands on her knees, peering in. Her tie-dye bag swung between them, Tamagotchi spinning violently enough to make me seasick for the poor little digital creature.

"For reference," she said. "Pick up is at 2:40. It's hard for students to respect school rules if adults don't lead by example."

"Oh, okay." Dad rested a self-assured arm on the steering wheel. "I get the outfit now. You want your students to be hippy-looking crackheads? You sure set a good example."

Mrs. Banks stepped back like she'd taken a hit to the chin.

"I've never taken drugs in my . . . " She looked at her skirt, then me. "That's how you talk in front of your daughter, Mr. Grayson?"

"You started it. Ripping me down."

"That's not what I—"

"Loralay! Put that rock down. We're leaving!"

"Where's Mom?" I asked, tossing a yellow ladybug back into the pile.

"I said get in!"

Mrs. Banks looked between us, mentally dissecting our family life as Dad pointed to the passenger seat like I was a dog. I chucked my backpack on the floorboard.

"Goodbye, Loralay," she said, forcing a chipper voice as she tucked the origami bag in my hand. "Well, see you tomorrow. Don't forget your costume."

"What costume?" Dad asked as I got in.

"For Halloween," Mrs. Banks said.

Dad grinned, putting the car in drive.

"Lucky you!" He looked her over again. "You're already set!"

Before she could answer, he stamped the gas pedal to the floor. The passenger door slammed closed on its own, simultaneously knocking me into the dashboard.

"Bag lady," he muttered as I fastened my buckle as quickly as I could. "You know what bag ladies are? Homeless trash. Crazy old loonies living next to the bridge, walking around carrying God knows what. That's what that teacher of yours'll be. Already letting herself go."

Choice words climbed my throat like vomit, but I swallowed them down.

"You could've hurt her." I swiveled to check if Mrs. Banks was okay. I reached for my backpack, but we hit a turn, the strap sliding out of my fingers. Dad was driving too fast. Rich guy willing to get a ticket. We turned down a road I didn't recognize.

"Where are we going?" I asked, mentally rehearsing the bus schedule.

"Making money." He was baiting me to ask more.

"I need to get home."

"I need to get home!" Dad mocked. "Well, Lady-girl, money beats home. So, we're . . . " He let the words hang in the air, still trying to make me beg for information. I didn't bite. "Fine, I won't tell you," he said, like I'd lost out on the world's greatest secret, hitting the gas again to push me back in my seat. I pretended not to notice, but I had to hold the chicken handle when he made a turn.

When Dad slowed down, we were in a magazine cover instead of a neighborhood. The high end of town, where people owned little dogs, got their lawns and nails manicured.

We parked in front of a modern manor—streaks of lush green grass, shapely trees. Even though it was late October, only one dead leaf had escaped to the brick walkway.

Dad unplugged something from the cigarette lighter. I followed the coiled cord until I saw a palm-sized square in his hand. It was black, the word *Motorola* in gold.

I wasn't about to ask, but he saw me looking. That was enough.

"My new StarTAC mobile phone," he said proudly. "The best cellular phone in the world. Clamshell design, screen display, extendable antenna, and it can vibrate instead of ring." He polished an invisible smudge. "People with money trust other people with money. If you can't beat them, join them and then beat them."

"Great motto. Just don't *repair* this one," I muttered.

"What was that?" Dad was too busy cradling the phone into a belt clip to check what I'd said. I watched an elderly jogger out the window, the fabric of her velvet jumpsuit bounding along with her steps.

Dad got out, taking the keys with him.

"Hey!" I yelled, but only the jogger turned, Dad already down the sidewalk.

I should've left yesterday. But then I'd have missed two days of school. Dad crossed the sidewalk, knocking on an oak door. He leaned back on his heels, pretending to talk on his phone.

My hand slid off my lap, knocking into the middle console where Dad's book was open, spine cracked to chapter 5, "Door to Door."

"Oh no," I breathed. That was why I'd been left at school. He was doing cold calls. He hadn't mentioned them before, just random unexplained disappearances. Dad gone for the day, then back, sleeping on the couch. How long would this take? According to my watch, there were only two buses left.

A woman answered the door—crimped hair, bit of bangs slipping in front of her face. *That's what I was going for when I got bangs,* I thought. *Wispy, not poodle.* Maybe having money would've fixed my hair. I watched her nod, inviting Dad inside, the door shutting. He left me sitting there for sixteen painstaking minutes, watching time flash on my wrist, until he was back in the car.

"She had nice hair," I said, trying to lighten the mood. Dad didn't look up, messing with his keys. "Looks like it went well. We done?"

Dad sat back. He'd added a keychain to his keys. It looked like a dog paw with one too many toes and bigger claws.

"Just starting." He said.

Dad drove us around the block, parking in front of the next beautiful house without a gate.

"Can't you drop me off at home? I just—" He slammed the car door, running up the steps to ring a doorbell.

This time a man answered, shirtless with a towel around his neck. I couldn't hear them, but the body language was clear— Dad, ready to walk in the house like last time. Man, frowning, pointing at a no soliciting sign under his address. Dad held a business card out as the door closed.

The keys were still in the ignition. I squinted to read the inscription on Dad's new keychain, *Paw-some.*

"Freaking weird," I muttered, then I turned the key. The radio came on. I flicked the key back off and studied the street signs, trying to figure out where we were, but stealing the car was

67

hopeless because this stupid ten-year-old brain didn't know how to get to the buses from here. I grabbed a fistful of hair, moaning as Dad tried the next house. They immediately shut the door on him. He knocked again, like their first rejection wasn't convincing. I dug in my bag for an answer as if I'd find a teleporter or Batman's shark repellent. My hand landed on the little baggy of origami star strips. One of the stars in the bag was unraveling. Mrs. Banks had told us all about a little girl who folded paper to save the fallen stars, delivering them back to the sky. I couldn't even save my bus ride.

Dad was reaching past a flustered lady to put his card on a table. The first house wasn't bad, but now the entire neighborhood was willing us away with mental arsenic. I slumped in my seat. Maybe I could skip school in the morning? But mom usually watched me get on the bus.

Dad was yowling in pain. He'd literally stuck his foot in the door as the lady closed him out. Dad got his foot free then kicked a flowerpot, spewing soil across the lady's driveway.

He saw me staring.

"Start the car!" he yelled, coming back with a limp.

"I called the police!" the woman yelled from her window. "Hey! You kicked over my flowers? You can't—"

Dad cursed. Keys rattled, doors slammed, Dad's middle finger was out as we sped off. I hid my face in my hands.

"Didn't get my plates, did yeah, hag?" He punched the wheel, setting off the horn. "Bet she wishes she'd taken my card now." *Key-key-key.*

He did a U-turn in the middle of an empty street.

"Too many pranks this time of year," he muttered, running his fingers through his hair. "Stay in the game, Jay. People think

68

you're going to skin their cat or something, that's all."

"Are we going home now?" I asked, silently considering a duck and roll out of the car.

"Yeah? So?" He sputtered into his laugh. "What is it, Lady-girl, you need to get ready for Halloween that badly? Gonna dress up as a fairy princess?" He flicked my hair.

I flinched, curl knocking into my face. *Princess*, the last thing I wanted to be. Someone who waited around to be saved. I needed to be a hero, not Princess Nevermore.

"Miss ten-year-old going on forty?" He was laughing again, manic. That was true. I was still just a kid. Maybe I was just a helpless princess. "Listen," he said, voice grave. "Keep this little outing between you and me. Your mom doesn't need to hear about those stuck-ups."

"Sure." I was willing to agree to anything that'd get us home. No wonder he didn't mention what he'd been up to.

Dad turned on the headlights as the daylight faded out. "I'll buy you the prettiest princess dress money can buy, right now."

"Uh, no thanks. Home, please." One bus left. For the first time, I was glad he drove too fast.

"What about a CD player?" Dad said. "No more tapes for you, huh? Oh, look, an ice-cream place. We'll get ice cream."

"No."

"Shut up. You love ice cream." He pulled in the drive-through.

A block away from home, I checked my watch. Twelve minutes left before the last bus was gone. The uneaten cone dripped on my lap. When we came to our driveway, Mom was in the window, lit up like a TV screen against the night sky. She came out to greet us, tiptoeing in slippers.

"Where have you been!"

"Ice-cream date with the Lady-girl," Dad said.

"Ice cream this whole time?" She made a sideways glance at the lines of ice cream weeping down my arm. "Oh! I'm so glad, Loralay, getting things back to normal with your Dad."

I eyed my bike, waiting in the yard.

"He asked this morning if he could pick you up! Isn't that sweet? It worried me sick when it took so long, but look at you with your little treat!"

I attempted a smile so she'd let me go, then started for the house.

Dad called after me. "Don't eat too much ice cream, Lady-girl. You'll get fat!" *Key-key-key.*

I tossed the ice cream in the kitchen trash, wiped my arm on the dishtowel, and slipped off to my bedroom. Window open, I dropped my backpack on the ground outside.

When I hit the grass, I didn't check if they could see me. I just grabbed my bike and rode. I made it to the shelter, people still checking the water warped schedule—ditching my bike by the public bathroom.

When the bus pulled up, I stuffed my fair in the bucket and sat next to a woman old enough to be a mom. Before she could start a conversation, I put my Walkman headphones on.

I sat back, my gut a pinball machine of emotions. Drew. My Drew. Tomorrow.

"I'll show you stubborn," I mumbled so the woman next to me couldn't hear. But I was sure Death heard, even if I couldn't see him.

70

Chapter Seven

HOME

From Cannery Brooks to Trrayton, from Trrayton to Lewis, and finally Oak Ridge. My eyes were closed, but I could still feel it. Each turn in the roads, slowing down before a stop sign. Left, right, then left again. Home. No other road felt like this—a thumbprint formed on the swirl of a map. There should be a word for that feeling. A relief or a dread, but always the same awareness, a sense you're going where you belong.

I got off in the dark. Just me. The bus driver didn't give a second glance before he pulled the lever, doors swiveling closed. The mother inside me blistered. He'd left a ten-year-old girl unattended in the middle of nowhere! I started to memorize his license plate, to make an angry phone call until I remembered *I* was that girl. I stopped reading the numbers and watched the glow from his headlights pivot around a bend in the road, disappearing.

I'd been dropped at the old gas station pad. Shapes cut out of the concrete where the convenience store and pumps once stood, burned down long before I'd been here.

This used to be the town's main entrance, but Oak Ridge shriveled at the edges once Lewis boomed, leaving decrepit structures to be reclaimed by the wilderness.

I could've gotten off near the school. That was where the buildings and sidewalks were, lights other than the celestial kind, but that meant people who'd want to know where my parents were. Besides, this was closer to where I needed to be—the concrete, trees, all of it my own backyard.

I hugged myself, wind picking up, but I was smiling.

It wasn't just the taste of petrichor on my tongue or the crickets coming to life in the dense shrubbery. I was walking through a dream, and I didn't want to wake up. I used to ride my bike down here. Fifteen, sixteen, seventeen, always meeting up with Drew, tires crunching over gravel, sometimes with Julius, or just us alone. The twelve-minute walk could have taken hours, but I wouldn't have noticed.

There it was. White with a wraparound porch, old swing rocking ghostly in the wind. I was so ready to be here that I forgot I'd lived through anything else.

Then I saw how dark it was. A for-sale sign pounded in the grass, reminding me what path I was on.

It wasn't hard to break in. The basement windows were still single pane. I dug around in the sawdust bed that circled the house until I found a jagged rock. The initial crack stopped the crickets, but Grandma's house was set back from the cul-de-sac of her street, so I didn't worry about neighbors. I pulled shards of broken glass out. Splinters of grille wood coming with them, only a few jagged triangles left. I took one last look around the yard, then slid through.

It was too fast. Backpack strap caught on my shoe, instinct forcing me to grab the ledge mid-fall. There was a cracking sound below, then I hit the floor. I knew I'd cut my arm before the pain. Scrapes on my palms and one long gash from elbow to wrist. No cat scratch, the real deal. The kind that makes nurses raise their eyebrows.

"Oooowh-ah!" I half yelled, half whispered, doing a little dance. Glass crunched under my shoes as I reached for my bag, fingers touching something wet. "Aw, come on!" The Snapple bottle I'd packed had cracked on impact. I started to pull out the broken glass, but a dark red stripe dripped from my fingers.

My mind worked in funny ways, more worried about staining the carpets than the injury. I held my already dripping bag under my also dripping arm, attempting to collect the blood as I ran upstairs. I flicked a light switch with my good elbow, but the power stayed off. Of course, the water was probably out too.

I sucked in a breath; the pain getting worse. All I could see were walls and shadows, but I hurried toward the bathroom from memory, half expecting to stumble over Grandma's body even though she'd already been buried.

I tripped, falling to my knees, foot caught on something. I was sure it was Grandma for a split second, but it was just a blanket, coiled on the living room floor.

73

"Are you kidding me?" I asked aloud, balancing my bag and bloody arm, kicking until I'd untangled myself with one hand. "Who the heck leaves a blanket on the ground!"

I stopped. That was a good question. Grandma's house was pristine when we'd moved in. I gingerly clicked the light on my now bloody watch, using the glowing numbers as a flashlight. It was ridiculously dim, but I could make out the jumble of things around me. Beer bottle tops on the carpet, an empty peanut butter jar with a plastic fork inside.

Squatters.

I stayed still, gritting my teeth to the pain. I needed to do something, but I was defenseless.

"Get out of my house," I yelled. No one answered. No bump or shuffle. "I'm only going to call the cops if you don't get out."

Still quiet.

I didn't know it until right then, but I'd wanted someone to answer, like this squatter was me, all those nights we'd slept in the rental houses. I knew better. Not every homeless person was a sob story. There were dangerous people on the streets. Even riskier were those bold enough to break into homes. Still, Mom didn't remember those things anymore, and I wanted someone who understood.

My arm dripped. I needed patching up, squatter or not.

Swiveling the watch light, I hurried through, finding more trash on the ground. The glow on my wrist went black as I reached for the bathroom doorknob, but there was nothing in front of me. The bathroom was already open.

The only sound was me, drip, dripping on the floor from my bag and blood.

74

I tossed the bag in the bathtub and tried to find something helpful on the counter. Partially used toothpaste, decorative soap still shrink-wrapped next to the dispenser—a hand towel. I ripped it off its rung, pressing it to my arm.

And I smelled him. Dad. He'd been here, spritzing that cologne like he'd marked his territory. Dad the squatter, in his own bachelor pad.

"Well, he can't get mad at me for breaking in," I said. "Like father, like daughter." But I didn't like the sound of that.

I knelt by the bathtub, feeling around the wet mass of backpack for the flashlight. I tried to flick it on—nothing. It must've busted in the fall.

I left my mess in the tub, bumping my way back to the living room, opening curtains. Moonlight flooded in from the large bay windows, making the abandoned peanut butter jar glow sliver-gold. I let my eyes adjust, seeing gooseneck lamps with magnifier attachments, wicker baskets full of unread magazines, and the low couch with plastic on the upholstery.

I sat, vinyl crinkling, holding my arm to my chest.

"Drew, tomorrow," I said, comforting myself before falling asleep, dreaming in orange.

"Loralay," my grandmother was saying, but it was Death inside, wearing her. A woman I'd only seen in pictures, holding my arm to bandage it. "Welcome home."

Chapter Eight

THE DAY I MET DREW

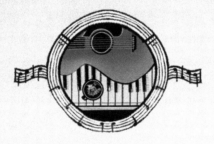

Sunlight seared my eyes. I vaulted up, looking for Death.

The room was empty. Only now I could see the still-life paintings that decorated each of Grandma's walls.

My arm hurt. No bandage, the towel now sticking to the cut.

I was cold, my neck ached, and one leg was numb, trapped sideways by the coffee table. None of that mattered. I'd slept better than I had in years.

Home.

I stretched, readjusting the towel to grab another throw blanket. This one had been inches from my face the whole chilly night, hidden by the dark. I wrapped it around me like a king's robe and went back to the bathroom to open the blinds, bringing in enough light to see the blush-pink toilet, tub, and counters. Now it was easy to find a handful of cotton balls and a roll of elastic bandage under the sink.

I let the blanket fall. There in the mirror was my haggard little body. Breathing through my teeth, I worked the towel away, a flow of bright blood oozing over dry. I sprinkled cotton balls across the gash, most of them landing on the floor. Using my chin to keep the wrap in place, I hooked each of the tiny metal prongs that came with the bandage, clipping it closed.

It was tight. Probably too tight, cotton puffs bulging in odd places, but I didn't want to risk opening it again.

I leaned over the side of the tub, my things strung out in murky puddles.

The Walkman, my symbol of fate, now dripping blood-tainted Snapple. I set it on the side of the tub and searched through. Soggy mush of sack lunch, wet clothes—even the money in the side pocket was soaked. Rummaging through the lunch, I found a few things protected by plastic. I chewed on a slice of cheese, leaving the tub to raid Grandma's closet.

I felt weird that she'd been here so recently, but this had been my bedroom in the Nevermore. It was the biggest room, all pink and lace. The antique bedcover was a mess, thanks to Dad, but I didn't care anymore because there was the piano.

My grandmother's upright sat under a circular window next to the bed. Grandma didn't play piano, but it didn't matter because this was a 1920's Themola London Pianola. There were bookshelves full of rolls, a library of songs you could feed into its belly, and the piano would spit out music like magic. I used to put my fingers on the concave keys, slowly playing along.

I wanted to touch it, even though I knew the skill was gone. *I'll learn again,* I thought. *I'll fix things, then I can focus on whatever I want.* It was an empty promise. I couldn't dedicate myself to fumbling through music practice. There was too much I needed to do. Besides, the way I learned was ridiculous, playing songs before I had form, having to retrain throughout college. I only had time for being an idiot in the Nevermore.

I pulled my hand away, turning back to the closet.

Flower print muumuus, shirts with Native American embroidery, these had been our clothes. We had so little when we'd moved that we'd slipped into Grandma's life like she'd been our placeholder.

I tossed each outfit on Grandma's crumpled bedspread until I'd picked out a green velvet tank top. Its darts proved it was intended for an adult, but it was the most reasonable thing I could find. I ignored the matching shrug with shoulder padding and grabbed a pleather jacket, gingerly sliding my bandaged arm through. I checked the mirror. Other than the sleeves running past my fingertips, it would do. For all I knew, it might have been what I'd actually worn, and at least Drew wouldn't see my homely first aid.

"Would've been nice if you really did bandage it for me," I muttered to Death as I rolled up the jacket sleeves to my wrists.

I was still hungry. Nothing in the kitchen looked safe, mold growing in the bread bags, unknown things in the fridge, so I dug through my backpack again, regretting throwing away yesterday's ice cream as I rubbed an apple down, making sure it was glass free.

The light dimmed outside. At first, I thought it was a patch of clouds, then my watch beeped.

"No, no, no, no, no, no, no, no!"

Five-forty. I'd slept like the dead. I wasn't sure when the talent show was over, but there was no way it was going past seven on a school night.

I ran out of the house—apple on the counter, bloody backpack in the bathroom. I didn't care. I had to go. I cut through Grandma's lawn, past the for-sale sign, making it to the end of the yard where the cul-de-sac did its round. From there, I could see the forest path just beyond the cul-de-sac. I shivered, seeing it. But I didn't need to go that way. Drew wouldn't be home.

Two witches and a goth passed me. I wasn't the only kid out, but I was the only one without a costume. The community center was a twenty-minute walk from my house; I made it in fourteen. The cut in my arm throbbed every time my feet hit the pavement, but I didn't have time to care. There were cars parked all around, people of every age dressed in synthetic wigs and cheap fabrics, carrying orange pumpkin baskets. Someone was selling glowsticks from a charity booth. A butcher paper banner hung above the community center door, multicolored handprints around the edges: *Tricky Talents, Harvest Party and Bazaar*

I went in, breathing hard from my run.

"Ticket for the raffle?" a woman asked me.

I looked up to say no, but the words didn't come. It was Mrs. Esmer, the elderly librarian. She used to crochet with my mom, but she died when I was in college.

"It's a doozy!" she said, pointing to the quilt behind her. "I made the patch on the bottom left corner, scout's honor." She held up three fingers, chuckled, then turned back to the crowds. "Tickets! Come an get 'em!"

I backed up. I knew these people. Some just a familiar face, others like family, and all of them so much younger than I remembered. My bandaged elbow hit my high school music teacher, Mrs. Corrin, and pain shot up my arm.

I zigzagged through, avoiding everyone's faces so I could focus —past a collection of folding tables lathered with crafts from Dracula cookies to oven mitts until I was through the double doors of the auditorium.

The room swooped down, rows of theater chairs circling the stage. There was a band playing "Monster Mash" to a mosh pit of ten. The audience was half full, talent show in swing. I cut through chairs, folding seats smacking my calves as I hurried.

I glued my eyes to the room at the back—big blue door. He'd be in there, only a few rows away.

Then I saw her.

Sally Sue Small, Sal for short. Or as I'd often heard, Sow, for cruelty's sake. She wasn't fat, only fleshy, but that wasn't reason enough for the name not to stick. I didn't remember her being here, just another body in the seats back then. Sal was an expert at shrinking herself down to blend in. But I still had an inkling of her dad at our door, selling jars of strawberry jam. And then her face had been plastered on every television when I was seventeen.

Sal was sitting alone in the front row, picking the caramel off a candy apple, hair in two lank braids, a red triangle painted on her nose. I was close enough to see the face paint was cracking, flakes blooming on her upper lip, like the pimples she'd one day be covered in. So close that if she turned, she could've reached out and touched me with her apple stick. But she didn't look up. Her long fingernails picked away at the caramel, leaving skinless pockmarks all over her treat.

"That was Shackled-Mundane," the speakers boomed. I didn't realize I was standing so close, ears ringing. I went behind the blue door.

The sound still raged, but it was muted—narrow walls lined with shelves, black instrument cases randomly scattered along the rows. A girl sat on a brown metal chair, cleaning out her flute. Two boys sat on the gray carpet, thumb wrestling over the top of a piano stool, neither of them Drew.

I ran through the possibilities. Right room, wrong time? Maybe he'd already played and gone home?

The door opened.

"Excuse me," Drew said. He wasn't looking directly at me, keeping his dad's guitar case from banging into the wall. I didn't move, drinking him in all at once. Brown, silky hair falling over thick eyebrows and dark lashes. His skin was olive tan, melting pink on his lips. So very, very young. He noticed I wasn't moving and smiled at me. "Sorry, just need to get through."

Oh. His voice hadn't changed yet. Much higher than I remembered. Wasn't expecting that.

"Yeah. Okay. Sorry." I stepped out of the way. My first words to Drew. *Yeah, okay,* and *sorry. Wow, Loralay, way to leave an impression.*

I leaned into the shelving to let him pass, hitting my arm.

"Ow!" I yelled. Everyone looked at me.

"You okay?" flute girl asked.

"Yep," I said, forcing chipper. When everyone went back to what they were doing, I realized how moronic it was not to have planned something to say. Bus trip, break-in, mad dash here, all wasted.

Should I even try to say something interesting? Would that deviate from our past? But then, what the heck *had* we talked about? All I remembered was we were laughing over something at the end.

I turned to Drew, ready to say anything that came to mind, when I saw he was sitting on a metal folding chair, pulling out the guitar. Ivory binding, sunburst finish, from yellow to orange, then black. I couldn't speak. Mind's eye watching my husband playing that very same guitar over Makenzie's crib.

"You play?" Drew asked, too respectful to mention I was in his personal space.

I backed up a step. "It's beautiful." I blushed when I realized I hadn't answered the question he'd just asked me.

"Thanks. It's my dad's." He rested it on his narrow knee, emphasizing that he was quite a few growth spurts away from the man I knew. "He's letting me borrow it until I get my own."

He strummed it once, frowned, twisted a knob, tried again.

"I don't," I said.

He seemed surprised I was still there. "What?"

"Play. I don't play. You asked if I did." Gah, why was I such an idiot?

"Everybody plays something." Drew grinned. Not the laugh I needed, but it was a start.

"No, they don't," I said. "I mean, I want to play piano, but I don't have one. Yet."

Drew's smile switched to a smirk. "You play the radio, don't you?"

The boys on the floor burst into laughter. I'd forgotten they were there the moment Drew walked in. I gawked, connecting that one of them was Julius, Drew's best friend.

"You know, *playing* it? The radio?" Drew prompted. Oh man, we both thought I was an idiot.

"That's cute," I said, cheeks like stove burners.

"Cu-ute," Julius mocked. *Yep, I should've seen that coming.*

"I'm Drew, by the way."

"I'm—" I started, but the door opened again, bringing in the sounds of the auditorium.

"You kids should keep it down back here," Mr. Neer said. "You'll want to hear when they announce you."

Mr. Neer, Drew's dad, alive again. A miracle only I appreciated.

"Still out of tune?" he asked, taking the guitar from Drew so he could expertly twist the machine head and fingerpick something folky.

I had a wild urge to ask him why he'd taken his own life. I was afraid I would—some crazy girl pounding her fists on an adult's chest, begging for answers. But I just stood there, aching over things that hadn't happened yet. He leaned in, locking eyes with Drew.

"You nervous?"

"No," Drew lied.

"No, sir, you say."

"No, sir."

Mr. Neer ruffled Drew's hair, handing the guitar back.

"Julius? Your mama know you're back here? I could've sworn I saw her searching the corn maze for you."

"Probably," Julius said, rolling his eyes. "Hey, Mr. Neer, can I sleep over tonight? We don't have homework."

Mr. Neer hunched his shoulders, making a big show of rubbing his forehead. "Can't we get rid of you for once, Jules, my boy? We might as well slap a Neer name tag on you."

"Thanks!" Jules said, running out the door.

"Don't tell my wife I said yes! And ask your mother for once!" He turned to Drew. "Did you tell him we're waking up at four thirty tomorrow for drills?"

Drew shook his head.

"Don't. It'll be my pleasure."

I watched them, a fly on the wall, intruding on their moment. These were their golden years, Mr. Neer finally sober, focusing on Drew instead of the bottle. And then I saw it was just the three of us. I'd missed when the other boy and flute girl left.

"You came here to hear him play?" Mr. Neer asked me.

I froze.

"Da-d!" Drew moaned. His neck rolled back like it was broken.

"I told you that's how it works," Mr. Neer said. "Play guitar and the girls come flocking. Isn't that right, Missy?"

Come on, think of something. You're an adult. "Don't know," I said. "But giving your son a name like *Drew* Neer, it's like you were pretty desperate to get girls in *close*. *Drawing* them in *Neer*."

Silence. I held my breath.

84

Drew looked at his Dad, eyes wide. "No!" Drew said. "Are you serious?"

Mr. Neer frowned, thinking. "How did I not notice . . . " he muttered. "I never . . . all those baby name books, saying it out loud." His stomach bounced, snickers escaping. "I guess we did hustle you out."

"My name is a freaking sentence?" Drew howled, turning beat red. I'd remembered shocking Drew back in the Nevermore when I'd teased him about it. I didn't know if it really was funny or if it was just the element of surprise.

Then I panicked, trying to remember if I'd heard his first and last name in our conversation or if I'd known too much, making myself suspicious. All three of us were laughing, me a ball of nerves.

"Oh, that was good," Mr. Neer breathed. "Too funny."

The door opened again. Sal was there, watching us.

"They told me you're on next, Drew," she said, eyes on me, quietly sizing up the newcomer.

"*Drew Neer,* that is," Mr. Neer said through a giggle, wiping his eye. Drew moaned.

Sal seemed confused, searching our expressions to understand what she'd missed.

I did the thing I'd always wished I'd done. I smiled at her, biglike she'd been in on our joke all along. It wasn't much, but it was a start.

"Hustle boy!" Mr. Neer said, pushing Drew out the door. "Go *draw* them in." He chuckled again, looking down at me. "What a spitfire."

I could hardly contain my glee as I found a seat in the back.

Drew climbed on stage, smiling like always, guitar bouncing on his nervous knee. Someone lowered the mic, and he strummed. Too fast, too soft, but Mr. Neer clapped in beat, proud enough to burst. His encouragement was a dose of bravery because Drew didn't play for himself. He did it for his dad.

Drew was singing "Help" by the Beatles. I looked up at the auditorium entrance. A police officer was talking to Mrs. Esmer. I didn't think it would come so fast. I got out of my seat and went to them, determined not to make a scene. The officer did a double take.

"You the Grayson girl?"

I nodded.

"Help!" Drew sang as the officer led me out by a shoulder. I craned my neck, to see Drew, lost in the performance, holding his hands up for everyone to join. "He-lp!" the room sang back.

I wondered if I'd done enough. He'd laughed, but was it our moment? Would he remember? Drew and I didn't go to the same junior high, so I wouldn't be seeing him for a few years.

I could only hope he would.

In the Nevermore these were the years I slept in a bed again, learned to play piano. Now I'd started high school in the wrong town, and I had the best Mom could manage, parenting by handing me over to someone else—a rotation of counselors. I'd smile, answer questions, then get them talking about treating mental illness—obsession, depression, books they'd recommend. They'd smile back sadly, thinking I was talking about Mom. I felt guilty letting them assume, but the truth would've gotten me committed.

"There's no reason to continue, Mrs. Grayson," one counselor said. "She's an exceptional child. But there's no shame in you having a few sessions of your own. I could recommend someone for you if you'd like? Parenting is overwhelming, especially when you don't have support from your spouse."

"Jay's as supportive as they come," Mom said too loud, hugging her purse as a shield. "I came so you'd help my daughter."

The counselors all gave up, but Mom didn't quit. The one time she'd shown some moxie, was when I needed her manageable.

The worst part was Mom was right. I wasn't okay. My head was a wire cage, locking me in. Save Drew. Save Mr. Neer. Save Sal. Memories throbbed in my skull, migraines burst behind my eyes, and Mom kept whisking me off to another office, desperately scraping the family counseling barrel until she found rock bottom with Doctor Julia.

Chapter Nine

COUNSELING

"We're all old souls," Doctor Turner said, or Doctor Julia, as she wanted me to call her. She dressed in airy eastern pantsuits and spiritual jewelry: wire, crystals, chunks of wood. At least I thought that's what she was wearing; I had to squint through the gloom and incense. We were in a dark, earth-toned room. The only sources of light were a few candles and a window covered with an array of sheer curtains—thin wisps of tan, sage, and muddy red, layered in mass and braided in waves that probably looked stunning—if you could see.

Fifteen hadn't been nice to me, my body only starting to fill in, summer heat turning my hair to frizz. I glared at the curtains, praying for a breeze to blow through.

"All is new, every time the sun hits our chakras. New perspectives, a new position," Doctor Julia exhaled the words, stretching herself across the yoga mat she was on. She'd offered me a mat when I came in, keeping them stacked by the door in a vase the way some people keep umbrellas. I'd been in a few hippy sessions with other counselors, none like Doctor Julia's brand of New Age. I preferred the couch.

"Lora-laay," Doctor Julia sang, causing me to look up. "As I was saying, we're going to connect with your past life."

I nearly choked on my own spit. "Mm—m" I cleared my throat. "My past life?"

"Yes. Amazing, isn't it? We'll run some tests and ultimately unlock your divinity."

Oh, thank God, I thought. *It's just more holistic healing crap.*

"And how, exactly, do you test for that?"

"Well, there're a few methods. We'll listen to music from different periods to see what era resonates with you," She gestured to a CD collection on the bookshelf.

Maybe this wouldn't be so bad.

"And we'll smell various aromas to ignite the inner self." She pointed one ledge higher where a vast collection of test tubes sat, each filled with powders, liquids and . . . I squinted. One seemed to consist of torn scraps of paper and . . . a gummy bear?

"Do you have any inklings you've been here before?" Doctor Julia asked.

"Wouldn't someone just *know* they lived before," I hedged. "Instead of having inklings?"

"Oh, no. These bodies are too weak to house our inner self."

You're telling me, I thought.

"If you shut your eyes, you can feel it." She moved into lotus pose, closing her eyes, chin resting on her chest. "Sense that?" She hummed. My eyes darted around the room, waiting for her to finish *sensing*.

"We can trust our instincts for guidance," she said. "Because we've lived it all before. Empowering, isn't it?"

"No," I said. "That's depressing."

She opened her eyes but didn't move her head, glaring by default. "And why is that?"

"Everybody's lived before, but this is it? Broken society, poverty, hunger. After all that, we're back to screw it up again?" At least I was making a difference with my second try.

"Cynicism. Imbalance of the Root Chakra," Doctor Julia diagnosed. "Leading with Root is a dolphin trait, you know." She smiled an irritated smile, like a teacher waiting on tenure. When I'd first come in, she'd told me she had a turquoise aura, a calming spirit. I understood that to mean she was breezy, but apparently, it meant she constantly needed to calm down.

I leaned in, squinting like I was interested when really the incense was making my eyes water. At least it's not cigarette smoke.

" . . . and that's how dolphins form a community. Tissue?" She nodded toward the coffee table between us. "Dolphins make me weep too."

On the table there was a bowl of wax fruit: artificial apples, pears, and scones with a tissue box buried in the center.

I frowned at the tissues. I'd never cry here, but people did. Real people came to get gumball colors assigned to their souls, listen to sixties music, and smell gummy bears, digging through fake fruit to get a tissue. All of that happened often enough that she'd made a living.

Doctor Julia checked her watch. "Your mother's late. No more talk. We'll practice breathing as we wait. Put your head backward and drink the air. Imagine oxygen being poured in your nose, like milk in a glass."

I watched her throw her head back. It seemed fitting that milk up the nostrils was her idea of calm imagery.

There was a knock at the door.

"Come into the healing circle, Sandy!" Doctor Julia called.

Mom came in, ready for her half. A one-hour session cut to thirty-minute chunks. First, me being talked to, then the two of them discussing me, in front of me, as if I were one of the wax apples.

"Oh, my. Dark, isn't it?" Mom tittered, out of her element around Julia, not that she had much of an element anyway.

"It is. That's why there are candles," Doctor Julia said a little too sweetly, softening her scorn. "Won't you take a mat?"

"Oh, don't mind if I do." Mom pulled out a small, squishy pink one meant for a child. Doctor Julia lowered her lids but said nothing.

Mom sat, bringing the waft of cigarettes. Doctor Julia didn't say anything about that either, but she made her opinion known, lighting another incense stick, the acceptable form of smoking. I rubbed my poor eyes in anticipation.

"You're late," she hummed. "It's 11:30, not 11:33. Now, tell me, Sandy, how is your heart feeling."

"Oh." Mom let out a splatter of giggles that made the candles flicker. "I'm a tad bit overwhelmed, to be honest."

"Tell me about it. Is it Jay?"

Already? I thought. I'd assumed Doctor Julia was a hack, but she was getting to the actual issue pretty fast.

"Oh, no, no, no. Jay's a peach."

"Yes, he seems lovely." Doctor Julia nodded encouragingly.

Nope, she's a hack.

"Well," Mom added. "He's been so busy with his realtor work, trying to provide for us. It's a hard job, realty."

"*Easy* money," I said under my breath.

"No, can't complain. He's just a peach," she repeated.

I closed my eyes, back to reliving my only moment with Drew.

"I did something, though. I don't know if it was right of me."

My eyes flicked back open.

"That's what my guidance is for," Doctor Julia said.

"Right." Mom took a deep breath, fingers twitching for a cigarette. "I found these in Loralay's room." She reached into her bra, pulling out papers she'd folded next to her heart.

92

I stood up like a Jack in the Box. "You went in my room?" Never, not in any memory I had, did she ever search my things. This was a breach of unwritten contract. But then again, I was used to the woman she'd been.

Mom shifted on her mat to glance at me, but Doctor Julia put a hand on my mother's knee, drawing her attention back.

"Remember, this is your session time, Sandy. We're witnessing your truth. Loralay is only an observer, don't engage until the final act." Doctor Julia was pulling the papers out of Mom's hands, opening them for herself.

I grabbed the hem of my shirt, crumpling it between sweaty palms. I knew what they were.

"She's got a diary too," Mom added. "I didn't feel right about reading it, but I brought it in case you think we should."

"What?" I yelled.

"It's just . . . I don't know what's going on with you." Mom squeezed her knees to her chest.

I sat back down, so mad I was sucking air through my teeth.

"Yes, Loralay, good," Doctor Julia said. "Keep practicing your breathing!"

"I'm not," I said.

Doctor Julia clutched her crystal necklace as she read.

"Requirements for emancipation? It fits with my suspicions."

"Why would she do it?" Mom asked Doctor Julia, still sneaking worried looks at me. "Fifteen and planning for emancipation?"

I wasn't, not really, just a backup plan. We were five years late, one year late for Drew's and my second meeting.

"How did she even know what emancipation is?" Mom whined, unaware of how the internet worked.

Thank God for the school computer.

"I'm worried she'll just up and run away again. It's been all this time, but I can't stop thinking about it. When we found her, she'd broken into that house, made a mess—"

"That wasn't me!" I said, starting the age-old argument to nowhere. "Dad did it." But he wouldn't admit it, not when my scandal provided an alibi.

"And then she hurt herself," Mom said.

That shut me up. I still had the scar across my arm. No one at the doctor's office had been impressed with my savvy first aid, plus I really didn't enjoy all the tiny wisps of cotton fluff getting tweezed out of the cut. I shuddered at the memory.

"I still can't fathom how . . . she just knows things there's not a reason in the whole wide world for her to know. Obsessed with that town. She's a smart kid. Skipped a whole grade."

That was true, but it wasn't from being smart. I was trying to make sure I'd graduate the same year Drew did, so we'd leave for college at the same time. "She still doesn't have any friends. Got invited to a pool party, but she didn't go. I loved swimming at her age! But more than that, it was a boy-girl party. Shouldn't that be normal? Trying to meet boys?"

Ah, the irony, seeing that meeting a boy was exactly what I'd been trying to do.

"But no, she just sits in her room, writing things like this so she can get away from me." Mom sobbed.

"Come on. It's not like that." I mustered my sympathy. This was where I got to shine, supportive daughter, a pillar of calm.

94

"Can I smoke in here?" Mom asked, rocking a bit. "It's just my nerves."

"Well, I can't be sure, but I believe I have answers for you." Doctor Julia's voice was low, divine tones, pointedly ignoring the smoking question. "I'm coming to understand that Loralay is an *indigo* child."

This was new. Mom leaned in, eating the words up.

"Many children get their auras mislabeled as mental illness," Doctor Julia added. "But for me, the signs are all there. Strong willed, intuitive beyond her years, aware of energy fields that the rest of us can't see."

"Energy fields?" Mom asked, lips parted in awe. "What on earth are those?"

"Ah!" Doctor Julia lifted her hands.

I didn't try to smile anymore, realizing I'd probably read more books on psychology than this woman owned for show.

"An indigo child would feel the pulse of the earth. That's what answers her awareness of things she shouldn't know, like the location of your hometown. The supernatural obviously led her. Did something happen there that was unfinished? Drawing her there?"

"Couldn't be. She's never been there before."

"But the energy could've been from you, passed on through your family line. A traumatic memory?"

Mom's eyes went wide.

"Dealing with those fields would explain her behavior."

"So," Mom said. "She's not sick?"

"I wouldn't go that far. If I'm right, her indigo is dark. Too close to black for comfort. I have a program we can put her through. It's attached to my deluxe package. The price on that would be steeper than our agreed-upon rate."

I'd gotten something out of the other visits, but this was a waste of time—my time. Somewhere out there, Drew was living his life without me. Doctor Julia dropped her hands.

"Aura realignment is an advanced labyrinth, but if we apply my methods correctly, I can guarantee a metamorphosis."

"Mom, let's go home."

Mom bit her bottom lip.

"Well!" Doctor Julia said. "Things are more drastic than I suspected. Let's have a look at that diary. Do you have it with you, Sandy?"

"What?" I screeched. *Stupid teenage brain,* I thought. *Calm down! You're telling her what you're worried about, just like Dad with the computer!*

"You're suffering," Doctor Julia simpered, about as kindly as the nurse at my deathbed. "It's only natural you'd block us from touching your wounds, but you need treatment."

"Are you sure?" Mom asked. "I don't know."

"You brought it here to me, didn't you? I'm at your service, for Loralay."

"Give me back my diary," I said, speaking slow and clear, making it obvious who the actual adult was. Mom looked between us, trying to decide. Putting up with Dad was one thing, but I hadn't lived twice for this. "Mom, where is it?"

"It's in my purse. I left it out there."

Doctor Julia was off her mat, heading for the door. "I'll get it," she assured Mom. "We'll only read it if she doesn't apply herself."

I was up, yanking the door open.

"Come back!" Doctor Julia huffed, but I was already down the stairs.

I made it into the empty waiting room, where Enya played over the speakers. Scanning the seats, I spied Mom's purse, leaning next to the plug-in waterfall. Only my mother would leave her things unattended, trusting the world not to cheat her.

I yanked the purse flap open, pulling my diary out.

"Loralay?" Mom asked, slinking after me.

"No," Doctor Julia cooed. "Don't speak to her. It's best not to engage an indigo when they're in the passions. Let this play out and see what she needs." I grabbed the keys, tossing Mom's purse back in the chair.

"Wow," I said, hand on the door. "You feel that? Those energy fields are leading me to the van."

The sunlight was blinding. I got in the car, scorching my fingers on the hot seatbelt. Mom opened the door after me, hand shading her eyes, looking like a puppy at a kill shelter. I leaned over my seat to stick the keys in the ignition for her.

"Lora—"

I pointed at her seat, a little too much like Dad. She exhaled, then shut up and slid in, purse on her lap.

"You shouldn't have gone through my stuff," I said.

"I'm sorry. It's my fault."

My heart hit the ground. I wasn't really like him, was I? "Don't, Mom. Just don't."

Doctor Julia knocked on the glass. I rolled my window down a crack. She hurried to my side, lips to the gap.

"Sandy! We can end our session here. It's been a long day. Let's regroup and—" I rolled the window back up, leaning into my seat.

More knocking.

"That wasn't very nice," Mom said. Her hands fidgeted with her purse straps, so flustered she couldn't look at me. "Doctor Julia just wants to help."

Why was I the bad guy? I'd put up with so many different counselors; wasn't this enough? All I'd done was save her money.

"We're never coming back," I said.

Mom put the van in reverse, and Doctor Julia backed away, standing by the sign in front of her clinic.

Mom was crying. I could hear it in the unsteady breaths, but I stared forward, Nevermore plaguing my head.

I could see us in the maternity ward, Mom reaching out to hold Makenzie for the first time, wrapping the granny square blanket she'd made over the warm little lump of my daughter. *"She's everything,"* Mom had said. Children were like that, giving you hope. But then they grew up, and you failed them, over and over. Death said I was stubborn, but I wasn't. I was just a mom. Even before I had Makenzie, I was a mother to the woman who should've been a mother to me. And I was failing her, over and over.

Mom gulped for air. "We're done for today, but maybe Doctor Julia could help you get less . . . blue," she said. "You're closed minded because she's *alternative*."

"Mom! You can't be this dense. That's not the problem. It's a scam no matter how many crystals she ties to it!"

She didn't answer. Too many pieces missing between us to build a bridge.

Chapter Ten

MY CASSETTE TAPE

I rubbed my face so I wouldn't cry, feeling the turns that meant we were almost home—the wrong home.

Dad wasn't there when we pulled up. He never was anymore, becoming background noise. The sound of him showering in the morning, the jingle of his keys as he tossed on his blazer, and then his snore in the middle of the night. It surprised me he hadn't given realty up yet.

Mom pulled up slowly, looking at his empty spot in the garage.

He'll leave anyway, then when the old mom's back, I'll take over and get us to Oak Ridge. But that was a wicked thought, wishing her to weave that misery nest.

"He's going door to door," I said to her. I'd said it a thousand times.

"I know he is." Her voice made it clear she didn't.

"He doesn't like to talk about what he's doing because he's horrible at it. It's like he's *fixing* that computer all over again."

Mom glared at me. Keeping her happy was like trying to keep a toddler from outlets, the thankless fun of not letting someone kill themselves.

"I'm going to make dinner," Mom announced. I checked my watch. Two o'clock?

"Ok-ay," I said with a clip. Then, feeling like a jerk, I added, "that's good. Thanks for that."

She went inside, and I waited, watching the garage door close behind her. I opened my diary.

Last resort: Emancipation. Legal at sixteen. Dad's enough of a liability that I should get a clean shot out. Possibly claim asthma over smoking? I can't breathe in this house anymo—

I ripped the page out, revealing the one behind it.

Senior year:

May 1, the last day I saw Sal,

May 15, Prom

Summer—Sal and family missing.

101

It'd been so dumb to leave a paper trail. Teenager dumb.

"This is getting old," I said to the empty car, to Death. "What are you trying to prove? I get I made a mistake with Dad. I don't know *how* I could've done it better, but you told me to wait and think."

Rip.

I pulled out more pages, littering my lap with secrets.

"I've thought it through now," I said. "I'm doing my part. But you promised this wouldn't take my daughter, so you'd better fix it."

Out came another page, the one with Drew's initials in a heart.

That made me think about Anita, Drew's first girlfriend. They'd be dating now, wouldn't they? Was she writing his name on her notebooks, kissing my husband with her cherry balm lips?

Rip. Out came a page scribbled with number combinations, failed attempts at remembering how to get ahold of him. Anita was probably getting ahold of him pretty fine all on her own.

Rip.

Rip.

Rip.

I tore the last in a fistful, only the cardboard cover left. I turned in my seat, going through the cleaning supplies until I found Rosie's smallest lavender trash liners, taking one for myself.

"What do you want me to say?" I asked, stuffing the papers in the bag. "You were right? I learned my lesson? I should've thought things through when you dropped me in the middle of a seven-year-old body without warning? Fine! I'm sorry!"

Something moved in the corner of my eye. I swiveled, eyes searching the garage, but there was nothing. My mind could've been playing tricks on me, but I was sure Death was there. I leaned my head on the car window, facing the direction I thought I'd seen him, my breath fogging the glass.

"Please. Don't go back on your word. I need Makenzie."

He didn't answer me, but there was nothing else to say and I'd finished cleaning up, so I got out of the car and went inside.

Mom stood over a pot, stirring. I edged past her, heading for the junk drawer. Bag behind my back, stuffed full of Nevermore. All I needed was the lighter.

"Loralay?" Mom asked.

"Uh-huh," I said, fingers tight on the plastic. "Need something?"

"Hand me the big spoon. The rice'll burn if I can't reach the bottom."

"Uh, yep." I smiled as I reached for the drawer I was already going for.

And then, on time to ruin my life, Dad walked in.

"Aw, look at this! My picture-perfect Honey and my beautiful Lady-girl." He folded something that looked like a receipt, sticking it in his jeans before he kissed the top of Mom's head. "What's with the long faces?"

Behind my back I crushed the bag, air emptying between my fingers. The last thing I needed was Dad interested in my diary, even if it was shredded. I was inches from the junk drawer. If I'd taken it a second sooner, the lighter would've been safe in my hands.

"Where were you, Jay?" Mom asked, abandoning the rice pot to hug him. "We missed you."

Speak for yourself, I thought. But I'd done enough damage, so I didn't dare say it.

"Where were *you*?" he said.

"You know, the counselor," she said, voice insect small.

"Oh! The one with the fruit bowl!" He shook his head. "*Art*," he sputtered sarcastically.

"*Counseling*," I said back in the same tone before I caught myself.

"Good one!" *Key-key-key*, he laughed, slapping my arm with the back of his hand.

I shuttered. "So, that's where we were. *You*?" I asked, showing I hadn't fallen for his little bait and switch. I was sick of the way he kept refusing to keep her updated.

"Oh, just working on some gooood neeews!"

Dang it, he came in looking for attention and I was giving it to him.

"Oh, Jay!" Mom squealed. "What've you been up to?" She fluffed her hair like a photographer was about to come in. Dad went back to the door.

"Close your eyes," he commanded. Mom did, and as an unusual kindness, Dad didn't comment when I kept mine open.

"You'll like this one, Lady-girl," he said.

Was he my buddy now? It worried me. I readied myself, determined not to make another scene, or at least less of one.

Mom stepped back. I had to turn so she wouldn't see the bag. Dad might've seen it, but he didn't question me, too busy tossing the doorknob with a flourish. He stepped out of the way for us to see past the frame.

There was a U-Haul in his parking spot.

"Open 'em!" he yelled.

Mom's eyes shot wide with a giggle, but the laughter slowed as she tried to understand. The only sound was the rice boiling. "Jay?"

Dad's focus was on me. It felt like he was beating a nail in my head, holding me in place until he guaranteed an audience of two.

"We're going to put our family back on track. Look at us, living in this hell hole." He held his arms out wide. Mom muttered she could clean up, but Dad cut over her. "We're not a unit anymore. This isn't what we wanted, Sandy. It's not nurturing. We need to think of the legacy we're leaving. It's time to make compromises."

I didn't know what he was smoking, but I wished he'd keep to the cigarettes. I could almost hear Doctor Julia telling me to practice breathing.

Mom went to the junk drawer, pulling the lighter out, unconsciously flaunting it in front of me. She lit her cigarette, tossed it back on the counter, and to my surprise, she wasn't dancing to his song this time.

"I can't do this today, Jay. Couldn't we just have a nice night? I'm making curry for dinner, just like you like." Long, deep puffs. She was sucking it down in a race to the filter.

"So, we're moving?" I asked. "Hawaii, Las Vegas?" My last resort was quickly becoming plan A. Whatever state he was taking us would mean different emancipation laws.

"Oh, just a little town called Oak Ridge."

"Jay!" Mom shrieked.

I didn't dare move, waiting for the floor to fall out from under me.

Dad dropped his hands, letting them collapse along with the friendly facade he'd been holding up. "Don't start, Sandy. I'm doing it for us."

"You promised!"

"I'm trying," he growled at the floor.

I looked between them, attempting to piece together the subtext, sure I'd heard him wrong.

"The people around here don't understand business," Dad said. "Loralay's right. It's just sitting there. Empty house falling apart. Besides, it's a bull market! We live there for a while, fix it up, make double the profit!"

"But you said we should sell now!" Her eyes shot from me back to Dad, like I was in on it. "You promised I wouldn't have to live there again! You *promised*!"

"Don't you trust me?" Dad said. "It's a detour!"

She'd almost finished her cigarette, reaching for a new one. I was happy to see her fidget; it meant she had nothing else to say.

Death heard me.

"It's fate," I said, too awestruck to watch my tongue.

"Jay!" Mom cried. "Listen to her! She's sick. She's got a . . . navy blue soul or something. I don't know, but it's all wrong—" She jumped, first cigarette burning down to her fingers before she'd switched. Moaning, she tossed the butt in the sink.

Dad swooped in on her distraction. "And keep pushing her away? Our Lady-girl?" He was standing behind me, hand on my shoulders, a human shield. "Our girl's committed to that town.

106

Shouldn't we support her? You said it was a nice neighborhood, didn't you?"

"That was eighteen years ago! You can't—"

"You're right, Sandy. But you're worried about the past when I'm talking about our future. You want us here, or living well?" His banter was making more sense than usual. But it was too fast, too perfect, too Dad.

Still, I needed this.

"I don't need much," Mom said. "I even put the past behind me working on things with *her*." Something told me this *her* wasn't me. Her as in Grandma? Was she talking about the handouts all those years? "I didn't cause any fuss."

"You've put up with a lot. I understand."

"Thank you." Mom nodded.

"It's okay if that's as much as you can do."

"Jay! You know I always stand by you."

"Until you can't," he said. "And that's okay."

"No!" Mom yelled, loud enough that I accidentally leaned into Dad. "Always Jay, I'm always going to stand by you!"

"Done!" Dad yelled, pulling us both in. Mom's mouth fell as she tried to piece together how she'd managed to agree. "We pack tonight. It's a big step, Sandy. I'm proud of you."

"Tonight?" I said, getting myself out of the circle. Dad was flying more red flags then a Tibetan field.

"Why not? Pull the Band-Aid off! We've only got this truck for . . . " He took the paper out of his pocket. "Three days! Who needs boxes? I've got boxes!"

Dad held his keys up by the bear paw key chain he'd gotten when he was out soliciting. I looked at the truck again, an image of a pale horse on the side. Something seriously wrong was going on. But it didn't matter how I got there; I just needed to make it work.

Mom muttered protests as thin as tissue paper.

"I'll take a box," I said, cutting over her. Ready for any reason to sneak outside. No one noticed the lighter I'd slid in my pocket.

"New rule," I said, my diary scraps burning on the grill, paper curling. "Don't write anything down." I scooped the ashes in a broken beer can, the urn of my stupidity. I had a desire to scatter it over a cliff like a cremated relative, but I settled for tossing in the front yard garbage can so I could hurry and pack.

In less than an hour, I was looking around my room, sure I'd missed something. Three boxes. One box lined with books on true crime and mental health, some recommended by counselors. One bulging box with clothes nicer than anything Nevermore Loralay owned, and third, a half-full box of everything else. I picked up my butterfly slammer, shocked I owned so little. My room was a hotel.

"It was," I said as I pushed my things over the ledge of the truck's cargo bed. "And now I'm moving on."

Dad came up as I wrote my name across my boxes in Sharpie.

"Here, throw this away. Garbage's over there."

I hefted the load, scooting around the broken rocking chair Dad always said he'd fix. I started to dump it all when I saw a shoe box on top of the trash can.

"Dad?" I called. "Did you throw these away?"

He hopped down from the back to look.

"Oh, yeah." He picked up the box, opening the top. "Old comic books. My uncles passed them down to me when I was a kid. Worthless, you only get money for the mint ones." He tossed the box back down.

I knew they weren't mint. They were loved. Fingerprints in the margins, clear tape over the rips to keep the pages whole. Original me found this box in my parents' closet, uncovered when we'd gone homeless. Mom ripped apart her bedroom to fit what we could in the van, downsizing even her underwear. Bras littered her bed, piles of keep and toss with me in-between, kicking my legs in the air, reading about heroes that never lost. That shoe box had been in my lap when we drove away, fitting perfectly under my seat. Every panel telling me that someday I'd win too.

"They're the golden age of Superman," I said, ripping them back out of the trash. "The 1950s Superman. Not the watered-down version. These are the ones where he could do anything! Mind control, shooting a mini replica of himself out of his hand!"

"You want to know a real superpower?" Dad asked. "Money, Loralay. Money's a superpower. Keeping trash doesn't get you money. Let's get a move on," he called as he walked away. "I want to take the first load tonight!" He took the box, dropping it back in.

"Superman doesn't need money," I muttered back, checking he wasn't watching as I picked the box back up. Underneath it I saw the ash-can I'd thrown in earlier and a paperback book, *Rags to Riches, Realtor!*

Well, it was about time he gave up. Maybe Mom would stop freaking out about him being gone all the—

109

My stomach sank, wishing I could undo what I'd seen. We'd be staying in Oak Ridge. He wasn't going to sell the house. He was giving up without telling her. And I wouldn't tell her either. "This isn't just for me," I told myself. "I can't let my parents get in the way."

"What was that?" Dad called.

"Nothing!" I yelled back, hugging the shoe box to my chest. I dumped the kitchen junk bin over Dad's book and my diary ashes, our secrets buried together.

I t was dark when we got to Grandma's house.

"Sandy! Hurry up getting in here." Dad stepped into the living room, now with working lights. He turned to me. "Pick your room, Lady-girl. You've already seen them all, haven't you?"

"I'll take Grandma's room." It'd been mine in the Nevermore. Mom couldn't sleep in there.

"The biggest room? Hell no. That's my room. Sandy!" Dad called all the louder. "Lady-girl wants the big room" Dad said. "I thought my offspring would've been smarter. You sure she's not the milkman's kid?"

Mom came in, back straight like she was off to death row.

"Oh, no, Jay. Please, not my mother's room. I feel weird enough being—"

"You can decorate," Dad told her, putting his poker chips on the mantle. "Then it won't be the same."

Mom turned back outside to get another box or to cry. It surprised me I wouldn't be getting my old bedroom back, but Dad and I, we were smiling.

Chapter Eleven

THE FIRST DAY OF HIGH SCHOOL

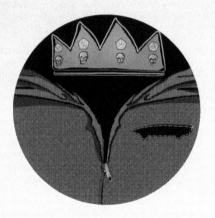

D ead leaves, conifer cones, paper-thin tree debris, all decomposing in the dirt across the lunch courtyard. I'd been waiting two-and-a-half months for this day, trying to prepare myself. It was here. *I* was here—holding an orange tray with a miniature carton of milk, butterflies too strong to let me eat anything else. Walking slowly, like a bride down the aisle when the music starts to play. There was the bike rack that was too rusted to use. There was the bench with cuss words carved by ballpoint pen. I was full. Full of life, full of joy, full of emotions to heal the yearning disease inside me.

Freshmen compared class schedules, looking for a social tribe to join. Upperclassmen greeting old friends, considering new ones. I was looking for someone too.

I hadn't seen Drew yet, and I wouldn't. He and Julius had their lunch in the music room.

I scanned the courtyard, looking for Sal.

She was at a lunch table, not entirely by herself, but turned to the side. Homeless in the horde. That was part of why I'd avoided her before. Nevermore Loralay was a refugee from the same lonesome shunning that Sal worked so hard to surround herself in.

I set my tray across from hers. She didn't look up.

"Hi!" I said.

Nothing.

I leaned in, grabbing her attention by violating the wall she'd built.

"Hey. Hi! I'm Loralay."

Sal jerked up, but her back stayed hunched, like an abused dog, cowering even at affection. The pimples were here now, skin jagged with stigma. The rest of her was put together with a fine-tooth comb. Hair slicked back in a thin, yellow bun. Not pretty, just perfect. The look of someone dressed by their mother.

"Laura?" Her voice cracked from underuse. Poor girl was petrified, but we had to start somewhere.

"Lora-lay," I corrected with a smile, sitting down. "It's weird, I know. You're not eating either?" I nodded to her tray. "Me too.

Nerves. I figure it's better not to force it instead of throwing up on the first day. You know what I mean?"

Sal's mouth bobbed like a fish for a second, but I just smiled all the wider as I waited.

"I-I don't like to eat here," she managed to say.

"Yeah, I hear you. It's hard on a first—"

"Sally Sow!" A boy called from down the table. *Really?* I thought. *Day one?* But with the juvenile hierarchy in chaos, we were fresh meat for those seeking to set the chain of command.

"First day," I finished, ignoring the boy. "I mean, I couldn't even figure out what to wear."

"What's that smell?" He sniffed the air.

Sal watched him, but I held up my sweater to grab her attention back.

"What do you think? Too warm? I mean, it is, but I really liked the way it fits."

She tried to answer, but there was oinking now.

I glanced at him, pretending not to know what he was on about. "Ooh, that kid's weird," I mutter to Sal. "Poor guy sounds like a pig. How embarrassing for *him*."

Sal tore her eyes away to frown at me, not picking up my hint on how to deal with the situation. The kid was up and on his heels, marching our way. Oh man, it was Douglas Milenhill. Not ol' Duggie. He was a bully, but he'd grow out of it when he took over managing the local gas station. He used to give Makenzie Dum Dums whenever we'd fill up.

It was strange watching the same kids who held candles at Sal's memorial, making her life hell. It couldn't have really been like this, could it? Doug just needed a buzz cut, and we'd be set for an anti-bullying video. But the hardest sting wasn't name-calling. It was slices of social agony because no one defended her. Were these really my peers? I was too hard on them. I hadn't done anything either. No, I wasn't a kid, and I'd been trained by the best bully of them all. *If you can't beat them, join them, then beat them.*

Doug leaned over, pretending to smell us, then doubled back.

"What have you been rollin' in Sow? Mud doesn't smell that bad!"

I laughed. Sal withered, attempting to use her power and manifest a sinkhole in the earth's crust so it could swallow her up, but I was her kryptonite.

First, play along.

"I wouldn't say that too loud," I sang, raising an eyebrow and a smile. "He who smelt it dealt it." Easy brown-bag joke. I'd surprised him. He even laughed a little, but not enough.

"Yeah, but you can't help smelling a sow!" he called, attempting to rally the troops. "Who else smells that?"

"We talked about this a second ago, remember? It's puberty, Duggie. Body odor."

"You know me?"

Next, keep up the redirect.

"By the smell." I nodded. "But don't worry, there's a remedy. It's called deodorant." I reached out and capped a hand on his shoulder in fake concern. "Don't you need to use those powers for good, not evil? Save the rest of your exhaust for the bad guys, Captain Puberty. But for us . . . " I mouthed the word *deodorant* again, still tapping his shoulder.

"Maybe it was you I was smelling," he said.

I nodded. Flat-out denial would only strengthen him.

"That's my power. I'm amplifying you, buddy. Giving your funk the reach of its full potential. But all the glory goes to you."

Duggie wasn't bad at the game himself, saving face by playing into it. He lifted his arms high in the air.

"Smell me! I'm pubescent!" He yelled without missing a beat, running around the table to chase down a group of girls wearing fuzzy earrings and glitter eyeshadow. "*Pew-pew*, Captain Puberty!" he called as they ran away from him, earning spatters of laughter and screams.

Sal was gone. I swiveled, looking for her. To Douglas, attention was all the same, negative or positive. For Sal, there was only one kind.

She'd already made it to the courtyard doors, slinking back to safety. I sat back down to my milk, not sure how helpful I'd been. *Oh well, it's a start.*

"That was baller," someone said next to me. Stephen Ray. It took a deal of restraint not to let out an audible *aw* at seeing him. Such a good, old friend. The troublemaking kid with doe like Chinese eyes, a love of graffiti, and wild parties. Here he was, a picture-perfect thug baby. Beanie slouched over his ears, an oversized Superman necklace, and baggy jeans that showcased his Fruit of the Loom.

"Wassup? Name's Stephen," he said, holding out a fist.

"Loralay."

Our knuckles hit. I held back a giggle at his gentlemen's attempt.

Sal was always young in my mind, the fate of all who die early, but my mental Stephen had chin stubble and an early streak of gray. We'd gone to college together and beyond, close enough that Makenzie called him Uncle. He'd get her sketchbooks every Christmas, drawing her as a superhero on the first page of every one.

"You stuck up for her," Stephen said, looking in the direction Sal had disappeared. "Legit." Anyone else might have thought I was playing around, but Stephen saw things other people missed, an artist. "What grade you at?"

"Sophomore."

"Same, tight. What classes you got?" he asked, nodding his head like a gangster. I bit my lip so I wouldn't crack. *Oh, Stephen,* I thought. *You little heartbreaker.* His hooligan's swagger was so cute.

We compared our freshly printed schedules, concluding that we had nothing together, but he still walked with me to the door when the bell rang.

We passed other people I knew, Melanie the lackey, Shawn the hyperactive. I even spotted Julius for a second.

I went through the day in a delicious dream. I'd been worried I'd missed too much in the last three years to make it work, but this was perfection. The most fun I'd had since before I'd died, floating through a fantasy version of who I'd always wished I'd be. I knew it was a dangerous head trip, so I kept the spectacle low, an undercurrent of my ideal—Superman, but still Clark Kent with my glasses on.

Until the busses.

"Dad!" Drew called, climbing up two steps on the second bus so he could talk to Mr. Neer.

I walked up behind Drew. He'd grown so much in the last five years. Taller, broader, sweatshirt stretching across the muscles of

117

his back. He smelled too good to be true. Calvin Klein One, I'd forgotten he used to afford that stuff, so much better than lemon pomade. I drank in all of him. First day of school haircut, tossing a water bottle between his hands. *Slosh, slosh, slosh.* I even let my eyes flick down to look at his thighs tightly in his jeans. My fingers ached to touch him. Slide my hands into the curve of his back pocket. Great, now I was drunk on hormones. I bit my lip.

Drew didn't see me, too busy looking at his dad—Mr. Neer, football coach, bus driver. It was a mystery that the school board didn't have him on the payroll as a janitor, secretary, and teacher. If there was anything in Oak Ridge Mr. Neer could stick his fingers into, he did. Sometimes it seemed like he lived at the school, dragging Drew right along with him. Drew hated it, quietly, existing as his dad's vicarious voodoo doll. Up at dawn, tag along to every academic venture, never awake enough to stay up past nine. He'd been drinking black coffee since I'd known him.

"Julius is coming over," Drew told him.

"You're not even asking me now?" Mr. Neer said. "When did that start?"

"Whatever works, Dad," Drew joked, but Mr. Neer was in one of his moods.

"Don't *whatever* me. I thought Julius was quitting the team." Ah. Mr. Neer wasn't mad. He was football mad—his own special brand of irritation.

"No," Drew said, trapped in an argument he didn't start. "He just didn't like that we're doing doubles on Sundays?"

"Why?"

"I don't know. He said that's not normal."

"He doesn't like taking Monday off? Well, I'm not here to make everyone happy."

"It's not really off. I mean, we have school."

"Oh? Your teachers having you run drills?"

Drew shrugged, tossing the water bottle faster.

Mr. Neer sighed.

"I don't care if he stays over, but we're going for a run in the morning. No sleepin' in." Mr. Neer spotted me, waiting to get on. "Head's up, Drew, your blocking the line."

I wished he hadn't said that. I'd been soaking up the moment, the bliss of Calvin Klein and bus fumes.

"Sorry," Drew said to me. There was a second where we made eye contact, but he only moved out of my way. I climbed the bus steps, sitting in the first seat so I could still see him.

Mr. Neer lowered his voice. I had to strain to hear.

"Julius is a fun kid, but if he's threatening your potential, you have to make a decision."

No, I thought. Mr. Neer would make all the decisions for him. But I had to fold my thoughts up, trunking them in my gut. In the Nevermore, I'd stepped in too much. Cocky girl who didn't think about consequences, I supported him dropping everything— football, scholarships, tuition. We regretted it when Makenzie was born. Bills stacking up, Drew putting on that factory uniform. And Mr. Neer, the man that had wanted Drew's life all to himself, fading from our lives. One day he left his guitar on our step. Then after three missed calls, no message, Mr. Neer killed himself.

"Okay," Drew said.

"You say yes, sir."

"Yes, sir."

"That kid'll be the death of me if you don't kill me first."

I cringed.

Julius got on, hamming it up by bowing low to Mr. Neer.

"Oh, all right," Mr. Neer said, face in palm, able to drop the tension by making himself even more melodramatic than Julius. "Just get back there and stay quiet so I can forget you exist."

"Quiet as camo," Drew said, walking to the back of the bus.

"What?" Julius laughed, holding two seats so he could leap through the isle.

"'Cause camo's invisible, so you can't see it."

"I don't think that's coming out as smart as you think it is," Julius said, his voice drowning in the sound of everyone else getting on.

I shouldn't have sat in the front. Drew always rode in back. We used to sit together on the days he wasn't stuck to his dad's hip. Drew and I, close, careful Mr. Neer didn't see us holding hands. I considered getting back up, but the flow of students was getting thick. I spotted Sal halfway down the line. Crap, I intended to tell her to sit with me, but I'd missed my chance.

As soon as the bus was full, we took off past farms and fields toward Drew's house, where he, Julius, and Sal got off.

In Drew's senior year, my junior, we were together in those back seats. Drew whispering in my ear that he wished he lived further from the school, to sit by me a little longer. "Shut up." I'd roll my eyes, giggling. "It's one stop over." Then Julius would whine about being third wheel.

We parked right in front of their houses, the big hand-painted U-Pick Strawberries sign in front of the Smalls' place like a bus stop.

Sal got off and walked toward the white manufactured home with the broken awning and Mickey Mouse blankets tacked up as curtains. Drew and Julius walked to the two-story brick house he'd been brought up in.

Sal watched Drew, only seven steps behind the popular boys. How many times had she stood behind Drew and me? We'd all known she'd had a crush on him in the Nevermore. Sometimes I'd joke she'd sweep Drew off his feet, and they'd run away together. I was cruel, saying it just so I could see the embarrassment on his face. Chop her down, thinking it was okay because I'd never said it to her face. In the end, my intent didn't take the guilt away. How could you forget that you'd cut someone metaphorically when that had been their physical end too?

Mr. Neer watched to see they all made it across the street. I watched too, trying to pinpoint where it all went wrong. What pieces of our story strengthened us and what broke us in the end?

I leaned back in my seat, the buzz of my fairytale day dissolving like sugar in water, too diluted to taste sweet.

"Welcome home," I told myself.

Chapter Twelve

BUTTERFLY WINGS

D ad was sprawled on our old flower couch. It replaced Grandma's plastic-covered one when he'd deemed hers uncomfortable. I felt strange every time I saw it there, along with the paintings he'd taken down. Like the mess he'd left in Grandma's house, everything was unfamiliar and nostalgic at the same time.

That couch he was sitting on should've been left behind. I looked at it sometimes, wondering about the butterfly effect. Had some soul's life changed forever because they hadn't found this couch at their local thrift shop? How could everything be fate's cassette tapes if Dad being here changed so much? But thinking that way bothered me, so I didn't let those thoughts settle.

"Loralay?" Dad said without looking away from the television. "Be my Lady-girl and get my wallet."

So much for hello. I sighed. "I haven't even taken my backpack off yet. And Mom made me rake the front yard before I came in."

"You were supposed to rake yesterday!" Mom yelled from the kitchen, her voice on edge but forced sweet. At least she sounded like a normal mom.

"It's in my room," Dad muttered, leaning in to focus on a news report blaring on the TV.

"Why do you even need it?" I whined.

"Beer."

I flung my backpack on a chair, giving up.

I didn't go to my old room much—another change, another butterfly wing.

It was a mess—bed in a tangle, Dad's pants on the floor with the underwear still inside. I stepped around a pile of shoes, ready to dig through his discarded clothes, when I saw the piano. A beer bottle left on the key cover? I stormed over, ripping the bottle off to drop it on the nightstand with prejudice. I ran my hand over the wood, checking if he'd left a water ring. My fingers came back with dust.

"Come on," I said, rolling my eyes and sitting down at the bench that was home to a dirty sock. I pushed the sock off, touching it as little as possible, then used my sleeve to clean away the neglect. "So, freaking, annoying," I muttered, lifting the lid to see those cracked ivory keys that were turning old paperback yellow. "Careless disregard for . . . " My hands were in position, ready to play. "What the . . . "

Here I was, learning algebra, even though I remembered graduating, unable to drive, even though I could vividly access the feeling of speeding down a dirt road.

But the piano, somehow it was still mine.

I left my fingers hovering, afraid to try, afraid I was wrong. And then I pressed, ever so softly, tapping soundlessly, until I trusted myself to let a song ring out. Filling the air with my own ragtime version of "Say It Ain't So" by Weezer, Drew's favorite song to play together. Our song.

"How . . . " I asked.

"I didn't take that one," Death said.

And the room was orange.

He was back to his thousand faces—old, young, man, woman, but always Death at the pupil. Six years, finally. I wasn't crazy.

I stood up, trying to make my mouth form words. The room was a mess, but Death didn't step over Dad's clothes when he came toward me. He stepped through them like a hologram. Only he was realer than anything else, the rest of the world unhinged in this pale, bittersweet color.

"I requested it on your behalf," Death said, voice hardly above a whisper but clear with no other sound competing for my ears. "It seemed too cruel to touch."

"The piano?" I looked back at it, confused. "You're okay taking my life, but you didn't want to touch my music?"

"Still so stubborn."

"Take it back! I don't care if I never play another song! I'll figure out another career. Just give me a life in trade."

His thousand faces were placid, tugging his gloves free from one finger at a time—the orange tint flaking away as he put them down on the nightstand. The sound of them falling, *pat*, *pat*, like the last beats of a heart. I could've sworn they were older, a little more worn.

"You just want to save a life? Last you told me you only wanted Makenzie."

"So, it *was* you!" I said. "You heard me." But that meant Death was always listening, my privacy stolen. I opened my mouth then closed it, a silly little girl in hysterics. At least I wasn't crying for once. *I need to act like him,* I thought. *Be in control of the room.*

"No, you don't," he said. "You were gifted with emotion to fuel your compassion, not to hide who you are."

My knees gave out, flopping me back down on the bench.

"You can hear my private thoughts?"

"You assume there's such a thing as privacy."

No, I couldn't believe it. I looked around for something to think at him. *Your gloves.* I thought. *What are they?*

"They're time," Death said, nodding to the nightstand. *So much for thinking I'm not crazy.* "Eternity is reality," Death said. "Time is just a cover to the endlessness. The soul lives on as the body decomposes. Mankind wearing life in a body, then laying it aside as they come through me. Here you live by cause and effect, but one day you'll see they're the same."

"But, how . . . " I started, but I had as many questions as Death had faces.

"You asked if you stepped on a beetle, would your daughter never be born, as if life was as trivial as that. You still hold on to the illusion of control because you believe time is the solid, not the eternity it covers. But you won't understand me yet. Your next gift waits."

"You mean I know something else? A hidden ability? Like piano?"

"No. A new gift. One given to you in its proper season."

"You're so aggravating! You can tell me you wear time gloves, but you can't tell me anything helpful about my life. I'm trying to save people! What am I supposed to be thankful for? Fantastic, I can still play piano. That'll be sure to save Sal!"

"I gave you what you need."

"I need a piano? Someone needs to brush up on Maslow's hierarchy of needs, then. Oh, my word! You're kidding me. Why do I know that? I didn't learn about that until I wasted a credit on that stupid Exploring Human Behavior class. You gave me college psychology too? That's my next gift? This is insane."

"I didn't. You're retaining your old self when I'm here, the eternal you waits—re-meeting your death. Music will follow you outside of this point, a gift to hold you through the treachery."

"Re-meeting *my* death when you kill me?"

Death didn't answer, hollow pupils, beckoning me to fall into their black center.

"I don't need your pity!" I said. "Everything I'm doing matters! I *will* make my own ending."

He met my bellows with a hush that tickled the hairs of my skin. "It always mattered. You just don't see. You still haven't answered the question."

126

"What question? You didn't ask—"

The color flickered, leaving me alone.

"You playing piano?" Dad called. "When did you learn that?"

I was still as a painting, cut off from my argument with Death so quickly I didn't know what to do with myself. I could hear him coming in, but Mom made it to the door first.

"No, Jay, it's a player piano." She picked up Dad's clothes. "I'm surprised you figured out how to set it up on your own, though. Got the tempo right and everything. Intuitive of you." She squeezed my cheek, forcing happy, even though I could tell she was exhausted. *I'm sorry, Mom, but you don't even know how bad it could've been.*

"Don't look so worried, sweetie," she said, tugging at my curls. "I'm not mad you got the piano started." She reached around, hand almost on the empty slider cabinet. "What song was that? I don't remember it from the rolls. Your grandma used to listen to them every nigh—"

"Player piano, huh?" Dad said, coming in. "Oh, I thought you were doing something interesting for once."

Mom turned, distracted by Dad. She handed him the wallet that she'd just found in his pants. He pocketed it without looking away from the piano.

"How much you think a player piano's worth?" he knocked on the side, listening to the wood like he knew what he was doing.

"Jay! That's been in my family for years!"

I couldn't rile myself to care if he sold it, my senses sapped by Death showing up again. Dad scowled at her, making a point to keep tapping at the wood.

"Might as well know what it's worth," he said.

There was a knocking sound that didn't come from him. His head tilted, looking at the piano like it'd come alive.

"Did you hear that?" he asked.

Mom leaned in. The knocking came again on its own. "Oh! It's the door, Jay! You're so silly, tricking me!" She hit him with his own sock.

"Yeah," Dad said, chuckling weekly. "Got you there." He shook his head clear as he left for the door.

Mom's happy mask faded. "Turn it back on," she said. "That song was so lively. It made me feel, I don't know, adventurous!"

That word was so far from anything describing her that it sounded weird coming from her mouth. She frowned and tsked. "I was sure I knew every roll! What's it called?"

I started giggling like an idiot, wracked by the absurdity of it all. The truth was so wild it didn't matter what she believed.

"What?" Mom fussed. I was half tempted to play that song again for her right then and there.

But then—

"Selling jam?" I heard Dad ask. My body ran cold.

"What is it, Loralay?" Mom asked, but I was up, running for the door, tripping over Dad's shoes.

"Loralay? Honey!" Mom called. I zipped around the corner until I could flatten myself against Dad's back, peeking over his shoulder.

"Whoa there, Loralay. What's gotten into you," Dad said.

And I saw him. Mr. Small.

I had to duck back behind Dad, looking for shelter from the monster in the white button-down shirt.

"Sorry about that," Dad said.

I blinked, but he was still there in my mind—pasty skin, rosy on the crown of his head. The hair he didn't have was compensated by those bushy eyebrows and the wireframe glasses.

I should've known Death would follow this man, the man who killed his family.

Sal was standing back by the curb, pulling the jam wagon. Staying strictly still.

"It's homemade, all natural," he said. "We grow the strawberries ourselves to keep a second income. Times are hard."

"I understand that," Dad said. "Tell you what, I don't have my wallet with me, but I'm interested. Why not give us a sample and come back around once we've tested the quality?"

"Fair enough," Mr. Small said. "Sally Sue, bring a jar up."

Sal jumped to life, fetching one of the old jars in her wagon. She handed it to her Dad—a masking tape label with a neat pencil printing of the contents and date.

"Is that a pickle jar?" Dad asked, taking it from Mr. Small.

"It is. It's clean. We recycle community jars. In fact, should you ever have a jar supply, we'd be mighty happy to take them off your hands. Just leave 'em out on the doorstep and give the Smalls a call. Find us in the phone book. Small's General Store next to the pharmacy."

I was running out of time. I needed to be brave.

"Welp, we'll give it a try and—"

"Sally?" I said, ducking under Dad's arm. I brushed past the murderer, every hair on my body standing on end. "It is you!" I called, arms outstretched like I was about to hug her. Sally's face turned as white as her wide eyes.

"You know my girl?" Mr. Small asked me. "Sally Sue, you know this child?"

Oh, Mr. Small, I thought. *I am no child.*

"We just met today," Sal said, looking relieved when I put my arms down. I stood next to her with a pasted grin. Close enough that I was sure I could physically feel her mind coming unglued with stress.

"You made a *friend?*" Mom shouted, blowing past Dad to come down the steps in such glee she looked like a prom princess. Dad did a double take. I almost joined him, wondering who this new version of Mom was.

"Hi, there!" She held a hand out to Sal. Trapped, Sal shook Mom's hand, looking like she'd touched a joy buzzer. "You should stay! All of you! Come on in!" She was ditching the wet blanket because she was excited for me? Maybe she really did care, more worried about us moving for my sake than her own scorn for Oak Ridge? I could've kissed my mother for fully coming through if I wasn't terrified that she'd just invited a homicidal lunatic into our home.

"No can do," Mr. Small said. "We have to finish our rounds."

I exhaled, relief like a warm bath.

"Just one cup of coffee," Mom pushed, dunking me in cold water.

"We couldn't intrude," Mr. Small said.

"Could Sal stay?" I asked, making Mom glow all the brighter, so happy I had a friend that she still hadn't noticed Sal stood in torment.

"No, thank you," Mr. Small said, a hand to his head. He nodded like he'd tipped a hat. "We have work to do. Maybe we'll make things social after you've tried the jam. I'm sure you'll like it. It's a local favorite."

They were leaving, ready to circle the rest of the cul-de-sac. How could I let her walk away with that man? But how do you condemn a murder when he hasn't yet committed his crime? I had three more years. I had to let it go.

"He's a nice man," Mom said, sounding like every person interviewed about the Smalls. *Such a very nice man.* But Mom wasn't interviewed in the Nevermore. We didn't know them much. No, they interviewed the neighbors.

They interviewed the Neers.

I watched the wagon bump past our walk, Mr. Small picking up the rake I'd accidentally left out, so the wagon could roll past.

"Oh. I'll get that!" Mom said, chasing after them to take the rake.

Dad handed me the jam jar. He'd already unscrewed the lid, taking a heap with his finger. He coughed a raspy hack.

"Didn't expect that." He spat in the sawdust near the house. "So much sugar, it's like chewing sand. Good thing I didn't pay."

"Where're you going?" I asked. He'd stuck around for a while when we first moved, but he was disappearing again. Only now I knew he wasn't on cold calls.

"Beer," he said, but he didn't leave. He leaned in, putting an arm around me. I tried to act natural with Mr. Small so close by.

"Lady-girl, see that place?" He pointed to a house across from us on the cul-de-sac, a brick-and-plaster building with a steep red roof. There was a for-sale sign in front of the lawn. "Nice house," he said.

I nodded, completely confused about what that had to do with me. "Probably going to get new neighbors then. Oh, Loralay, I almost forgot . . . " Dad said.

I watched Mom, rake in hand, giggling at something Mr. Small was saying. My trusting mother, the kind of woman who left her purse in a waiting room.

She didn't know him. She *shouldn't* know him. We never bought the jam.

"I wanted to thank you," Dad said. He was looking at his keys, thumbing the paw key chain he'd gotten out on cold calls.

"What?"

"You were right about moving here. It's just what I needed."

I hugged the jar. No matter what I told Death, all my plans smelled of anarchy. Plucking butterfly wings like daisy petals, letting them fall where they may.

Chapter Thirteen

THE DAY OF MUSIC

Early morning, the kind that makes your stomach hurt. I knew the weather was changing because I'd woken up to my hair demanding moisturizer like the Aztecs wanted blood. After a lucky thirteen different hair products, I'd run out of time and had to throw it all in a ponytail that, no matter what I did, looked like I'd glued a matted pom-pom to the back of my head.

"Can't you even be a nice pom-pom?" I begged it. But, just like everything else I'd tried, my hair didn't respond to whining.

And in the end, I'd spent so much time trying to appease my curls that I hadn't thought about *how* the weather changed. I rushed to the curb in a pair of thin khakis and a quarter-sleeve shirt.

Naturally, it was getting colder—a windy, why-didn't-I-bring-a-jacket kind of day. It was going to rain. Not too cloudy yet—but my hair, it knew.

I held my backpack in front of me as a barrier, stamping my feet at the bus stop, trying to stay warm.

When Mr. Neer pulled up, I discovered the bus wasn't much warmer. Drew was sitting in the back with Julius, watching the world pass out the foggy windows. I wished I could take a photo of them, my guys, legs up on the seats, drinking their coffee in silence, faces still red from their run. I imagined nuzzling myself into Drew's chest, talking to Jillian as Drew hugged me with hands toasty from holding his drink. Instead, I hugged myself, looking for a seat.

"Morning," I said, scooting next to Sal. She didn't look surprised this time, just wary.

"Hi," She mouthed, then nothing.

My legs bounced on their own with the cold. Sal was eyeing my jittering. She had a coat and a plain little scarf. I tried to play my shivers off like I was hyper and not the girl who'd hydrated her built-in weather detector while she'd forgotten to dress accordingly.

"So, do you help make the jam?" I asked. "Or is it just your parent's thing?"

Sal's hands tightened into claws on her knees. "What's your deal?" She wasn't loud, but her words jabbed callous like an ice pick. "What do you want from me? Telling my dad we're *friends* when I don't know you."

Wow, where was this sunshine-sucking vampire hiding? Our conversations last life had been short-lived, but I'd accepted the persona we all saw, meek and weak. I'd never thought a seething cyclone was brewing underneath.

"Sorry? I'd only said we'd met. My *mom* was the one who said we're friends."

"What is it then? Say whatever you want so you can *leave!*"

I mentally begged her to keep her voice down, glancing around the bus to see Sal had already attracted the attention of a girl two seats over. Mr. Neer pulled over, picking up more kids, more potential humiliation.

"I don't like it," Sal said. "You think you can just push me into being best friends?"

"Sorry. I just wanted to talk," I said. What was I doing? I didn't even know her, and now I expected her to take what I was selling? Foot in the door, forcing business cards and kicking over flowerpots. Sal was more than my good Samaritan story. "Do you want me to leave you alone?" I asked, guilty that I didn't really want to sit next to her anymore.

Sal unclenched, hunching lower in her seat.

"What do you mean, you're sorry? You haven't done anything. You're just nice. I'm such an idiot." She was clawing at her own arm—red lines with papery skin coming up on the edges. The mother in me couldn't watch. I put my hand over hers.

"Sal, stop."

"Don't touch me!" Sal yelled. Now everyone was looking at us, even Mr. Neer from his rectangular mirror. Sal turned a monochrome of reds, lowering her head. I hated myself for thinking this would be easy.

"Everything okay back there?" Mr. Neer called. Sal didn't answer, still hunched over. I couldn't think of anything to say. Mr. Neer probably didn't remember me from three years ago, and now his first recollection would be of a delinquent kid on the bus. "Why don't you separate," he said.

I got up, taking the walk of shame two rows back. I took one quick glance at Drew. Our eyes met. His head darted back to watching the world pass by. *He was looking at me? Fantastic, I'd made a spectacle.*

When we pulled up to school, Sal was off like a shot toward the doors. I started to follow.

"You. Stay in your seat," Mr. Neer said. "I wanna talk to you."

"Ooh," Julius said as he and Drew passed me.

Mr. Neer waited until the bus was empty, drawing out the dread. The floor rocked, a draft seeping through the cracks of the windows.

"All right, come on up," Mr. Neer called. Unfortunately, he wasn't in a good mood.

"I'm Mr. Neer," he introduced himself. I nodded, stepping closer, discovering the heater vents. Two over-sized air pockets of bliss pointed directly at Mr. Neer because apparently, only the driver needed to be warm. "Some say I'm an easy-going man, but there are three things I don't tolerate: a low bid, a lowball, and a low-down loss."

I was getting a football speech? Drew was always quoting it, but I'd never been on the receiving end. I inched my feet closer to the waves of heat. For the love of every hot spell, I hoped he talked long enough for me to warm up. I was watching a kid try

136

to get inside the school, his body wind bent, leaning like a constant fall, never hitting the ground. "Never bid yourself too low, because you're going to pay for it later. Never let someone lowball your worth because you'll live up to their expectations, and never get involved in a low-down loss. You get one try in life."

Two, I mentally corrected him.

"And what you don't want is a legacy of low-down losses. Bullying the Small girl? That's a low-down loss."

"What? No, I wouldn't—"

Mr. Neer held up a hand. "Save your piece," he said. "That girl doesn't need no more trouble, and you don't want to look back years from now thinking you caused her a handful of pain. Find a way to be kind. For your own sake. Now, off my bus." He pulled the door lever, a gust of air swirling inside. I took a deep breath like I was about to dive underwater, stepping back out in the wind.

My shirt attempted to transform into a kite as I stood there, thinking Mr. Neer was coming down too so I could say the things he'd told me to hold, but the bus pulled away, and another took its place, putting me in the bottleneck of the morning flow.

"Wait back there for your buddies," the new driver said, assuming I was holding up the line because I was looking for someone.

Friends, I thought. *That'd be nice right about now.* To think I'd woken up excited. The first class I'd have with Drew, Music Basics 101.

I was running down the side path as another gust hit, roughing up my ponytail. My hair slipped free of its pom-pom cage, slapping me in the face. My last hair tie rolled like a tumbleweed across the yard.

"No!" I yelled, doubling back to catch it. The cold cut through my clothes, but I had to go back. I'd only grabbed one hair tie, one!

Stephen was in front of me, saying something I couldn't hear over the gusts around us, his Superman necklace flicking around his neck as the wind caught it.

"What?" I yelled.

"What's wrong with you? Trying to turn into an ice cube?"

"My hair tie," I screeched, pointing at . . . nothing. It was gone.

"School's this way!" he yelled back, grabbing both my arms to turn me around. "Dang, girl! You're ten degrees below freezing!"

I started to answer, but Stephen shook his head at me, dropping his boulder-sized backpack on the ground and taking his hoodie off.

"No!" I said when I realized what he was doing. But he yanked it over my head anyway. It covered me like a tent, coming down to my thighs, and just like Stephen, it was warm inside. "But you'll be cold," I said.

"Shut up," he said, smoothing back his black hair as it danced around his head. Now the only thing covering his torso was a short-sleeved shirt and Superman bling.

"But—"

He pulled the cords on the hood, so it smashed my hair down like insulation for my ears, tugging until only my eyes and nose poked through.

"Chillax, I'm not postal. I got a coat in my locker. Come on, it's hella cold!" He led me toward the school's double doors, but the music classes were in the detached music building.

"I have music class Tuesday and Thursday!" I yelled through the fabric over my mouth, but I realized he was already heading that way.

"I know, genius, I saw your schedule."

He remembered my classes? I only remembered he didn't have a class with me. We turned at the fork in the path, coming up to the second building in the schoolyard. The structures matched, red brick with efflorescence spilling down from the roof, windowsills like sugar icing on a bunt cake. When we passed the lichen-covered bust of Franz Schubert at the end of the pavement, I reached up, putting my hand on top of his head, like Drew and I used to do before walking into the leaky vestibule.

Stephen yanked the door closed behind us, sealing out the cold, locking us in the smell of wet brick and rotting wood. I loved this school. Nothing was new, all of it built in better-off times, but those times must've been amazing. Well, maybe not the ceiling tiles. They screamed asbestos.

"Why'd you grab that nasty dude's head?" Stephen asked.

"What? The bust of Franz Schubert?" I took off the hood and shrugged, surprised by the question. "I don't know, it's tradition?"

"You been here two days, and you've got traditions?"

Watch yourself, Loralay. "Well, it should be," I said, smoothing my hair, trying not to think about how hard it would be to comb it all out. "Here," I added as I started taking off his sweater. "Thanks, Stephen. It was so sweet of you to—" he put his hand on my head, locking the hood in place.

139

"Spaz. You're trippin' if you think I'm going through my day knowing you're an iceberg. Bring it back tomorrow. And don't even think of being all, 'Ooh, it's mine now.' That's *my* Element duds. You hear me?"

I nodded, looking down at the skater logo. I felt small inside his clothes, and I didn't think that was just the size of them. Stephen turned, hands in his pockets, arms stiff as popsicle sticks. "I gotta bounce before Mrs. Lamont marks me absent. She's homies with my mom, so everything I do in there comes around."

"Thank you!" I called after him.

He shrugged without looking back, door banging shut behind him.

Stupid girl. Why'd you think you didn't have friends?

I found my way to the right classroom, steps echoing in the quiet: white walls, whiteboard, a row of guitars hanging from their necks. Bongos and congas pushed in the corner. No desks or chairs, but carpeted steps as seats, like a sunken living room turned auditorium, and all of it to myself.

I was early. Mrs. Corrin was probably huffing to the staff room to get the TV trolley so we could watch *Intro to Music*.

I stood at the school piano. An upright on wheels made to roll from choir room to stage. Dented edges and a sticky key on the end, but I'd never been picky when it came to pianos.

I sat at the bench, pulling Stephen's sweater sleeves up to my elbows before playing a few measures of Der Erlkönig to the empty room. Inspired by ol' Franz Schubert himself. I jumped right into the seventh verse, and the room vibrated with notes crisper than the cold outside. All my training was there. No recollection of algebra or history, but piano came back as clear as my—regrets.

I stopped playing. What was I doing? Der Erlkönig was about a father struggling to save his son. A tragedy. The boy killed by the Elf King. Death gave me one stupid thing back, and I play his victory theme?

"Lovely!" Mrs. Corrin said, purple scarves and silver bangles waving as she clapped.

She was back with the trolley, a few students in tow, including Drew.

I threw my hands up to my hair, wishing I'd done something about it before they came back.

"Nice," Drew said, nodding as he passed me.

"Thanks," I said back, but my brain was reeling because Anita was under his arm, casually holding my husband's hip. I knew it was coming, but there wasn't much preparing for the way they so naturally slid together.

Anita broke away from Drew, standing in front of the piano to lean over the casing. She practically climbed the thing to look down at my hands on the keys. Her long brown ponytail flipped next to my face.

"Hi?" I asked, leaning back.

"Hi," Anita said, hardly glancing up from my hands. She seemed to be searching for something.

"What is it?" Drew asked her, looking over the piano too. He was smirking at Anita in a *you're so adorable* way before smiling at me apologetically and reaching between us to pull her hair up. I was almost thankful, but he kept sliding his hands through that ponytail, her straight, flat hair slipping between his fingers as easily as sand.

"Nothing," Anita cooed. "Just looking."

"Then get back here and leave the nice pianist alone," Drew laughed, tickling her ribs.

She jumped back, stumbling into him while simultaneously heel-stomping my heart.

I'd never been through this. Nevermore Loralay only crushed on Drew when he was available.

"I was just trying to see where the music sheet was," she said.

"You don't always need music," Drew said. "She played it by heart."

Yep, the same heart you're smashing into the carpet, I thought.

I needed to get ahold of myself. Drew *wasn't* dating me. That was okay. In fact, they were right on track. He and I were going to be best friends, and they were doomed before Thanksgiving. But all I could think about was the way he looked at her.

"I've just never heard anyone play like that," she said. "Like, unless it was on a CD or something."

No, don't be nice, I want to hate you!

I smiled at her, too wide, trying to convince us both I wasn't out to steal her boyfriend. Anita smiled back, pulling thoughtlessly at her puka shell necklace.

"Can you play it faster?" she asked.

"Uh, maybe?" I said. "Erlkönig's pretty fast all on its own."

"Go on!" Mrs. Corrin said, still setting up the TV. "We're eager listeners!"

Maybe Mrs. Corrin was eager, but Drew and Anita were distracted by a weird little flirting game that involved Drew poking a bit of muffin top skin above Anita's jeans and Anita

142

giggling as she slapped his hand away. Poke, poke, giggle, poke, poke.

For the love of—

"Drew?" Mrs. Corrin said, unintentionally saving me. "Be a dear and get the extension cord hooked up."

I jammed my hands down, jumping into an overly hyper ragtime version of *our* song, even if Drew didn't know it was.

"Don't even need to look at the keys, do we?" Mrs. Corrin yelled over my excessive jabbing. "I'm keeping mental notes on you!" She wriggled a finger playfully in my direction, bangles chiming. "Just need to work on your dazzle. Now, where's a smile, huh?"

I didn't smile. I wasn't playing it for her.

Drew unwrapped the extension cord, but he was slowing down, leaning in, listening to our language. "Is that Weezer?" he asked.

"You know it." It wasn't a question, but he thought it was.

"Yeah, I do! I love them!"

"Why don't you sing it then? Here, I'll lead you in."

He shook his head, embarrassed, but I plodded on, playing the beginning in a flow until he found his place. Drew's voice, intimate with my fingers. Improvised and magic. His boyish pitch replaced by a deeper tenor since I'd last heard him. Sometimes he held a note too long because he hadn't heard our version, but Drew caught on fast.

I never wanted the moment to stop, itching to slow the tempo so we could make it last. Drew pressed into my piano with Anita, but to me, she wasn't there anymore. The vibrations of sound shared only between us. I was starting to cry, stupid girl, playing music to her unrequited love.

"Ooh!" Mrs. Corrin squealed, but I didn't look up, throwing myself into the last few notes we had left.

When it was over, I lowered my head so I could secretly wipe my face, but I didn't think I fooled anyone. I looked up. The morning gathering had grown. More than half the steps were lined with kids, an audience surrounding Drew and me. It felt like they'd caught us necking.

"Come on then!" Mrs. Corrin said to the class. "Let's give them a *bravo*."

There was a forced attempt at applause. Honestly, it was too early for this kind of thing. "And bow! Always bow!" she demanded.

I got up, not intending to play along, but Drew took my hand in his, championing us in a theatrical bow.

The warmth of his skin, what it did to me. If only he knew.

The first bell rang. Anita stopped clapping and groaned in annoyance as she stomped behind Mrs. Corrin's desk to grab a pink backpack that must have been hers.

She didn't have music class with us? Huh, come to think of it, I didn't remember her there, but she seemed like the kind of girl who'd want her boyfriend escorting her, not the other way around. And then it came back to me. She was Anita *Corrin*, Mrs. Corrin's daughter.

I climbed to the top step, getting myself to the back of the room, next to the bongos. I made a point of not watching Drew and Anita's goodbyes, too jealous to exist in my own skin. I was so busy not noticing that I didn't know Drew sat next to me until I was breathing a heavenly cloud of Calvin Klein. He smiled a *hey* at me, making a cool little two-fingered wave.

I was aware I was being run by a billion hormones, but knowing *why* I melted when the boy with the chestnut hair smiled at me didn't mean I experienced it any less. I rubbed my palm, still feeling the place his hand had touched mine.

The rest of class was dedicated to watching painfully old computer graphics with horizontal lines in the image as we all got our "intro to music."

"The content is still valid!" Mrs. Corrin hollered over our complaints.

Drew yawned, horsing around with a paper, folding it into a frog. He pulled out a pencil, writing something on the frog's head. Then balanced his binder to make a launchpad, flicking the frog into my lap.

It landed upside down. I flipped it over, reading the note:

Why would you need intro to music? Are you going to switch classes?

I didn't have an answer, but even if I did, Mr. Corrin was already at our row, taking the frog from me with a nasty glare.

"My bad," Drew muttered when she turned her back. I smiled to show him I didn't care.

I wanted to feel happy.

But Drew was right.

On the way out of class, Mrs. Corrin cornered me.

"*Lora* then *lay* together, is it?" she asked, looking at her roll call sheet. "Well, Lora*lay*, I'm going to be removing you from this class."

"Why?" I asked, but I knew.

"You're clearly above the basics. Can't even keep your mind on what we're learning." She handed the frog back to me. I pocketed it. "But don't worry, I'll be moving you to my advanced classes." She said it like she was giving me a treat.

"I'd rather have this one," I said. "No pianist is above working on the basics."

"Darling," she cooed, patting my shoulders. "A student such as yourself shouldn't be left behind. The emotion you play with! Don't think I didn't see how moved you were by the music. Actual tears! At your age too! I can teach, but no one teaches that."

Great, I thought. *So everyone saw me?* I wanted to slap Death all over again.

I thanked her but left with my arms crossed. Drew wouldn't be in advanced classes until his senior year. Last time he helped me, maybe I could tutor him this time so we could—Drew was standing outside the classroom. He'd stayed? Waiting for me?

"Hey," he said. "That was awesome back there."

I opened my mouth, unsure how to answer. *I'm in love with you, please marry me, our daughter is going to be beautiful,* seemed like the wrong direction to take the conversation.

We were walking together, keeping pace, side by side.

"You look familiar."

My heart skipped. He remembered me!

"Kind of like my cousin Sara."

"Oh?"

Fantastic, not only did I remind him of someone he was related to, abolishing any chance he was contemplating kissing me, I

146

looked like that annoying girl who called herself a thespian and drank too much every Thanksgiving. That was a new, unpleasant little something to overthink.

"That song," he said. "It gets me too. The lyrics, they're all about drinking, you know. Well, my dad . . . " He sighed, letting his shoulders relax. "Everyone knows, so it's okay to say it, but he was an alcoholic. He's sobered up now and all, but I remember it pretty well. The way you play that song, all fast and happy?"

"Ragtime."

"Yeah! It feels—I don't know . . . "

"Hopeful?" I asked, but I already knew.

"Yeah! Like I can make it okay. All on my own, I mean. I wish I could play like that."

"You will," I said, probably too clairvoyant for my own good, but he took it as encouragement.

"Oh, I don't play piano."

"No, I know. You play guitar. I saw you at the talent show."

Drew frowned at me. "What talent . . . wait, the Halloween one? No way, that was a long time ago. How long have you lived around here?"

"Oh, I was just visiting then," I said. "But you're good."

"Thanks. I mean, I have to be good at everything if my Dad has anything to say about it."

There it was. *Oh, Drew.*

"What?" I asked, pretending I didn't know.

"My dad pushes everything: football, grades, community service. I'm a walking college application. You wouldn't believe it, but he even put up a sticker chart on the fridge for weightlifting,"

Oh, I believed it. But only because I'd seen that chart with my own eyes. Little gold stars and extra points for cardio.

"This music class? He'd never let me do it if he hadn't played back in the day. But there's nothing I can do that'll be good enough. He doesn't see what I do. He only sees what I could've done. He used to be funny, and everyone talks about how nice he is, but he's an ass at home." Drew looked me over like it surprised him I was there. "I don't know why I'm telling you this. Sorry. That freaking song—It's messing with me."

"No. It's okay. I get it," I said, but Drew was still worn down. "Your dad, he's a dry drunk."

"A what?" He laughed.

"It means he probably drank to deal with something else in his life, and now that he's not drinking, he's focusing on you. You're his . . . " I almost said vodka, but I stopped before I rattled off Mr. Neer's favorite drink. "Beer, or whatever."

We'd come to the door out, wind waiting for us. But Drew was still absorbing what I'd said. He leaned into the brick, eyes flicking through his thoughts.

"Whoa, you serious right now? That's a thing? Like he's getting into my life instead of . . . and I'm filling that void, or whatever?"

I nodded. I knew I'd hit him with an information arrow, but he needed to know, and I was holding back from telling him so much more.

"How do you know about that?"

"I read a lot of psychology books in my free time." Drew tilted his head at me, mouth hanging open. How was it that every expression on his face made me want to kiss him?

"So, he's not sober? Like what does that even mean?"

The bell rang.

"Sorry," I said. "That was way too much to dump on you."

"No, it's good. You're good."

I blushed.

"Seriously, we should play again sometime. I'll bring the guitar. Maybe you could tell me more about those psychology books you read."

Oh, the things I could tell you, Drew Neer.

"I'd like that," I said, smiling at my husband.

Chapter Fourteen

BLACK DAY COFFEE

I dressed warmer the next morning. My hair was right. It'd rained in the middle of the night and hadn't quit. Sweater, rain jacket, scarf, hair stuffed under a beanie. I'd decided my curls and I needed some time away from each other, reconsider our relationship.

Water absorbed into my clothes, pelting my backpack with a *ping, ping, ping* as I stood at the bus stop.

"Rain, rain, go away," I sang. But I shouldn't have. Piano skills didn't translate to vocal ones. That was Drew's thing.

Mr. Neer pulled up.

"Good Morning," he said like it was a warning.

"Morning," I said, my eyes sweeping over the bus to pick a drama-free seat. Sal hadn't ridden home yesterday, but she was here now, scooted next to the window, smiling at me. I did a double take, trying to figure out what that was about.

"Hey, Piano Girl!" Drew called, waving me to the back.

Sal's head turned faster than mine, and Mr. Neer made an unhappy little grunt. I shook my head just a little, unconsciously trying to warn Drew about the landmines he was missing. Sal's head shot back to me, her smile gone. *I don't even know how to untangle the things going on in your life, girl.*

"Pick a seat," Mr. Neer said. "Hurry up."

I took that as approval, even though I knew it wasn't.

"Hi," I said to Sal as I walked by, trying to keep things light. Drew and Julius were drinking their morning coffee, but this time it was in paper to-go cups from the local coffee stand, Black Day's Coffee. That meant they'd been forced on another morning run, Mr. Neer picking them up only when they made it to the stand. I tried to sit down, but Julius had his feet up, blocking the seat I was trying to take.

"This spot's taken," Julius said, stretching his legs to cover more area. Drew knocked them off, nearly making Julius hit the ground too. "Classy," Julius mumbled, taking a sip of his coffee like nothing happened. Was he always this big a jerk or was that the morning run talking?

Drew wiped away a bit of rubble left over by Julius's shoes and patted the seat for me to sit down.

The bus jolted. Mr. Neer finished waiting. I sat down fast, right between them. Julius made a loud grunt like I'd gut-punched him, even though I'd only bumped his elbow.

"This is Julius," Drew said. "He's a moron, so be ready for that."

"Takes one to know one." Julius sighed.

"And Julius, this is the girl I was telling you about."

That flattered me until I realized Drew didn't know my name. "Loralay."

Drew said the name back to himself, nodding, but Julius eyed me like I'd made it up on the spot. Funny boy, we'd soon be best friends. I guess first impressions really weren't worth much.

"Did you bring a psychology book with you?" Drew leaned on his knees, looking from his dad to me.

"No, but I was studying them again last night." That was true, but mostly because I was trying to understand Sal. "I was reading about social anxiety and—"

Sal got up out of her seat, coming toward us.

"Do not get up when the bus is moving!" Mr. Neer called, but she was already sitting down again, one seat in front of Drew.

"Hi guys!" she said. "What're we talking about?"

We all adjusted ourselves. Even Julius sat up, looking at Sal like she'd gone science fiction on us.

"Talking?" I said. "About . . . um . . . ?" The awkwardness was corporeal. Even Julius had nothing to say.

Drew, sweetheart of the ages, only went stiff for a second before recovering.

"Loralay was talking about psychology." He shrugged at me.

"Yeah. I like psychology." My brain was catching fire trying to think. I couldn't push Sal away. Her life depended on me. I couldn't talk about the kind of psychology Drew was interested in. That was too personal. "And piano. I love piano. Really," I added lamely.

"Oh yeah," Drew said, knocking my leg with a knuckle. "Wanna come to the music room at lunch? Julius, Anita, and I, we're all going to hang out there. We could play something together."

"That'd be fun!" Sal said as if he'd invited her.

"What are you doing?" Julius asked. He hadn't looked away from Sal.

"What?" Sal asked, shrinking back, hands slipping over her perfect hair bun, checking that it was in place. "Just thought I'd say hello."

Drew and I glared at Julius, watching him unravel the polite facade we'd created.

"Watch it, Julius." Drew sounded way too much like his dad, causing me to look up and see Mr. Neer's eyes on us all.

"I'd love to play together," I said, trying to bring things back down. We were almost at the school, only a few seconds left to salvage everything.

"Oh, yeah?" Julius's coffee spilled over his thumb. "Why don't we invite everyone? Who else wants a piece of your time?" He flicked the coffee off. Some of it hit my leg, a brown dot spreading across my jeans. He cursed, wiped off his hands on his own pants, then jumped up, storming off toward the bus door.

"Whoa, whoa, whoa!" Mr. Neer yelled and parked the bus. "What's with you kids today?"

Drew waited for his dad to stop, then hopped up, chasing after Julius. In his hustle, he'd forgotten his disposable cup. It sat next to me, tipped, empty.

Sal and I didn't move, the rest of the bus clearing around us.

"I'm sorry," Sal said. "And I'm sorry about earlier. You were nice, and I don't know, I just lost it." She pressed her lips tight, keeping her chin steady.

Sal was more than a red flag. She was a crimson plane skywriting in neon red vapor, *Warning*. She needed someone.

"Don't worry about it."

She scooted closer like she thought I was trying to get away.

I wished I could tell her it was okay. I was here now. She wouldn't be abandoned anymore.

She reached across me, picking up Drew's cup. It was sweet of her, taking care of his trash so Mr. Neer wouldn't get mad. "No. You're nice, and I'm so weird."

"Hey, I get it," I said. "You don't know me. I could be a jerk." *Like Julius.*

We both heard the words I didn't say.

"Julius is usually nice to me," She said.

I blinked. Maybe she just had a different scale than the rest of us.

"My dad," Sal added. "He says I should invite you to dinner."

And then I wondered if the anger was just Sal trying to save *me* all along.

Chapter Fifteen

THE CARD

I should've been glad. This was more than lucky. It was exactly what I needed. A chance to get inside their home, see what was going on, but all I could think about was sitting at a table, inches away from *him*.

"Is six thirty too late?" Mom asked Mr. Small as she balanced seven jars of jam none of us would eat. Dad hated it, Mom was dieting, and it tasted like blood to me. I'd already caught her secretly spooning the last jar down the sink, chunks of strawberries collecting in the drain, so she could sham a reason to buy more. "I'm just dying to meet your wife," she finished, burdening the entire stockpile into my hands and giggling when I nearly dropped the lot. "Careful, Loralay!"

I didn't know when the dinner had become a family gathering, but now there was no backing out.

"That'll work. Store closes at five. Vikki will enjoy company," Mr. Small said. He always answered that way. Sentences that were inches from natural but too formal to sit right.

Mom hummed to herself as they pulled the little wagon out of view. I knew there wasn't any putting it off anymore.

Sal's mom, Vikki, called my mom to confirm. Dates set, calendars marked. It was like we were in grade school again. I didn't think anyone ever went through such a rigid ritual for something as small as a dinner. Even after all that, Sal gave me a card at school.

"What's this?" I asked, shifting the thermos I was carrying to open the envelope. She'd sealed it with a horse sticker, hand-drawn flowers, grass around the hooves.

"You'll see." Sal waited, putting her hand on the bust of Franz Schubert, following the tradition I'd apparently started. Inside the envelope was a piece of cardstock stamped with a teddy bear tea party. A homemade invitation, like I was coming to her fifth birthday. Her handwriting was hard to read, tiny words in cursive.

You are invited to: Dinner.

Time: Tomorrow night.

Don't forget: A smile!

There wasn't any sun out, but Sal was beaming in its place. She got up close to me, bumping into my side.

"Like it?" she asked.

The bottom of the card had the letters *BFF*.

"I can tell you spent a lot of time on this. Thanks." I smiled, too wide, like the dentist told me to say *E*. It was enough to fool Sal.

"My mom let me use her stamps," she said as we walked to the music building. "I colored them in, see? It's gel pen. This one sparkles."

The more time I spent with her, the clearer it was we had little in common, but that wasn't anything new. Even before I'd become Princess Nevermore, I didn't have much in common with anyone.

"I don't take nature shots," Sal said.

"What?" I asked before I realized she was continuing an old conversation, sans the lead-in. Her lack of social skills was daunting.

"After high school, remember? Jeez, sometimes you're so slow."

I sighed. I had to remember she didn't have nice interactions to build on. This was how she thought people talked. But Sal's disparaging comments became more common as she got comfortable with me.

"Nope, I'm not slow," I said softly, then closed my mouth tight so I wouldn't add anything regrettable.

"Well, sometimes you are. Anyway, I take candid portraits."

I coughed, hiding my cringe. I knew all about her kind of pictures, but that was only because I'd lived before. And we were going to skip all that weird stuff this time.

"I can make my little brother smile for the camera. He likes getting his picture taken with me. I'd make a good photographer."

"You will," I said, vowing that her life would have an *after school*.

I held the music room door open for her, and we went inside. Sal's constant presence hadn't changed much about this part of my life. She parked herself in the back, watching us over her homework, taking pictures on her camera. I'd tried to include her more, but she resisted, seeking the safety of a wallflower.

"Salutations." Drew strummed a school guitar along with the word. Julius joined him by doing a lick on the pathetic school drum kit.

I put my thermos of soup on the floor, sitting next to Anita, who had taken up residence at the far side of the piano bench. This morning she was tapping a cowbell, the sound muffled by her hand. I joined in, playing chords for the impromptu welcome song that sounded suspiciously like something by Everclear.

"Is that, like, easy?" Anita asked as she murdered the rhythm. "Hello?" She waved a drumstick in my face. It took a second to connect that she was talking to me. I'd been drifting, looking at Drew. "That song," Anita prompted. "How did you know it? Like, is that basic stuff?"

"Uh . . . " I blushed at being caught. "Well?"

"Maybe for Loralay it is," Mrs. Corrin chortled, coming over to stand behind us. "But *she's* a prodigy!"

"No, I'm not."

Mrs. Corrin had my head between her palms, bangles jingling next to my ears as she shook my skull in what I assumed was affection.

"Oh, you! Fake modesty doesn't change that some people are born with it, and others can't manage "Hot Cross Buns" on a penny whistle."

Anita shot her mom a dirty look.

"No, no, Anita, honey." She let go of me, a few strands of my hair yanked out by one of her many rings. She grabbed Anita's head next.

Anita wasn't having it. She whacked her mom away.

"I wasn't talking about you! You're talented in other ways." She paused, thinking. "Your little chants, for example!"

"It's called Cheer, and it's a sport, Mom."

"There you go!" Mrs. Corrin nodded encouragingly at her daughter, managing the opposite. No one was talking. I tried to think of something to say, anything, but it was all too patronizing. I pressed my foot down on the damper pedal, softly playing "The Sound of Silence." Only Drew got my joke, looking up to smirk at me.

"Did your parents force you?" Anita asked, still glaring at Mrs. Corrin. "My mom tried to make me take flute once. I didn't like it. I memorized the whole *Titanic* song on piano, though. Can I play next?"

"I'll tie you down with my scarf before I listen to "My Heart Will Go On" one more time, Anita. We all have our place in this world. You, calling for team spirit."

Drew fingerpicked Nirvana and both of us snickered.

"Loralay's talent is *Music*," Mrs' Corrin continued, oblivious to our joke. "Music with a capital *M*! The personification of mastery. The perfection of—"

"Talent's worthless," I said. That made the room quiet. "You can be anything with practice." Mrs. Corrin cleared her throat, but I didn't care. lumping my efforts together as something inborn instead of work was demeaning. "I played for hours every night, and when I couldn't play, I did scales and arpeggios in my mind. Anything can be a piano, a table, the back of a chair." But none of that existed anymore. I had some sort of undead zombie talent, back from the grave.

"Dedication! It's inspiring!" Mrs. Corrin bellowed.

"I can do a double hook," Anita said, jetting her chin out. "It's not like that was easy."

"Right. Practice," I said, rubbing my temple. "That's how you do cheer stunts and how I got better." I started to suggest we should do just that, but Mrs. Corrin slapped my shoulder with her scarf tassels.

"There are some things you can't learn, like falling in love with the music."

My eyes flicked to Drew, wondering what things about love I could force. Anita almost caught my glace. I was a prodigy now, no matter what I thought of the label. And worse than that was the way I could see Anita shriveling as I stole her boyfriend's attention and now her mom. I thought this would feel special, but it was vomit in my mouth.

I started playing. Loud. Smashing out Drew's and my song, making sure there wouldn't be any more conversations.

Drew followed my lead, tossing the guitar strap over his shoulder and standing up. I rocked in time, comforting myself as Drew walked toward me. He was getting so much better, pushing himself in ways he never had in the Nevermore. He wasn't playing songs. He was playing inside songs, using them to express himself.

Julius joined in, a novice drummer, but Drew and I made the beat so clear even Anita couldn't play out of time. Our music was alive.

We were in love. Maybe not now, but Death told me time was just a cover to the endlessness. Seeing the truth of it was beautiful, filling me.

"You're so hot," Anita said to Drew when we'd finished. The most wrong thing to say about the music, about Drew's connection to the song.

"Not for my ears!" Mrs. Corrin moaned, grading papers at her desk.

Drew smiled and nodded. A polite nod, not the kind she was hoping for. Anita swallowed, fidgeting in her seat. And for the first time, I noticed that Julius was doing the same thing, only he was looking at Anita.

I tried to think who Julius dated in high school. That girl named Melanie had been around for a while, but never Anita. Maybe I could help with that.

I ran scenarios over in my head, trying to think if that would change too much, but it seemed to fit. It could get me back in Julius's good graces. And maybe I wouldn't feel so guilty about what I was doing to Anita.

But then I saw Sal with her gooey eyes, just as moved by Drew's song, watching my husband sweep his hair back. I couldn't fix everyone's crush.

The bell rang.

"Fates, but why?" Mrs. Corrin howled. "Alas, my love, you do me wrong! Ah well. I'll see you all soon."

I got up, gathering my bag and the thermos of soup I'd forgotten to scarf down.

"Hey, can I, like, talk with you?" Anita asked or announced, seeing that she'd grabbed my arm like we were besties. She'd jostled me until my bag dropped off my shoulder, slipping to my elbow. When had being the music geek gotten attention from Anita? But the answer was obvious. And popularity wasn't working in my favor.

"Yeah, sure." I shared a long look with Drew as she led the way out the hall. Sal came too, the girls swarming me like bees.

"You're so, like, pretty," said Anita.

Like Pretty? I had a feeling that *like* wasn't due to her routine overuse of the word. Anita whined, flicking one of my renegade curls.

"And, bitchy, but the good kind. You're totally, like, the new Miss Thing! It's so not fair."

It wasn't a compliment. It was a three-point threat checklist. She'd caught those glances at Drew, and now her arm was tightening around me with tentacle strength.

Sal trailed behind. I grabbed her shoulder, tucking her neatly under my arm. She made a mousy little squeak, but I yanked her in closer. There was no way she was leaving me to deal with Anita on my own. But Sal was glowing, just as flustered as I was for being accepted into the feminine fold, drinking it in like oxygen. I smiled back at her. Us misfits were rewriting history together.

"I wish I was like you," Anita cooed. She was too busy pulling out her lip balm again to even look at me. Was her voice genuinely this feral cat pitch all the time? "You could have any guy you wanted. Like, maybe a guy like Drew."

Sal went stiff under my arm.

Was I sweating?

"Not that you can have him," Anita added, unhooking her arm. The girl should've quit cheer for drama club. She already had dramatic pause down to a *T*. "Drew's my boyfriend. But you already knew that, *right?*" She stuffed her lip balm back in her jeans pocket. Her pants were so tight I could make out the shape of the tube pressing into her skin. "That's why I said you could have any guy *like* Drew. Get it?"

I get it, Miss Mafia. Leave him alone, or I'll swim with the fishes. Princess Nevermore found her nemesis. Anita's pushing tempted me to make Drew into a trophy, but I was above this. Little Anita was sixteen, almost half my mental age. *If only I could get these teenage emotions to play fair.*

"Right, like Julius or Stephen. They're cute," I said, desperate to talk about anyone that wasn't destined to marry me and maybe set a seed for Julius in her mind.

"Julius creeps me outTotal perv. And Stephen? Um, no thank you," Anita moaned. "Unless you like long-distance calls from juvie. He's so totally going to, like, end up in prison."

"He's a lot more than that," I said. "Stephen's an artist."

"Is that what you call tagging?" She bit her lip. "Guess we know who Loralay wants."

There was a splatter of giggles from Anita and Sal, but Sal's sounded nervous. "At least someone wants him, seeing that his mom didn't," Anita added.

I inwardly congratulated myself on never befriending Anita in the Nevermore.

"It's funny to you he was adopted?" I asked. "Like that makes you better than him?"

Anita dug her cherry lip balm out again. Was lip balm addiction a thing?

"Okay, okay, sorry," she snorted. "Whatever."

We were stopped in the hall, Anita layering her lips, Sal twitching under my arm from the prolonged contact.

"You don't want to do that," I said, keeping my voice as low as Death's. "Ripping him down to feel better about yourself. Believe me." I hugged Sal a little closer.

"I said I was sorry! Jeez! That's, like, so not even what I wanted to talk about. I was just trying to, like, help you. Yeah know, hook you up. I know all the football players." She had a pen out, writing on my arm. "I know Stephen too, if that's your flavor. Call me sometime, yeah? I'll, like, *She's All That* you, it'll be fun. Kay?"

I frowned, trying to understand the reference. I was too busy to watch movies this life, and pop culture wasn't part of my retained memories package. Anita was looking over my face, way too close.

"You're going to scream when you see how good your hair looks when I straighten it." She blew me a kiss and left, popping her hip like she was practicing a dance move.

"Have you watched that movie?" I asked Sal.

She shook her head.

I did a double take of the phone number, Anita's name above it, the letter I dotted with a bubbly heart. Then I laughed at the absurdity of it all. Anita and I, both trying to set each other up.

Sal didn't join me, and the sound died out.

164

On the bus ride home, Drew wasn't there. I'd seen him in the office on my way out, printing papers for Mrs. Corrin, waiting for football practice as an after-school TA until his Dad was back.

But Julius was on the bus, brooding. I didn't know what that was about. Whatever it was, Mr. Neer didn't look amused. I sat one seat ahead of Julius in case he'd talk with me. He didn't.

When Mr. Neer got to Sal and Drew's stop, Sal got off. Julius was right behind her.

"Not staying?" Mr. Neer asked.

"No," Julius said.

"No, sir," Mr. Neer corrected. Julius mumbled an echo. "When I told your mom you could stay over on football nights, I thought you'd be playing football, kid."

I could barely hear Julius's response, but no one else wanted to make a sound when Mr. Neer used that voice, so I could still make it out.

"What's the point. I don't want to play. I quit."

But that wasn't right. Julius always threatened it, but he never quit. He played all the way through, even when Drew was done. Drew and I'd gone to his games, cheering him on.

"Well, you know where the key is. We'll be home later."

Julius got off, walking up to the Neers' house.

And then there was Sal, standing on her porch. She was looking at Julius, so she missed me wave when we drove away.

And I wondered if she really believed I liked Stephen.

165

Chapter Sixteen

DINNER

At first, it was stomach aches. Getting physically sick by the idea of eating at Mr. Smalls' table. I started questioning everything. I'd never been to her house before. What if this dinner changed our timeline? But that was dumb. I needed it to change. I just wanted it to happen without having to get my hands dirty. There were some things we knew about Mr. Small, but there were also pieces missing. Was he a wife beater? Emotionally abusive? He had to be something, the kind of something that wouldn't be pretty to uncover.

So far, I'd had a nice distraction of a day. Anita had a cheer squad meeting, so there was less talking through our lunch music session. Drew ended up sitting next to me, sharing my bench. I had to stretch to reach the piano keys, but it reminded me of our wedding. Campsite venue by the bay. Sky and water dressed in gray to match the black and white of tux and lace. Everyone was still raw from the Smalls, so Drew and I rushed our wedding, looking for a reason to smile, a way to escape.

Other than poor Mrs. Esmer's attempt at Wagner's "Bridal Chorus," we played at our own reception. Drew hired a moving company to get a piano on the flat turf near the water. We slapped at mosquitoes, eyes stinging from bonfire smoke, but we turned those campgrounds into a twilight dance hall until Stephen drunkenly declared he wouldn't let us miss our first dance, taking over to conduct with a solo cup, leading everyone in an off-key version of "All Star." When he jumped on top of a folding chair to belt the chorus, Drew was laughing so hard, we tripped over a picnic table, falling into a sandbank. And then Drew kissed me, missing my mouth in the dark, lips landing on my ear. A delicious blunder that brought him to whisper, "Lifetime of this to come."

But he was wrong. We were cheated.

And just like that, our time together was cut off again, this time by a bell. Drew hardly said goodbye, rushing to class. I had such little time with him, and there I went, reminiscing instead of enjoying it.

Drew wasn't on the bus home either. There wasn't football practice, so he was probably on his way to Julius's house.

I held my bag on my lap, hugging it over my, again, hurting stomach. Sal was looking at me sideways like she was worried I'd make an excuse, but I kept quiet, too busy trying to keep my insides from imploding.

I gave Mr. Neer the note that allowed me to get off at first stop. I flattened it in my palms before handing it over because of all the times I'd rolled and unrolled that page, turning it into a twisted mess. He eyed the paper and nodded, throwing away my last chance to wriggle out.

Sal got off first. As I was about to follow, Mr. Neer had my shoulder.

"I've been watching you two for a while now, and I've meant to say, I'm glad you took our little talk about the Small girl to heart. Sometimes you can't tell with kids, who they're gonna be, what parts matter. It's nice that you listened to this old man's lecture."

I sighed, hating how wrong he was about me and how right he was about how much we all don't know about the people around us, settling somewhere in the nothing-to-say-back middle.

"Thanks," I tried, but it was too shallow to help.

"No problem, kiddo."

I got off, joining Sal as we walked up to her house.

It'd rained again earlier, the crisp air kind, a last goodbye to the sunshine. Sal's house was a low income, broken down single wide, haunted by living ghosts. *I don't want to be here, I don't want to be here, I don't want to*—but I kept moving one foot in front of the other.

When we passed the Neers' place, I didn't allow myself even a glance in its direction, worried Sal would notice my wishful yearning.

The Smalls' awning was still broken, but now the U-pick sign had been stored away until the next harvest, and the Mickey Mouse blanket curtains had been removed. We walked around the burn barrel in the front yard, and Sal opened the whiny screen door, discreetly tucking a busted bit of weathering strip back around the edging before going inside.

Heat and the smell of cooking strawberries hit us like a wall.

It was dark inside their living room. No fixture above head, only a couple of lamps around a lumpy tweed couch and a broken ceiling fan—wood-paneled walls stained by finger smudges and cobwebs. Thumbtack holes covered where the curtain rods should've been, and now that the blankets were removed, the window frame was naked. Dusty light streaming through like a missing tooth in the room's face.

Distress draped over me, realizing Dad would hate every second at the Smalls' house. This was too close to how our family used to live, like putting on dirty clothes after a shower. Dad craved monetary sanitation.

The room was empty except for a tiny figure squatting on the floor next to a TV that'd been propped up on a broken-backed chair. He turned to look at us, mouth hanging open in a television stupor. Heath Hennery Small, only about one and a half years old.

He frowned, sizing me up.

"Hi," I said, trying to reassure him. I had an overwhelming urge to grab him and run, never letting go.

"Sally, is that you?" a voice called from the back of the house. Vikki Small came in. Picture-perfect homemaker in a plain plaid dress and linen apron with a stirring spoon in the pocket.

In the Nevermore, when the news trucks came, and the documentary's started, it'd all been because of her. People die every day. Murder, even familicide, wasn't more than an odd blurb on the local news, but Vikki, she made it national with her hourglass waist and dimpled smile, blond hair dipping

169

around her shoulders. Picture-perfect victims made people care. Maybe if Sal had better skin, they'd have gotten even more publicity.

"Is it three thirty already? I completely lost track of time! It's so nice to meet you, Loralay!" She rubbed her hands on her apron before holding them out to me—callused, dainty fingers, patting my hand. "I need to start dinner! You girls play in your room. All right, Sally Sue? And can you bring Heath Hennery with you?" Her smile was electric. Blue eyes bright and wide next to apple blossom cheeks.

Sal hoisted Heath Hennery into her arms, and I held out mine, looking to hold him.

"Can I?" I said when Sal didn't hand him over.

"You sure? He doesn't like strangers," she said. Funny how that worked, seeing as I was safety and his own blood was the one to watch.

I shrugged, leaving my hands out to see if we could try. Sal handed him off. I supported his heavy little body on my hip, just like I had with Makenzie so long ago. Heath fussed, displeased with the unknown, but I bounced him up and down, distracting his senses.

"Looks like he likes me," I said, trying to hide my relief.

I followed Sal past the living room, through the kitchen arch where the two halves of the home had been connected. The L-shaped counter was an assembly line of jars at varying stages of recycling.

Sal's older sister Irene was at the far end, working off an old label, dunking a jar in bubbly sink water as steam rose around her.

"Irene, company's here," Vikki said. "This is Loralay, Sally Sue's friend from school. Loralay, that's Sally's sister, Irene Isabelle."

Irene Isabelle smiled a shy hello, sharing her mother's angelic shape and grace. I didn't remember Irene much, but I knew she graduated recently, living at home until the day she was killed. I smiled back, but as I adjusted to the room, the wallpaper caught my eye.

Every inch was covered in flowers. It couldn't have been real wallpaper though; no images repeated, and the colors were too vast—bunches of baby-blue hydrangeas, deep orange marigolds to pink tulips, veins of fuchsia on the petal's tips. Vikki noticed me looking.

"Oh, this." She seemed embarrassed. "My decorating project. Silly, isn't it? I've always been planning to redo this kitchen, even since the girls were little, but we've never had the funds. Anyway, we get seed magazines sent to the store all the time with glossy photos and, when the seasons change, I hate to see the old ones go to waste. So, I cut out my favorites. At first, it was just one or two. Liven the place up a bit, but I'm afraid it's gotten out of hand over the years."

I stepped closer. I'd never seen anything like it—a massive collage held in place by clear contact paper. Just the tenacity of cutting every bloom to make them fit seamlessly was overwhelming, like a mason selecting every stone. Vikki Small, battling a gritty life, making beauty in the hovel. It was a fact history had lost in the Nevermore.

Little Heath Hennery slapped his hand on an azalea. I'd forgotten I was holding him.

"It's beautiful," I said, even though that wasn't enough.

Vikki beamed at me.

171

"Aw! I'm so glad you like it! Now you girls run along and have some fun. Irene Isabelle and I'll finish this up. We have thirty pounds of strawberries defrosted and nowhere to put them till we're done." She exhaled, looking around. "After that, we'll get dinner going."

I realized this was Sal's normal. Washing jars, canning, cooking jam. No wonder the setup for our get-together had been so detailed. This dinner was more significant than all that; it was a gift of time they didn't have.

"I can help," I said. "I'd love to learn how it's done."

Vikki protested, but it didn't take long before I'd set Heath back down to watch television, and I sat at the kitchen table stirring a bowl of lumpy strawberries and bleached sugar. Sal was across from me, seeming more comfortable looking down; covering masking tape in small cursive dates.

"Hate to intrude on your fun," Vikki said, biting her lip as she watched us work. She didn't know sitting quietly was about as lively as we ever were.

By the time I'd heard parents arrive, we'd finished the jam, finished the vegetable soup, and helped make a loaf of strawberry bread. A car pulled up. I ran for the living room, ready to combat the negativity Dad would bring, but he wasn't there. It was Mr. Small, coming home from work, swooping to pick up his son, an owl over mouse.

I threw my arms out in Mr. Small's direction, body baring the way. "Oh, can I hold him?"

"Can't I hug my boy first?" he asked.

"Sure!" I chirped, arms still out as I waited. Mr. Small smiled, but it didn't reach his eyes. We both knew I was obnoxious, but I was determined to get that boy out of his arms.

172

"Teenage girls and babies," he chuckled, eyes tight. "Always want to hold 'em. Well, what do you think, Heath Hennery? You want this girl or your dad?"

I said a silent prayer that Heath wouldn't fuss as Mr. Small plopped him in my arms. Holding children was all about confidence. *Stay confident.* Heath pulled his head back, annoyed, but his face brushed my curls. He took hold, yanking on a clump. It hurt, but I'd smile through him pulling every strand out if it kept that boy away from Mr. Small.

Mr. Small seemed to sneer, but it disappeared too fast for me to be sure.

"Well, look at that. You've got some nice childbearing hips there," he said, like it was a compliment. It didn't seem like a normal thing to say. Maybe it was?

He patted his son's leg next to my thigh. I froze, feeling filthy at the idea of his eyes on my hips. He hadn't done it yet. He wasn't a murderer. Maybe I shouldn't have hated him. But how could I stop when I knew what he was capable of?

Vikki stood in the arch of the kitchen, watching.

"What's for dinner?" Mr. Small asked, walking past her. She watched her husband go, then came up to me, concerned.

"You all right, dear?" she asked. "He didn't mean any harm. You have a healthy frame, that's all. We're just so glad you're here."

Hearing her try to explain it only solidified the creepiness. Childbearing hips? A grown man saying that to a fifteen-year-old? Why defend him?

"Do you want me to take him?" Vikki held her hands out to her son.

"No, I've got him." I swiveled Heath Hennery out of reach. A knock came from the door. Vikki went to get it, and I tried to slow my breathing. I knew it was weird, keeping their son to myself, but the anger kept bubbling. This woman, explaining away her disturbing husband, wanting to hold the child she hadn't protected in the Nevermore.

When Vikki opened the door, Mom was alone on the step, Dad nowhere to be seen.

"Jay sends his regards," Mom said to Vikki. I was 79 percent sure the word *regards* wasn't in Dad's vocabulary.

We ate dinner without him. Mr. Small talked about the general store and its local history. Mom peppered Vikki with questions about the strawberry bread, *oohing* when she'd heard I helped. Mom's hands jittered, but she didn't excuse herself to smoke. It helped to draw attention away from my own tremors, but I couldn't figure out why she'd hide it. No one would miss the smell she wore like an overcoat of carnage.

I stayed busy studying their house, looking for anything that could be child endangering, an early reason to call the police. There just wasn't. The only oddity was Sal seeming more reserved, if that was even possible.

"That's enough yammering over bread, Vikki," Mr. Small said when dinner was over. Vikki eyed her lap, rubbing her wedding ring. "Adults to the living room. I would've enjoyed man talk after dinner, but you ladies will excuse me if I fall asleep while you chew the fat. Irene, clean up. Girls, make yourselves scarce."

We scattered. Sal, Heath, and I headed past a narrow hall into the room Sal shared with her sister. The Mickey Mouse blankets lay folded at the foot of each bed. There wasn't much: dressers, a few stuffed animals, and a closet, but like her mom, Sal had covered her walls with her happiness. Not flowers, but photographs.

"This one's mine," Sal said, pointing to the bed near the closet. I sat on Micky, looking out her window to the strawberry fields and a bit of Drew's backyard. If she stood by the edge of the sill, I bet she could see part of his house, maybe even his bedroom.

Heath reached for a stuffed turtle next to Sal's pillow.

"He can have that," Sal said, handing it to him. "Do you like Drew?" She spoke fast, like she'd broken a dam in her throat.

Say something. Now! "He's nice," I hedged. "Want to show me your pictures?" I pointed to the wall.

Sal stiffly held up her hand, putting them on display.

"No," I laughed. "Like tell me about them."

"This one's my brother eating pancakes. That one's . . . so, you don't like Drew?"

I coughed. "He doesn't like me like that."

Sal's shoulders relaxed. "I know."

You know? I thought. But I tried not to seem perturbed. *Cheeky little . . .*

She got up briefly and checked the hall to see if we were alone.

"What is it?" I asked, but she put her finger to her lips, quietly closing the door, going for the closet.

"I'll show you my real pictures," she said. And then I knew why she'd asked about Drew. She couldn't possibly be showing me, could she? We hardly knew one another. How could she think this is okay? But I was the closest thing she had to a friend. I just needed to teach her to confide in me, show her I was trustworthy,

175

and she'd tell me about the abuse one day. Then I could save her life.

She was back with a family-sized cereal box, masking tape over the pop-top—*Top Secret* written across the fold.

"This is the third one. There're more," she said.

Third one? What did that mean? Maybe I was wrong about what she was going to show me. But then she dumped them out on her bed, just like I'd been afraid of, only far worse than I'd imagined.

A hundred Drews in front of me. Drew taking out the trash, Drew getting off the bus, Drew playing guitar with me, and then one shot through the window with him sleeping in his bed.

Not one of them looking at the camera. Not one shot where she'd made herself known. These were the shots of a stalker. Candid.

"My pictures," she said.

Chapter Seventeen

NEVERMORE

I lay my head back in the water, the lowest it could go, warmth surrounding me as bubbles escaped my ears. Grandma must've been a looks-over-comfort sort of woman, seeing that she'd chosen an uncomfortably shallow tub that perfectly matched the pink counters, toilet, and sink.

"At least it'd be impossible to drown," I muttered, looking at my red knees. "Stop talking to yourself, Loralay. You sound insane." Chastising wouldn't help. I didn't want to stop. I was so lonely even my own voice comforted me.

That was what brought me to the bath in the first place: no one to talk to, seeking heat like a hug, rocking myself weightless as if someone held me. But even though I was turning darker than the Small family's jam, I couldn't lift the mental chill running over my shoulders.

My pictures, Sal's voice repeated again and again in my head. *There're more . . .*

I remembered the police taking Drew in for questioning in the Nevermore. He told me about the pictures then, but he never mentioned how many there were. I remembered the documentary that brought Oak Ridge its fame. The story of the murdered girl next door and her broken heart.

"Would you have dated her if you knew?" One reporter had asked Drew. But Mr. Neer had closed the door before Drew could answer. "Did you know he was hurting them?" the reporter called through the wood.

"Get off my property," Mr. Neer shouted back, his voice echoing as the documentary faded to black. And I'd never forgotten the words Drew had said when we'd taken our bikes far away from his house, all the way to the concrete pad so we could be alone together. "I didn't know," he'd said.

Maybe that wasn't much to most people, maybe a relief to some. He didn't know, wasn't involved, but to Drew, do-no-harm-Drew, he'd broken his core creed. We were guilty. Ignorance wasn't an excuse. It was the crime—missing details that mattered because we'd only cared about ourselves.

Sally Sue Small, unloved and unwanted. Things a child never should be. Her father, the man meant to protect her, brought his wife and kids into the woods, took their lives, then ended his own. Sal was stabbed nineteen times, more holes in her skin than years she'd lived. Cracked branches and blood smears showed she'd tried to get away. But no one came, and she died. All of them, the Smalls, gone on the same night. Blankets and cat litter covered the back compartment of their family van. The police had said they'd seen it before. Mr. Small had planned to dispose of their bodies, using litter to soak up the blood, blankets to cover his sins. Walk free, start his life over after he'd taken theirs. But when he'd gotten in the front seat of his car, he'd shot himself instead, leaving the whole thing for a few hikers to stumble on. It was over, but he couldn't accept what he'd done. Because death wasn't passive. It never was.

"He sends me messages," she'd said as I'd looked down at my husband's childish face surrounding me on Sal's bedspread. She pointed to a blurry picture of Drew pulling groceries out of the trunk of his mom's car. "Like this. Four bags, see? That's four words. It was a Friday, and that's the only day of the week with the letter I in it, so the first word is I."

"Sal—" I said, trying to ease her down, speaking her name so she'd remember who she was.

"That's right." She nodded, missing my intent. "One word was my name."

I wanted to blame her for the insanity of it all, but who could blame Sal for making up a story about that handsome boy who lived next door, the one with brown hair and pink lips that melted into olive skin? I'd done so much preparation, but I'd never studied this.

"But this one, that's in his bedroom, isn't it?"

"No." Sal lied. "You've never been in his bedroom, have you? How would you know?"

When Heath Hennery lost interest in the stuffed turtle, he reached for the pictures of Drew. Sal yanked the glossy images back, collecting them into her top-secret cereal box.

It had scared me. Not Mr. Small, not Sal, but the missing pieces inside her, so torn that she needed this world she'd made. So many pictures, so very many pictures.

I pulled myself out of the bathwater, trying not to think anymore, hair gathering around me like Lady Godiva. When had it grown so long? I pinched a damp lock, fanning it out as I checked for split ends, thinking about the days of little pigtails and jumbo bead hair ties. Time moved fast this life, speeding up the way it had when Makenzie was born. I'd thought I'd use my memories like stepping-stones, but instead, they'd been tied around my neck, dragging me down so I couldn't get air.

Maybe that's why Death called this life a burden.

One thing at a time, I thought.

I yanked the plug and got out, holding my breath as I dried off because my towel smelled like Dad's cologne.

Dad's toothbrush on the counter, Dad's socks next to the heater, Dad everywhere but always missing from home. He'd leave us again, I was sure. Not like he did in the Nevermore, this time slowly, like cancer.

Not only did I have to stop a murderer, fix Sal's weird obsession, but marriage patrol too? I slammed the lid on the hamper, resisting the urge to scream.

I needed the piano—my release.

I didn't care if Mom found out I could play. It didn't matter. As if she could ever connect the dots. Maybe it would even bring us together, give her something to be proud of.

I rushed through applying leave-in conditioner, wrapping my head in a towel even though I knew I'd hate myself in the morning for not maximizing my detangling now, but future me would just have to put up with it.

My parent's door was cracked open, Mom sitting on the bed, smoking hard for all the time she'd missed at the Smalls'. I came behind her as she dropped the last of her cigarette in an empty jar, once used for pickles, then for jam, now on her nightstand filled with dirty water—boated filters floating between us in the yellow liquid that was probably cleaner than her lungs. I was so busy looking at it, I didn't notice she was sitting there crying until I heard the telltale breath between her sobs.

"Mom?" I asked, shaking her shoulder. "Are you okay? Mom! What is it?"

She didn't respond, words sucked away by the convulsing. I sat next to her, but she didn't look up. I wrapped her arms around me. She leaned in, elbow slipping to dig into my lap.

"I'm sorry," she said. "It's just that they were all so happy."

"What are you talking about?" I asked, too worried about her to be soothing. "What's going on?"

She straightened, wiping her eyes on the back of her hands.

"That family, your friend." She coughed the words out, grabbing a throw blanket to cover her face. I peeled the blanket back enough that I could hear her. "She's so pretty, that Vikki. Those girls, so well behaved. Made me want to be respectable too—a lady."

"The Smalls?" I asked, in case she'd been at a different house for dinner than I was.

"Yeah." Mom sniffed, covering her face again as the sobs returned.

I guess she was right. If there was anything sinister about the Smalls, I would've noticed it, but they seemed as normal as everyone always said they did, except for the little things. The quietness, the family stress, and the "childbearing hips." In my mind, I was back to the day Grandma died, standing outside Rosie's lakeside cabin, looking at the man across the water as he fished. Strangers always looking so put together, as if their boulevard wasn't full of potholes.

"I always wanted us to be like that," Mom said. "I can't. I keep trying but it never works for me."

"Mom?" My mouth worked quicker than my mind. Some part of me put things together, the absences and dinner, this breakdown. What if he'd already . . . "Where's Dad?"

She kept her face hidden, voice a mummer from behind her hands. I pulled her fingers back.

"Downstairs."

"Are you sure?"

She frowned at me. "He's watching a poker tournament." Mom wiped her eyes. "It's a cable special he's been following. Runs until midnight. He wanted to stay and see how it ended. And don't you dare get him! I'm so embarrassing right now."

"He skipped dinner for that?"

She needed someone. I was too busy getting Sal to tell me about the abuse, convince Vikki that Mr. Small wasn't well, maybe get them all to the Lewis women's shelter. I couldn't trust Mom not to get tangled up with the Smalls. I needed to find her someone I knew would be safe.

I glanced at the player piano, mentally kicking myself for what I needed to say.

"Mom, I wanna learn piano," I said. Mom cocked her head. *Way to sound completely random, Loralay,* I thought, but I plowed on. "There's this elderly lady, Mrs. Esmer, and she gives lessons to kids. Could you sign me up? She'd come every Sunday. I think you'd like her."

"Okay?" she said, picking up the blanket to wipe her face some more. I couldn't play now, not even pretend I was a prodigy. Mrs. Esmer knew less about music than Julius. She mainly taught little kids, but she'd shown me the basics in the Nevermore. It wouldn't make sense for her to take me on as a student unless I was as poor a player as I'd once been. It made me angry that Mom wasn't grateful even though she didn't know what I'd sacrificed.

"I don't know," Mom added. "We'll have to see if we can afford it."

We were having financial problems too? How much damage had Dad done? I had to remember how she was: less self-reliant than a toddler. I didn't have time to watch her again.

"I can pay for lessons," I said. "I'll be getting my first job this summer anyway."

Mom nodded, too busy tapping at her cigarette pack to answer. She should've hugged me, talked about how I'd grown up, asked where I'd work. Instead, she was lighting up.

"Or maybe we could afford them if you quit smoking?"

"Loralay, stop." She sounded like Anita, childish and whiny. I half expected her to pop her hip and reapply lip gloss while she sucked tar.

"Did you know glass is in the filter? Shards hacking up your lungs." If I thought it'd help, I'd start tacking anti-smoking ads up in the house like boy band posters in a tween's bedroom. "Can't you quit for me?" *Can't you quit before Makenzie?*

"I can't right now. I'm too stressed out."

I readjusted myself, so we weren't as near to one another. I hated loving her more than she loved me back. "I guess you're going to need to know . . . " she said. "Your dad and I, we're going to marriage counseling."

"What?" I'd heard her, but the words didn't sink in, too unexpected to process.

"We've been going in the mornings when you were at school."

I couldn't picture Dad agreeing to that, let alone sitting in a counselor's office. Only I cared enough about Mom to put up with all that. I shook my head, taking it all in.

"Why?" I wondered what he was up to.

"You probably don't know, but things have always been hard between us." She paused there, and I kept my mouth closed tight, worried I'd say something sarcastic. "We wouldn't have been together if it wasn't for having you."

No, I thought. *You wouldn't have been.*

Chapter Eighteen

SUPERMAN

The year went by faster than I expected. Drew moved up to advanced music, and Stephen and I got classes together. I stayed close to Sal, supporting her, writing notes, trying to throttle her free of the fantasy world. But she got weirder when Drew broke up with Anita.

"Where're you going to work this summer?" I asked Stephen. It was the last day of school, and we were killing time in English, the old *To Kill A Mockingbird* movie playing in black and white. Stephen had the box of golden age superman comics I'd given him, using the panels as reference for his own sketch. He didn't look up from his drawing when he answered.

"Small's," he said. "And the Potbelly. I need some serious *cheese*." Even Stephen couldn't call money cheese without a smirk.

There were only three places in Oak Ridge that were a sure hire for teens. Bussing tables at the Potbelly Bowling Alley, bagger at the Small's General Store, and Oak Ridge's old folks' home, where Drew worked every summer between football camp and morning workouts. In the Nevermore, I'd spent my time off school at the Potbelly. I'd imagined I'd work with Drew this life, but dreaming was useless. I already knew where I needed to be because I knew about the catalyst to Mr. Small's inexcusable actions.

"Same," I said. "except for Potbelly. You too?" I asked, turning in my desk to look back at Julius.

"Serious?" Julius slumped on his desk. "You're both working at Small's with me? I should've known summer would suck."

"Nice." Stephen paused his shading of Superman's cape. "What's his problem?"

I didn't know. I'd gone over it so many times. Julius should've been my friend by now, but nothing I'd tried worked.

"What's my problem?" Julius asked, the hint of a laugh in his voice. "Don't you mean, 'Wassup with him, dawg?' Or are you finally gonna stop pretending you're black, Asian Boy? You're a Wang, Wong, Wanksta. Take off your bling before you talk to me."

Stephen looked down at his Superman necklace, then turned in his seat. "We got problems?"

"Excuse me?" the teacher called from the front of the room. "We're watching, not chatting."

I waited for her to look away.

"What's wrong with you, Julius?" I hissed. "Can't you stop being a jerk for like five seconds? You're not like this. You're a nice guy."

Stephen snorted.

"No, I'm serious," I said.

Julius leaned on his elbow, shaking his head at his desk. "I'm tired of being nice," he said. "Nobody dates the nice guy."

I closed my eyes, working hard to hold back a groan. It was so cliché, but worse, he meant it.

"Wait, you're the nice guy?" Stephen cracked, his laughter barreling through the room. "Are you for real?" he sputtered, dropping his pencil.

"What on earth is going on over there?" the teacher called.

Julius smashed his binder in his backpack, face turning three shades of red. "I'm going to the bathroom," he said over Stephen's laughter.

"Not with that attitude you're not. Sit back down, young ma—"

Julius kicked his desk, knocking it over. But Stephen couldn't take it. He fell out of his chair, doubling over on the floor.

"Julius!" the teacher yelled. "Get your stuff and go to the principal's office, now!"

Julius slammed his fist on a desk, storming out.

"Super nice guy." Stephen laughed all the harder.

Chapter Nineteen

THE DAYS WE WORKED

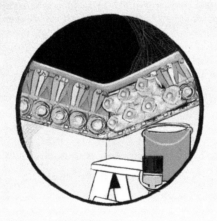

The Small's General Store was anything but general. It was a historic three-story brick building, a beloved hallmark, standing chunk of history, right down to a dedication plaque on the old iron doors and a black pit of debt.

To anyone on the outside, it might've seemed strange that such a large establishment left the Smalls in the red, but with the steady decline of the town, the cost of annual upkeep, and the expectations of every Oak Ridge native that their quaint brick buildings stayed pretty, a cash monster all on its own.

Logically, the high school should've been under the same expectations, yet when preservation was up to the taxpayers, just scraping by seemed acceptable.

Small's General Store didn't have that option. They survived off local shoppers choosing them instead of taking the short drive to Lewis town center. So, the Smalls paid to replace the single-pane Palladian windows, took out a loan to add a garden center out back, and paid double to gut the bathrooms without changing any of the cherished interior design. Anything to hold on to the look of success as they siphoned prophets from their U-pick fields and homemade jam into the bowels of a dying business.

The Nevermore consensus had been Mr. Small became too embarrassed by his failures to keep on living but unwilling to kill himself and leave his family to fend alone, deciding they were all better off dead.

"Good morning, Grayson girl," Mr. Small said when I walked in. He was behind the cash register, counting the till. He nodded the way he always did, like he'd tipped a hat. His glasses glinted in the light. "You work in the kitchen. Apron is back here."

The door shut behind me, setting off the bell above my head. Old wood floors smoothed by shoes, decorative plaster shaped into leaves and flowers. I passed the large handmade shelving units, each stuffed full of merchandise. Stephen was there, stocking shelves, still managing to look gangster with a baggy button-down shirt and apron. Or maybe it only appeared baggy. Western shirts tended to be loose on his frame.

I waved as he disappeared into the back of the store. I went behind the counter, hair on end like a trespasser, putting on the black employee apron that Mr. Small slid over to me. I kept my back to the wall in case he'd offer to help tie it. I never wanted his hands close to my hips again.

"Kitchen's through the door over there," Mr. Small said. "Vikki will be more than happy to have your help."

I nodded, looking over at Sal. She stood awkwardly still behind the photo lab next to the counter. There was a photo printer that looked like two industrial copy machines put together and a wobbly table for cracking open disposable cameras. Sal hardly acknowledged me. I'd done everything I could to show we were still friends. It was getting hard, keeping up both sides of our relationship. But who could blame her with Mr. Small there?

"I was so glad you put in an application!" Vikki said, putting down a package of bread so she could hand me a pair of gloves. The kitchen was out of the customers' view, making it a safe place to skimp. Plywood cupboards, dented metal sink. A clean hovel of a room that had once been grand.

The assembly line was similar to the Smalls' house, only now, instead of jam jars, there were plastic-wrapped sandwiches on Styrofoam trays, nestled with homemade cookies and a signature garnish of a single stick of mint gum. Irene Isabelle opened gum packs, dumping the individual pieces into a bowl, as Heath Hennery sat in a high chair, frowning at a slice of tomato— clearly not as enticing as the cookies stacked across from him.

"I hope we don't work you too hard!" Vikki said, leading me to the cookie tray to teach me to wrap. Heath put his hands out as if he wanted to be held. I didn't think it was as much to do with me as the big pile of cookies I was next to.

I stuffed two cookies in the bag.

"Only one, please, Loralay," Vikki said in a forced, upbeat tone. "We used to do two, but we're trying to cut costs."

I put the cookie back. Only two more years until she'd be murdered over those cutbacks not working, at least in the Nevermore.

"Oh, and one more thing." Her voice lowered and she leaned in. "It's probably not best you mention working in the kitchen if anyone asks. You don't have a food handler's license. But don't worry. There's too much work around here to get stuck on those things."

I tried to look unconcerned. I must've failed, judging by the looks Vikki and Irene were giving me.

"So," Vikki said with a little sigh. "Sally Sue told me you play piano!"

"Yeah." Fantastic. It only took one conversation between Vikki and my mother before I had no way to explain myself and no need of Mrs. Esmer. I tried to change the subject. "But I can't bake. I'd love to learn how you make these cookies. They look amazing."

"She says you're practically a professional."

Practically? I thought, wrapping the next cookie a little too tight. That had been my job. That had made me the definition of a professional.

"If only we had a piano here for you to play! I'd love to hear it! Wouldn't you, Irene?" Vikki nodded at her daughter. I nodded back, thankful that they didn't.

Julius came in wearing an apron that matched mine, pushing a hand truck of boxes in a corner.

"Julius," Vikki said. "Have you heard Loralay play piano?"

"Yeah?" he answered, leaning into the hand truck to scoot it out from the boxes. "So? It didn't change my life or anything."

Irene's head jerked, eyes darting back down to her work. Vikki mumbled something about taking Heath Hennery in back for a nap. I squeezed my lips together, trying not to smile. *Julius, you wonderful jerk*! He might have just saved me from them bringing it up again. But I could hear Sal in my mind. *Julius is usually nice to me*, she'd said.

How? Who was this kid anymore?

Vikki wasn't kidding when she talked about overworking me. Lunch making finished in a matter of minutes, and I was off to stock the shelves and haul fertilizer bags. Things slowed down when Vikki and Irene went home to finish canning jam. Mr. Small sent Stephen and me to the bathroom with two cans of expensive paint. The cost had something to do with being suitable for a historic home.

"Should we be doing this?" Stephen asked, brush in hand, looking up at the cornice molding. It looked like an ornate picture frame, all set with boxed ivy patterns displaying the empty ceiling. There was a patch of thickly carved plaster missing in one corner that Mr. Small had knocked out all the rest of the way, filling the hole with a cardboard egg carton cut to size, the closest thing he could find to match. Oddly enough, it matched in thickness, but the gray-brown paper gave it away. "I don't think we're qualified."

"No, you're not," Mr. Small said, bringing in a stepping stool. "But neither of you are old enough to sell alcohol. You can't run the till, and this needs doing before tomorrow. There's a potential buyer . . . " He paused, looking at the wall as if he questioned his choice just as much as Stephen.

I'd forgotten how many times they'd tried to sell in the Nevermore. But the people of Oak Ridge weren't stupid. No one wanted to take the dead weight on.

"I'll be in to fix whatever damage you two do." Mr. Small added before leaving us. "Don't let it drip. Make thin layers."

Stephen looked at me, raising his dark eyebrows. I raised mine back, afraid to make the first move.

"We should start high," he said. "That way, if it drips, we can catch it. Plus, that fugly egg carton gonna look a whole lot better painted."

"What made that hole?" I asked.

"Don't know. Mr. Small's wiggin' out that it was me or Julius and that one of us is too afraid to admit it. He's pulled me out four times now, trying to get me to confess."

"That's lame," I said. "He's hounding you to get a false confession?"

"I'll deal. But props," Stephen said, already uncapping the paint can, looking confident. Where I knew piano, Stephen knew paint.

"Thanks? What for?" I asked.

"For believin' I didn't do it."

I didn't know what to say to that. He didn't know I'd known him far longer than just this year. He'd done graffiti, but never as a vandal in the strictest sense of the word. I thought about that, wondering if I should tell him to give up tagging because I knew he'd move on to bigger things.

"I *had* a plan." Stephen was already standing on the stepping stool, carefully dabbing his brush to fill in the egg carton. "Make a mold of the junk carved over there, then fill the mold with plaster. We could make it look tight like the rest. You know what Mr. Small said to that? Not interested. Sayin' it was bad enough he had to pay for special paint. Yada yada."

"This place isn't worth your time for something like that." I stretched as high as I could to paint the other wall. "You should only spend your time on projects where you're wanted. You're an artist."

"Aiight, there she is!" Stephen laughed as he leaned over to catch a drip I'd made. "You huffin' paint fumes? You sound like my mama."

"Hey!" I dropped a glob of paint on my shoe that I hoped only I noticed. "Wait, I do?"

"Yeah, did she?" Julius asked in a mocking tone, coming in and sitting on the closed toilet seat. "I'm just dying to know."

Stephen turned, waving him out the door. "Get off that thing, man. Don't you have some shelves to stock?"

"No way," Julius said. "Mr. Small wanted me to check if you ladies are making any drips. Like that one." He pointed to my left. "I told him you'd be making out by now."

I grit my teeth. "I bet that sounded way funnier in your head," I said. "But now that you've heard it out loud with the rest of us, let's learn from our mistakes, okay?"

"*Ooh*," Stephen said. "Now she's your mom!"

Mr. Small came in. The laughter died. Julius stood up.

"Looks like you already took your break. I won't have Sally Sue cover for you then. You can sort those bottle returns out back."

"But those bags are old! I saw maggots in there!" Julius said.

"Better double glove."

I didn't see Julius again until the end of the night when we were heading home. Mr. Small had us stay after, deep cleaning for the buyer that would come to nothing. Stephen stayed behind, mopping up after us, and I went out back to the dusty parking lot. It was humbling there—the green metal dumpster and garden center out of place next to the base of the mountains. It seemed too sacred for the back end of a general store, the way the ground shot up, stretching out high above us, making Small's General Store insignificant in the grand scheme. It wasn't, though. The lives in this dying town were so much more. They were the people who pasted flowers on walls and made brick buildings into livelihoods. Until Death took it all, anyway.

Drew's bike leaned next to the garden center. I spotted Drew nearby, body sprawled across a patch of grass, holding his hand to his forehead to ward off what was left of the low summer sun.

I checked over my shoulder to make sure Sal wasn't around, then made a desperate attempt to fix myself up, smoothing my hair without a mirror.

Drew waved. I thought it was meant for me.

"I had to sort seven bags," Julius yelled, coming out from behind me, arms in the air like a gladiator.

I followed him, feeling awkward for going the same way even though there was nowhere else to go. Drew sat up when he saw us coming.

"Loralay! Hey," Drew said. "I was hoping you'd be working at the nursing home. They would've loved you playing for them. Dodged a bullet there. They only want Johnny Cash songs, nonstop." He stretched his fingers. "I think my hands are going to fall off."

I started to answer, but Julius swayed as he walked forward, moseying in to stand in front of me.

"I'm not talking about normal trash bags." Julius held his arms wide, blocking me just a little more. "These bags are like three or four feet tall. And way too many people in this town use cans for spitting chew. There's no way you had a worse day than me."

195

"I don't know," Drew said. "An entire day singing about cocaine and spousal abuse to senior citizens? But rap music, now that's immoral trash."

"You know it," Julius said, stepping out a little wider. I could only see a sliver of Drew now, completely cut from the conversation.

I didn't want to leave, but the last thing I needed to do was gawk at the cute boy, like Sal, watching them from her porch. I walked away. Drew was too busy arguing over who's day was hardest to notice me going. I was almost out of earshot when Drew got up and hollered my name.

"Hey, Loralay, we're heading the same way, right? Want to come with us?"

Yes, a thousand times yes.

Julius grabbed his bike, kicking the stand harder than he needed to, bending the rod. Drew pretended not to notice, but I saw him wince.

"Hi," Sal said from the doorway, waving at Drew.

Great, now I was one of two gawkers. "Thanks," I said to Drew. "But I can't. I don't have a bike."

I waited for an answer, but they seemed to have lost interest in me.

Julius tossed his bike down, back tire spinning in abandon as he angrily announced that he'd forgotten something inside.

Sal leaped back fast like he burned her. Stephen was in the way, baring Julius with his mop.

"Hold up there," Stephen said. "I just finished mopping this dump, and you over here lookin' like a tweaker took a bath in beer. No way you're going back in."

"What, you're a bouncer now?" Julius asked, coming at Stephen with his arms out. He looked like he was preparing for the worlds angriest hug. "I can go in. I work here!"

"Yeah, sure, come in," Stephen said. "Just strip down naked first. I'll hose you down."

I gave up watching. Julius wasn't the kid I remembered. Was I nostalgic, or had I done the unthinkable? When I switched his timeline, did I cause the change?

I walked down our cracked country boulevard, headed toward home. There wasn't much to look at. The sidewalk ahead was sprinkled with a few houses and closed businesses, all of it slanting ominously toward a ditch, turning orange.

Orange?

I stopped, glaring at the siding of the post office, waiting for Death to appear, but he didn't. It was only the sunset. I pulled my backpack tighter, wanting something to cover me.

I could hear tires speeding over asphalt.

"Hey." Drew slowed to a stop beside me. "I remembered you. At the talent show? It hit me last week. You're the girl that told me my name's a sentence."

"Yeah, that's me!" My stress shriveled. Not just because he cared, but because being close to Drew reminded me how important it all was.

"How'd you get so good at piano? You said you didn't know how to play back then, but now you're amazing in what, six years?"

"That's funny. You remember that?"

"Sure. You were all interested in my dad's guitar, but you wanted to play piano. Like this girl is crowding me when there's a piano right next to us she could've been checking out."

I replayed the moments in my mind. I didn't remember the piano.

"So, who'd you kill to get your superpowers?"

I had to lie, didn't I? but I didn't want to, not to Drew. "Do you know the feeling when you're driving home?" I asked, watching the road. "It's like a few blocks before you get there, and you feel it."

Drew laughed. "Okay, did you *not* hear the question I asked? Or are you changing the subject on purpose?"

"Stay with me," I said. "Even if your eyes are closed, you know where you're going because you've been there before. Like a dream."

"Sounds more like a movie."

"Yeah. I guess it belongs in one." I felt stupid. There wasn't a reason for him to believe me.

"No," Drew said. "Like a foreign film."

"What?"

"You know when you're watching a movie in a different language? Sometimes you read the subtitles too fast, and you know what's coming even though the actors aren't there yet."

"Dreaming in subtitles," I said.

"Deep."

"You're the one that came up with it."

"We came up with it," Drew corrected me. "We're good together."

I didn't dare breathe, wanting him to say it again, not trusting I'd heard right. We walked under the old bridge together, slats of light hatching across his face.

"I've never sounded better than when I'm playing music with you," Drew said. "It's like our brains are on the same wavelength." He pushed his bike along on his tiptoes, kicking a twig out of his way. "Or maybe you just play so good you make me sound better."

"No, it's us."

He didn't seem to notice my answer, busy looking back at the Small's General Store. Julius stood next to the dumpster, hands waving around like he was talking to someone. At first, I thought he was still arguing with Stephen, but as if in answer, Stephen passed us on the road, his mom driving him home.

"He doesn't look happy," I said.

"Julius? Naw, he's mad at me."

"Why?"

"Lately? He wanted me to work at Small's with him this summer, but my mom, she's a tax manager." It was an unwritten standard that Oak Ridge businesses paid teens under the table. The store was no exception, but the nursing home kept things on the up-and-up. "Don't worry. She's not gonna attack our neighbors, but she'd open a can on me if I worked there." Drew frowned. "You've got something in your hair."

"Where?" I felt around the static-stuffed mass on my head.

"Here," Drew said, tipping on one foot so he could pull a white glob out from my hair.

A car passed. Sal in the back seat of her family van, watching us. A single finger pressed against her window. Why did it have to be this hard? I couldn't avoid Drew. We had a life together. But as they pulled away, I knew I was a traitor. We didn't even have Julius with us to make things look natural.

"I think I got some hair with it, sorry." Drew held up a gummy chunk. He tossed it in the bushes beside us. "If you think about it, usually, you only volunteer at places like that, so it's amazing they pay at all. I just bring them dinner, play some songs, listen to them talk, and I get a better interview portfolio."

I could hear it. It wasn't a tone or a set of words. It was the emptiness in what he said. These were Mr. Neer's talking points, not his.

But I had to support it. "That's good. You're going to be so much happier if you don't quit."

"Who said anything about quitting?" Julius pulled up beside us, tires squealing, huffing air from how hard he'd pushed to catch up.

"What happened back there?" Drew asked.

"Nothing," Julius answered. "Now come on. Hurry up, or your dad's going to be mad you took so long, and he won't let us hang out after work anymore."

And then I connected the dots. Nevermore Julius and I were closer because we'd been an alliance. Both of us fighting to free Drew from his dad. Now that I defected, our friendship was a casualty.

"Yeah. Hey, Loralay, wanna come to my house sometime? Keep up the music practice? We don't have a piano, but Dad has an old keyboard."

"Hurry!" Julius called, pedaling harder like he planned to drag Drew with him.

Drew kicked off, turning his head to say one more thing as he picked up speed. "It's just that when we play together, everything makes sense to me."

"Yeah, let's do that." I called the words so he could hear me as he grew smaller in the distance.

Drew turned and smiled one more time before leaving me behind on my broken boulevard.

I'd agreed, even though I didn't know how that would work with him living next to Sal.

I had to do more than save her. I had to help her find a cure because Sal's obsession couldn't stand in the way of family.

Chapter Twenty

PIANO AND PAINT

Mrs. Esmer pulled a spiral-bound booklet out of her bag and positioned it on the family piano. I remembered this book, *Monty's Music Manual,* Mrs. Esmer's doctrine and Nevermore Loralay's torment.

In those days, I'd thought I was big stuff, playing songs I'd memorized to prove myself, but she'd patted my head and told me I needed the basics. This time I could've been the one teaching those basics to her.

She opened the booklet up to a cartoon of a parrot, oversized speech bubbles explaining what we'd be learning. I sucked on my cheek instead of saying anything.

"Scoot in then, dear," Mrs. Esmer said.

I *was* scooted. That wasn't the problem. The piano itself was what she was noticing—the entire thing was crookedly pressed into the wall because of Dad. As soon as he'd heard that some old lady would be coming into his bedroom to use the piano, he was off the couch, rolling up his sleeves and yanking it out.

"But Jay!" Mom had said, quickly clearing the way as he dragged the piano through. "The shelves in here were built around that pianola! It's meant to stay together!"

He was too busy huffing to answer as he got it next to the bay windows. I complained about the humidity, but he didn't budge until I explained that it would lower its value, leaving out the fact that our piano wasn't worth much in the first place. He moved it to the other side with repetitive grunts like an angry train, pushing it next to the fireplace. It didn't fit—the hearth got in the way—but he left it there. I tried to tell him the draft from the fireplace might be an issue, but he'd already gone back to the couch, nursing a beer, peeved with life until his poker tournament came back on.

I straightened the bench anyway. Mrs. Esmer sighed pointedly, seeing it hadn't made any difference, then she pulled out a sharpie pen from the same bag, taking each of my hands in turn, holding them between raisin soft fingers and drawing on my knuckles, like a thug's tattoo. Only instead of *love, hate,* or any other four-letter word, she wrote numbers, one through ten.

Great, I thought. I was hoping she'd check what I already knew, so we'd skip this bit, at least. I held my marked hands in my lap, ink bleeding into the cracks of my skin as she sat next to me to play the first lesson out in example.

When she moved over for me to play, I set my hands in position, using perfect form to hurry up the lesson, but she seemed to think it was her duty to prop them even higher.

"That's good." Her voice warbled. "Like you're holding a ball."

You mean a marble? I thought. I looked at the odd arch she'd created. I wasn't here to play well, I reminded myself, but I had too much pride to screw up "Hot Cross Buns."

The phone rang. I could hear my mother answering it in the kitchen. She should've been sitting with us like she had in the Nevermore. I glared at the ivory.

Hot cross buns. One a penny, two a penny . . .

I was holding myself back from busting out some "Flight of the Bumblebee" or freestyle Jazz, anything but this.

"Good enough," Mrs. Esmer said.

Good enough? I thought. Was she trying to get me prison time for assaulting an old woman with sheet music?

"You're a hothead, aren't cha? I can tell. Well, cool your jets. We'll make progress soon. Let's see what our friend Monty Feather has to say about finding middle C."

I had no idea it was going to be this hard, and Mom wasn't even trying to connect with the playmate I'd brought her.

"Loralay!" Mom called, coming in from the kitchen. "Sorry for interrupting, Mrs. Esmer."

"You're fine, dear," Mrs. Esmer said. "It'll take lots of time for this one to learn. We're in no hurry."

I looked at Mrs. Esmer, long and hard, thinking about how many times she'd screwed up playing at my wedding.

"That was Vikki Small on the phone. She wants you to come down to the store. She says it's urgent."

"But it's Sunday," Mrs. Esmer said. "Small's isn't open on Sundays."

It was fine by me. I'd break in—anything to make this stop. "Can you drive me, Mom?" I was already putting on my coat. "Sorry, Mrs. Esmer, next week, then?"

Mrs. Esmer patted *Monty's Music Manual*. She told me she'd leave it for me to practice if I promised to take care of her copy. I swore no harm would come to it, even though I was mentally taking Mom's lighter to have another book-burning session.

The public transportation bus wasn't back yet, and Mrs. Esmer didn't drive, so we had to give her a lift. Before she got in, Mom rushed to screw a lid on her dirty water jar, hiding the cigarette butts under the center console. Mrs. Esmer waved her hands.

"Tish tosh, don't worry about all that. I've seen it all before. My husband used to be a smoker."

Used to, I thought, tempted to ask how he died in case it was lung cancer. I shook my head instead, wondering how addled I was, berating a widow. She was a nice lady, a very nice, lousy piano-playing, tone-deaf, dreadful tempo-keeping lady that I appreciated very, very much. I was hopeless.

The car was quiet as we took the long turn of the cul-de-sac. So quiet I could hear the cigarette jar sloshing when we passed the red-roofed house with the for-sale sign.

"Mrs. Esmer works at the library," I prompted, but that didn't get much out of Mom. "And she crochets like you do. You both should get together and do that. Maybe you should pull out your yarn next week when I'm playing."

"Maybe," Mrs. Esmer said. "But we need to get you a good foundation first. You aren't going to learn as fast as some, starting up at your age. The piano takes hard work. Well, it does for most. Mrs. Corrin was in the library the other day, and she told me she has a real prodigy in her class."

"Oh," Mom said. "Wouldn't that be something!"

I slumped back in my seat, watching the road as they talked about me, without knowing it was me, until we dropped Mrs. Esmer off at her cottage house, little windmills in the front lawn.

"Come in for coffee and pie?" Mrs. Esmer asked. She slapped her forehead. "Oh, that's right, you've got to go."

As she shut the door, we waved and drove away.

"Why does Vikki want me at the store?"

"Can you imagine? Being a prodigy," Mom said, too glassy-eyed to listen.

I tapped my fingers on the armrest, making a mental estimate of how many times I'd be playing Monty's nursery rhymes before they'd buy I'd magically progressed. Probably not before someone put a name to our small-town prodigy. *Why no, Mrs. Esmer, the prodigy couldn't possibly be me, you're going senile. Can we practice Twinkle-Twinkle again? Pretty please?*

And then, I saw it.

"What on earth!" Mom said. The old bridge had been graffitied, a huge Superman symbol with yellow circles, breaking off the image in bubble art. "Superman? How did they get up there?"

It might as well have said *Stephen* across it. That settled it. I was screwing things up. Stephen had not done that last time. I was sure of it.

"Well," Mom said. "At least it's better than all those funny words people usually write. It was kind of pretty."

Yeah, that'll really impress the police.

Mom pulled our van over, about a block away from the store, in a shady spot where she could secretly smoke. I squinted at the Small's parking lot. A police car? No, it couldn't be.

And then I realized that police car was parked outside Small's General Store.

I unbuckled before Mom finished parking, flying out the door.

"Your shoe's untied." Her cigarette flipped around her mouth as she spoke.

I looked down, but I didn't see my foot, mind running through panicked flashes, images crystalizing in my brain.

All I could see were bodies.

No, come on, I reassured myself. It had to just be about Stephen. We were safe. Sal was safe. My brain slowed like a carnival ride on the decline until the only thing in front of me was my dirty shoelace coiled in the dirt.

PTSD for things that never happened. I was a mess.

"I'll be out here, taking a quick smoke." Mom missed my freak-out because she'd been putting her dirty jar back in its place.

"Why am I even here?" My voice was shaking. "There's a police car."

She leaned into the steering wheel, squinting so she could see.

207

"Oh, honey, I'm sure it's nothing. Cops shop too, you know."

"Small's is closed, Mom. What did Vikki say?"

Mom held up her hand, so she could finish inhaling. "Loralay—" my name came out in smoke. "I don't know what it's about. I'm sure it's nothing serious, but if you're so worried, I'll finish my cigarette and come in with you."

"Never mind," I said, trudging up to the store. "Cops shop too," I muttered to myself.

Whatever was going on, I didn't remember it, so it didn't involve me. Maybe they were here because someone shoplifted a candy bar or because of Stephen's graffiti.

I opened the door sharply, trying to hurry to the back of the store where I assumed everyone would be, only to accidentally clip the officer in the arm. He gave me a stern look.

"…painted a pentagram, right out back," he said. It took me a moment to realize he'd been in the middle of a sentence before I'd come barreling in. The officer pulled out a notebook. "Used the specialty paint purchased for the bathroom, and if I gather correctly, you were one of the employees in possession of that paint?" He'd turned to me now, leaning into the photo counter. Sal shrunk back out of his way, looking lumpy in an oversized sweater.

They were all there. Sal, Vikki, Irene holding Heath Hennery, Julius, and Mr. Small. All of them watching me.

"Like a star?" I asked stupidly.

"More or less," the officer said. "Would you know anything about that?"

"Sabotaged my chances of selling this place!" Mr. Small cut in.

208

"No, I don't," I said, and I meant it. Oak Ridge wasn't the town for that kind of thing.

"Why are we wasting time?" Mr. Small's mouth competed for the Indy 500. "Sally Sue, get out there and bring in the paint cans before they're ruined." Sal went out back at a run, Julius following close behind. "Now you, officer, you should be talking to the Rays. We both know it was that disrespectful boy they adopted. I'm not blaming them. They got him when he was seven, already set in his ways."

I was wrong. Everyone wasn't here. Stephen was missing.

"Always vandalizing. You see that graffiti on the bridge? He defaced it, just like everything else in this town!" Mr. Small leaned in, the wisps of hair on his balding head trembling with every shaky breath.

"Honey," Vikki whispered. She sounded like my mom, but my mom would've touched Dad, trying to hold him together. Vikki stayed back, out of arm's reach. "Heath Hennery's falling asleep. Maybe I should take him home?"

"No one's going anywhere until we get this fixed, Vikki!" Her name popped out of his mouth like the veins that were white on his red neck. "First, he busts the bathroom molding, now this. I need compensated! I need a lawyer!

Mr. Small's intensity slowed down, body running on idle.

"Well, Miss Grayson." The officer folded his arms. He was like one of the wooden bears in Rosie's house, only he wasn't smiling. "Would you happen to have seen—"

"It doesn't matter what she saw," Mr. Small cut in again. "I know who it was."

"I called her," Vikki said.

"I don't care! I didn't ask! I want the Ray boy held account—"

"The Rays said they're on the way," the officer said. "Until then, let's . . . hey, Vikki? How about those lunches you make, with the gum on top? Always loved those."

"Of course! We don't keep them over weekends, but I'll make you a fresh one."

"Very kind." The officer followed her toward the kitchen. "But it's not for me. It's for your husband. Maybe we can calm things down."

"I don't want a sandwich!"

They went into the kitchen, leaving Irene and me alone. Heath Hennery continued to sleep through the sound of Mr. Small yelling.

"Does he act like this a lot?" I asked Irene.

"He takes care of us," she said.

I didn't remember hearing her voice before. It was quiet, like Death.

"But no, he's not a happy man."

"Does he hurt you?" I couldn't help myself.

"No," she said, like it was a normal question, then busied herself adjusting Heath Hennery on her shoulder. I started to ask more, but she hurried into the kitchen.

I went out back, wanting to warn Stephen before he walked in.

There was the pentagram streaked across the brick. It was ugly. Not just the vandalism, but the method, globby lines dripping thick. One of the leftover paint cans was knocked over—a puddle of white, still wet, collecting dirt and a few unfortunate flies. If Stephen made a pentagram, which wasn't his style, it would've been with water-like fluidity.

"I don't know," Sal said from somewhere behind me.

I almost answered, but another voice spoke.

"It's like I told you, but you never listen."

I knew that voice. They were behind the dumpster, Sal and Julius, whispering.

"You promised," Sal said.

"No," Julius hissed. "I'm not giving you one more picture of him, not after what you've done."

"You told me to watch the signs," Sal said. "Drew told me I could talk to him. See? Sunset, day before yesterday, he paused when he was undoing his bike lock. Sunset means he's happy with me. The lock is our secretive love, and he undid the lock." There was a swishing sound, picture after picture passing by. "Here it is. Look. He's telling me we can be together soon. We're going to run away, and—"

"You brought them with you? Do you have any idea what other people would think if they saw those? I'm the only one who understands you."

I didn't dare move. Trying not to breathe, I exhaled so slowly like I was suffocating. Julius's voice was contaminated, moist, like a public bathroom.

"I know I acted wrong on the bus, but that was ages ago. And in the music room, Loralay kept asking me to sit close, and I didn't. But yesterday, he said I could!"

"I've got a bigger message," Julius said. "He's mad at you. You're only allowed to talk to Drew through me. The broken molding, the pentagram, your Dad yelling. It's your fault."

Sal made a desperate little squeak like when we'd walked arm and arm with Anita, only this time I was sure he scared her.

"Drew's mad at me again? I thought when he and Anita broke up—"

"Yeah, but you failed him. And now you're trying to get me to help you with nothing in return."

I was nauseated. Julius knew. He knew about the pictures, he knew about her stalking Drew, the obsession, and he was playing along, feeding it back to her in spoonsful of vomit. Why?

"It's . . . I don't like doing that stuff with you."

"Hey, it's not my fault. I'm just trying to help. You need to make it worth my while."

"Kissing, again?"

"More than that this time."

I couldn't take it.

"Julius!" I yelled, kicking the dumpster.

His head popped up like a prairie dog. He'd gone so pale he was two shades away from clear.

I couldn't speak, anger so hot it burned up the words trying to come out.

"Hey, Loralay," he nodded like he could weasel his way out.

"You!" the word escaped the fire of my mouth, still searing as it slammed into him.

He twitched like an insect, looking for a way out. *Calm down, Loralay*, I told myself. *He's a kid.* But he was old enough to know what he was doing.

"Come here," I said.

"What?" Julius asked. "Make me."

"It's in your interest," I said between deep breaths. "Not to make a scene. Seeing that a police officer is right inside."

He came around the dumpster, a little saunter in his step, making a point of standing his full height next to me. It only made me madder.

I grabbed his collar.

"What're you doing!" Julius growled, ducking under my arm, but he only managed to yank me with him.

I wouldn't be letting go.

"Your mom would be so disappointed," I said. He was starting to go blurry, so I scrunched my nose, trying to stop the tears before their ambush.

"What do you know about my mom?"

"Everything!" I said, shaking his shirt. He tried to dip again, but I'd rip a hole through it before he got it off. He'd done it in the Nevermore; I was sure of it. Only Mr. Small's slaughter hid it all. A messed-up girl dying before she got help. My Julius, the Nevermore Julius—did he feel guilty then? Did he let it eat away at him when the news came out? *I didn't know*, I could hear Drew saying in my mind, only there was so much more we'd missed.

"What do you want from me?" Julius whined. Whining, that's what a bully was. Weak-willed, begging for someone to think he was important. Knowing him so well only made it hurt more because I knew he could've been better than this.

"You're going to tell her what you've been doing," I said, walking toward Sal. Julius took two steps forward. I jerked him in for a third.

213

Sal hadn't moved, knees bent, fingertips peeking over the dumpster lid. She was ridiculous in that oversized sweater in the middle of summer. She was so ill. She needed so much more than I could give. Julius looked anywhere but at Sal, a criminal avoiding the crime scene.

I waited.

"What do you want me to say?" Julius asked.

"I'm not going to tell you what to say. That's not my job. You're going to use your own words. Whenever you're ready."

"Sorry," he said, without conviction. "Better?"

I didn't answer him. He didn't deserve it. "I didn't get a message."

Sal was like a field mouse, large eyes watching us, ready to run. Where was the cyclone when she needed it?

"It's a game, Sal," he said. "Just our little game, for fun."

This wasn't working. "That's a start," I said. "Now you're going to tell the officer what you did."

Julius looked at me. I could hear it, something inside him cracking. "Fine," he said, slow and cold. "Let's go."

"What?" I asked.

"I'm ready. You can let go of me."

"If you think for one second that I'm going to—"

But he didn't wait, already marching up to the store. Sal stood up the rest of the way, eyes darting. Julius walked fast. My grip pulled his shirt tight across his neck. I stumbled, tugging him backward, and accidentally let go, but Julius didn't change course. Sal and I trailed behind him.

We were inside again, walking into the middle of the kitchen, where the officer sat with the Smalls.

"There yeah go. Just the right amount of pickle," the officer said as Mr. Small popped the last bite in his mouth.

"You sure I can't make one for you?" Vikki asked, getting the bread out before he answered. Then the adults noticed us.

"I did it," Julius said.

My mouth dropped. *Was I really that persuasive, or did his conscience get to him?*

Sal edged back to hide behind the doorframe.

"Did what?" the officer asked.

"I painted the pentagram."

"What?" Mr. Small yelled, chair screeching as he stood up. "You have to be joking!" When Julius didn't back down, Mr. Small's bald spot went red. "I lost my buyer because of you!"

"Hold on," The officer said. "Sit down, Small, let him talk. Why'd you do that, son?"

"I thought it would help."

Mr. Small smacked a fist on the table. I backed up next to Sal, half hoping Mr. Small would attack Julius and get arrested, half wondering what Julius meant by *help*.

The officer put his hand up. "Go on."

"I wanted to help her." Julius pointed at Sal.

Oh no. This wasn't how this was supposed to go.

"She's stalking Drew, taking pictures of him. A whole stockpile of crazy. It's like every time I see her, she's got more!"

215

Sal was still trying to back away, but with one glance from her dad, she froze.

"Thought I could scare it out of her."

He was turning it on us. What was I thinking? Grab his shirt, and he'll confess? Julius played me, staying there just to weigh his options.

Sal fidgeted like she wanted out of her body, arms rubbing at her sides like an animal gnawing at its cage. I reached out to comfort her, but she didn't respond. It was like I wasn't there, and I guess I hadn't been.

"I caught her doing it a few years ago," Julius said. "But it's getting worse. I got desperate, tried to scare it out of her, but I'm done! It's your problem now."

He was walking out, right past us like he owned the place.

"Hey! Hey! Hold on!" The officer was calling, knocking over the chair as he got up. The officer grabbed his shoulder.

"Get off me!" Julius yelled. He punched the officer in the ribs.

"Whoa, whoa, whoa!" the officer said. He worked on bringing Julius down, but the more confined he was, the angrier Julius got. "You're assaulting an officer, son. Calm down, will you?"

Merchandise was falling off the handmade shelves. Julius came at Sal. I pulled her back, but he yanked on her sweater.

Vikki yelped, running toward us. Julius was already stepping back, holding something.

He'd pulled the photos from her back pocket. A glossy stack she'd been hiding there. Julius tossed them on the ground. The handcuffs came out.

"See!" he yelled as his arms were pulled behind his back. "Blame me all you want, but she's insane!" Drew covered the floor. Drew bending over his bike. Drew checking his lock, Drew riding away. "She's got more! Stacks and stacks!"

I was so caught up with the pictures of Drew, I almost missed Julius being taken outside.

"Loralay, I think you should go home now," Vikki said. "I'll walk you to your car."

I looked at Sal, unsure if she understood I was on her side, not knowing what I could do.

"I want to stay with Sal," I told her, but Vikki put an arm on my shoulder.

I didn't have any say. I was in their store, the only person left that wasn't family, but I didn't want to leave her with her dad.

Sal's fingers were twitching like they ached to pick her many Drews up.

Vikki stayed quiet as we came to the van. Mom stowed her cigarette as soon as she saw us.

Vikki thanked my mother for driving out, and we were gone.

"Big poker tournament tonight," Mom said. "You could watch with us."

"Can't. I work tomorrow," I said, wondering if I had a job.

"What was the emergency all about?"

"Pictures," I said.

"See, nothing to worry about."

"Yeah. Nothing."

Chapter Twenty-One

SENTINEL

My watch glowed up at me. It was six o'clock in the morning, and I was trudging through the woods, stumbling over sluggish feet, low light slipping through the trees in a dizzy blue-gray. All those hours watching Sal's house, scared it would all go wrong.

Waiting always seems like a simple thing until you're the one on standby. I'd spent the night hungry, alert at every nocturnal noise until my adrenaline burned black to empty.

On the way home from Julius's arrest, I'd sat in the car, mind unhinged. Why hadn't I stayed when Vikki told me to go? Why hadn't I dragged Sal with me? We'd deviated so far from the Nevermore that I was sure the dam of time had broken, all my nightmares spilling out. Maybe this was it, Mr. Small stabbing Sal as I waited for Mom to park.

So as soon as we made it home, I undid my detour.

It took little effort with a poker tournament going in the living room. I wouldn't have thought a bunch of people quietly playing cards was all that distracting on its own, but Dad's couch coaching escalated to yelling at the screen, and Mom was off to soothe him with beer and popcorn.

First, I raided the kitchen, getting Dad's old cell phone from the junk drawer and a kitchen knife, stuffing them in my backpack just in case. Then I snuck out. Running through the dark cul-de-sac to the patch of forest that used to lead me to Drew's house, the place Mr. Small had brought his family on a midnight hike.

I stayed Sunday night to five o'clock Monday morning. That was when the Smalls' house came back to life. Vikki loaded the car with the kids, Mr. Small, with a coffee mug in his hand, not smiling but nodding goodbye from the door. Sal didn't seem happy, but that wasn't surprising. I ducked behind the trees as their car rolled past. When I looked again, Mr. Small was already inside, leaving a hollow feeling in my gut and an empty street, telling me to go home. I had to work soon. Small's General Store opened at eight, but my sleep-deprived paranoia kept me a little longer. What if Mr. Small was cleaning his gun, biding his time? I stayed, just in case.

And then Mr. Small came back outside. This time he had a cereal box under his arm, a cup of coffee, and a lighter in the other. He tossed the box in the burn barrel, flicking the lighter.

I couldn't see it, but I imagined the lid igniting first, right above the words *Top Secret.*

The Neers' door opened. Drew sat on the step to tie his shoes before taking off down the road. Mr. Neer stood by the mailbox, stopwatch in hand.

The two fathers waved, Mr. Neer with his lanyard, Mr. Small with his coffee. Both of them burning Drew in their own way.

Then I really went home.

"Loralay? Is that you?" Mom called from the bathroom.

"Yeah, I'm sorry—" I started to say, but she didn't sound worried at all—no police call, no searching for an excuse.

"What are you sorry for?" she asked, coming out. She was wearing leopard print pants and a red T-shirt intended for someone less than half her age. "Were you outside? You look like you were rolling in leaves." She picked a tiny twig out of my hair, sauntering away to toss it in the trash. "You're just like your dad, always on some little adventure."

She didn't notice. Not that I was wearing yesterday's clothes, not that I hadn't slept, eaten, or talked to her since we got home. She didn't need an explanation, just poker and Jay. That was enough for her.

"Yeah, I was outside," I said, but she didn't stay to listen. "Are you getting ready for something?"

"Counseling appointment," she said from the bathroom. I came in to see her digging through a bin of lipstick, matching the color to her outfit. "Do you want some of my makeup? You look like you need it."

I waved her offer away, and she shrugged, turning back to make faces at the mirror as she applied a new red smile.

"Can you drop me off at work before you go?" I asked, leaning in the mirror with her to frown at the big purple bags under my bloodshot eyes. Mom nodded she would, then handed me a tube of liquid concealer that was two shades too light for me before fluffing her hair out with a comb to make the perfect circle. I wondered if she'd ever let it grow out or if those curls were a permanent part of her now. In the Nevermore, she'd taken on a wavy little bob that cupped her face.

Mom dropped me at the Small's General Store fifteen minutes late. She must've been late too, not putting out her cigarette before we got there. I pulled up my backpack straps and yanked on the shop handle. It came back locked. *That's not a good sign.* I turned around, but Mom was already gone.

"Perfect," I said. "Just beautiful."

I walked around back to check that door next. Mr. Small was there, standing in a soapy mess, wire brush in hand and a hose coiled at his feet like a snake, scrubbing at the pentagram.

My tongue went dry.

What if he knew I'd been watching his house?

No, you're paranoid from not sleeping, I told myself. But panic seeped guilty on my skin.

"The door's locked," I said before he acknowledged me. Why did I say anything? I could've left.

"Grayson girl." He dropped the brush in the pail. "Didn't expect anyone in after all . . . that."

I took a step back, realizing we were alone—no Julius, no Stephen, no Vikki and the kids. I'd thought they were driving here, coming in early for work, but they were gone. It was Mr. Small and me. I dug Dad's phone out of my backpack, just in case. It fit snugly in the palm of my hand. The knife was there too, but that felt stupid to have on me now like I was handing him a weapon.

"We're going to be making cuts," Mr. Small said.

Yeah, I know you are, I thought. *Nineteen of them.*

"Can't keep extra staff. Liquidating the gardening center and the delivery service. You'll have to find employment elsewhere. Sorry for any inconvenience. I shoulda' notified you."

Did he look sad? He didn't have a right to that emotion. I squeezed the phone, watching him pick the brush back up.

Wire to brick made an awful sound—a metallic milling, like teeth grinding into pavement. He hosed down the wet brick, putting his hand on the wall to scrub it all the harder, bits of paint and milky red clay foaming between the bristles, dripping down the wall and through the cracks of his fingers.

"Where's Sal?" I asked, walking further backward.

I didn't like his hand so red. *He's not a serial killer*, I told myself, but *only* being a family killer wasn't much comfort.

Mr. Small stopped scrubbing. He wiped his bald brow with his forearm, smudging some soapy brick mixture on the rim of his glasses. "She's going to be staying with Vikki's mother for a while. Taking time to clear her head." He paused. "You didn't know about all of this, did you?"

"Know about what?" My heart pounded. I wanted to run even though he was just a man cleaning a wall and I was just a friend of his daughter. The more time I spent with him, the more I felt some sort of uncanny space between him and reality.

"This," Mr. Small said, pointing to what was left of the paint. "The defacing."

"I didn't," I said, glad he wasn't asking about the pictures.

222

Mr. Small nodded, wiping his hand on his apron. He pulled out his wallet. "Almost forgot, Sal wanted you to have the number where she's staying. If you want to call her, that is."

"I do. Why wouldn't I?"

He nodded. "You're a good girl. Didn't expect so much. Coming in today, calling Sal."

He came closer, handing me a blank business card with a phone number written in ballpoint ink. I took it with one hand, the other holding the Motorola like a hand grenade, walking backward as naturally as I could. He'd left a wet thumbprint on the corner of the card, a bit of red clay showing the spiral of his thumb. I'd seen his family go, but what if he was moving things to a different location? Holding them all somewhere?

"I can put it in my phone," I flipped it open, but I didn't go to contacts, letting my thumb rest over send for an emergency call.

"Thank you for all you've done for us." Mr. Small watched me as I struggled for something to say, but my mouth was empty. He turned back to the wall.

I left, trying not to run but moving fast, continually checking that Mr. Small wasn't behind me.

The long walk home felt longer with the card in my hand. I kept it pinched between two fingers, not wanting to touch it but unable to let go—a lifeline to Sal.

The road ahead looked like a highway abandoned to nature, and the Small's General Store was far gone, but it felt like I'd carried it with me.

My chest was closing, even though I knew I was breathing fine. Birds chirped in the trees, not a car around.

And then I screamed.

I didn't even try to, but it came out of me, a fit of rage. *I hate him. I hate this life. I hate that . . .*

"I'm ashamed to exist!"

The birds went silent, then slowly, their sounds swelled again.

By the time I got home, my fingers were numb from pinching the card. I dropped it on the piano, the feeling of it still on my fingertips.

The house was just as empty as the road.

I locked the doors, then did it again, unsure if I felt the right kind of click. I wanted to check a third time, but I stumbled to the kitchen phone instead, dialing the number, counting the rings.

"Hello?" an elderly woman asked.

"Hi, is Sal there?" I tried to make the words as clear as possible, closing my eyes to relieve the burn behind them.

"Why no, dear," My eyes shot open. I panicked until she added, "She's not here yet. That's an eight-hour drive, sweetie. I can have her call you when she gets here. Is it an emergency?" I slumped into the counter, feeling the cool cupboard on my forehead. Eight hours away from Mr. Small.

"No, I'm sorry. I'll call back," I said, hearing the smile in my voice. I hung up, dragging myself to the living room, and flopped on the couch.

Every muscle in my body went instantly cozy. Sal was safe. Maybe all of them were going to stay with Grandma. Grandmas were wonderful things to have. I was already falling asleep with a final thought. I didn't need to work with Mr. Small anymore.

I must've slept, but it felt like I'd only closed my eyes when someone knocked. I tried to ignore it, but it was too late. I'd been ripped out of the sleep coma, unable to get comfortable again. I yanked myself up and stomped to the door, opening it, and—

"Drew?" I asked, even though he was clearly standing in front of me.

"No, it's Saint Nick." He forced a laugh even though he looked more tired than I was. How did he function like this? "Hey, listen, sorry for inviting myself, but I didn't have your number."

I didn't even nod before he kept talking.

"Listen, you work with Julius, right? Right, I mean, I know that. Do you know what happened to him yesterday?"

I opened my mouth to answer.

"Like, anything? My Dad said he got caught up in some sort of —" he paused to make air quotes. "*Illegal activity,* and he's trying to see if I know anything about it, and I don't, and now I'm trying to see if you know anything about it when you probably don't. No one tells me anything."

I started to answer, but he held up his hands.

"It's been a long day. I've been up since five, but when am I not up since five, so who cares?"

"Uh, hi," I said.

"Hi." He stuck his hands in his pockets. "Sorry, it's just that his mom called my house and said he wasn't coming over. She was crying . . . I don't know. It seemed serious."

"No, you're fine. I didn't sleep either. I know about it. Do you want to come in?" I held the door open for him.

"You know about it? Don't make me wait. What is it?"

"He painted a pentagram on the side of Small's General Store."

Drew raised an eyebrow like he thought I was trying to be funny.

"I'm serious," I said. "Do you want to come in now?"

"Yeah, I guess I should."

Drew was in my house for the first time, only not the way I'd pictured it happening. He sat down on my couch, hands on his knees.

"What's with the piano?" he asked, looking at its upsettingly disjointed placement.

"It's my dad—"

"Where are your parents?" he asked.

Ah, not only was it my first time with Drew in the house, it was my first visit *alone* with Drew in my house. That was fast.

"They're out," I answered distractedly, trying to think. There was so much to explain, but he had to know. I bit my lip, about to fix it, telling him everything so he wouldn't be in the dark. "Look." I sat next to him. "I don't know how to say this, so I'm just going to get it out there."

The words flaked off me like lead scales that'd grown over my skin. All their weight dropping off me, falling on him.

"You saw these pictures?" he asked after a long while. His lips pulled back like he was nauseated.

I'd gone too far. He wasn't ready for all of this.

"What did I do to make her think . . . no, hey, that can't be right, I would've seen her if she was taking that many."

"She was careful. They were taken at a distance." I wasn't going to mention Julius's help. *One thing at a time.* "And you're not the most vigilant person."

"I'm not?" Drew sat a little straighter.

I laughed, but then I saw how tense he was, so I cleared my throat instead.

"You're exhausted, Drew. How alert can someone be if they're always busy."

He nodded at the floor. "I've been thinking about quitting football. Just can't figure a way to do it."

I put my hand on his knee. It seemed platonic enough, but my nerve endings caught fire. Stupid hormones. That wasn't why we were here right now.

"What do I do?" Drew asked. "Should I talk to her? Let her know it's not real?"

I closed my eyes, trying to think back to the counselors I had when I was thirteen. Not Doctor Julia, but the good ones that I used to talk with, modeling how I thought they'd answer.

"I don't think you should. She doesn't have a crush on you. You don't really have anything to do with it. Obsession isn't about you. It's about Sal and the version of you she has in her head. All she has is a story where you're the stand-in. Her life sucks, so she made up this alternate reality."

Drew shuttered. "What's so wrong in her life that she needs me, or whatever. The *story* of me?"

"I don't know," I said.

Drew leaned back on my couch, running his hands through his hair, muscles twitching from sleep deprivation. I wanted to lay in his lap, both of us sleeping here alone, but I leaned into the armrest instead.

"I can't do all this," Drew said, still holding his head. "I'm too exhausted to take care of myself, now I've got Julius in trouble, and Sally Small." He dropped one hand, so he could see me out of the corner of his eye.

"I wish we were still playing. I'm practicing on my own, but it's not the same. You really get me, like, what I'm trying to do."

I smiled at him, a stupid toothy grin, but I was too drained to care.

"I lost my job today," I said.

He sat up, looking at me full on now.

"You serious? Because of this? Oh man, I'm sorry. I should've asked or something. I don't know. That's lame." I kept smiling at him. "What?"

"I'm wondering if the nursing home's hiring. I don't mind Johnny cash songs all that much."

Chapter Twenty-Two

POLISH

The smell of acetone, potpourri, and the elderly filled my nostrils. The nursing home's common room was done up for its monthly spa party. Artificial roses and decorated folding tables filled the room, and little old ladies scooted in snugly around nail files and bottles of polish.

I'd gotten up early and spent an extra hour getting ready for my first day of work. Putting my hair in a puffy braid, digging my best button-up shirt out from the laundry to wash it in time. Anything to make this day special. This was my day, my day with Drew.

So far, all I'd done was spend the morning being shuffled from room to room, getting my start-up paperwork settled, and watching a video on junior staff expectations. But luckily, they were understaffed due to a rogue flu, so when they gave me a pink lanyard that marked me as a junior staff member, I was thrown in without ado.

Drew was sitting with four residents who were waiting on him, his coffee by his side, cold and untouched as his hands kept hustling. I sat down, but he didn't notice, concentrating on the cuticle he was currently flooding with sunshine yellow.

"They said this would be easy . . . " he muttered, pulling out a fresh orange stick to fix his mistakes. "How am I doing, Doris?"

"Spotty," Doris said, but Drew was working his magic on her. When he struggled on her thumbnail, she pretended to cough so she could secretly tilt it for him.

One of the leading staff members came over to check on his progress.

"Almost done?" she asked, tapping her own acrylic nails on the table. "We need to be getting everyone through."

"Can you do this then?" Drew asked her, desperately trying to hand over the polish brush. "I don't do nails. They said they didn't have enough people, so they took me out of the rec room."

The leading staff member held her hands up like she was blocking an onslaught. "Oh no, I don't even do my own. I said we should do something easy, like footbaths. Christi was the one who picked mani day."

"Footbaths are a slipping hazard!" called another staff person from across the room, who I assumed was Christi.

"Anyway," The leading staff woman went on, looking at me. "New girl, give him a hand."

230

"Loralay!" Drew said, noticing me for the first time. He scooted his chair to include me in the circle. "Do you know how to do this?" he asked like nail polish application was a national secret. I nodded, trying hard not to laugh. "Mrs. Esmer?" Drew said, tapping the leg of a tiny woman. "This is Loralay. She'll be doing your nails while I finish Doris's."

This wasn't my Mrs. Esmer but the elderly mother of the woman I knew. Every part of her frame was hunched except for her rigged shoulders that swallowed up her neck.

"What color would you like, Mrs. Esmer?" Drew asked for me, scooping up vials of nail polish. The glass bottles clinked between his fingers, threatening to fall.

"Hurrmmma," she said.

"What?" Drew leaned in and dropped two bottles on the table.

"She said pink," I told Drew as if I knew. I took the color from his hand and helping him set the rest down, one nearly rolling off the edge of the table. I moved his coffee cup in front of him. He made a grateful sound, chugging it.

"Lovely," said the leading staff member, face saying the opposite. "Make it fast, but make it good. It's family dinner tonight. We don't want the families to think we don't care."

Drew's eyebrows shot up, glancing at me before diving back down on Doris's thumb.

Mrs. Esmer's hand was on the table, joints constricted in a claw, unable to lay flat. I wanted to tell her I understood, being trapped in her own body, holding onto that edgeless cavern as time pushed to force her free.

I took Mrs. Esmer's hand in mine, holding it steady. She squeezed back.

231

Christi was right. Manicures were a perfect idea—anything to get us close. People needed to be held. This was where I was meant to be. Close to Drew, fighting Death with piano playing and polish, soothing souls that longed for contact. If only I didn't have to feel so isolated all the time.

"Nice," Drew said as I finished a finger. "Everything's like piano to you, isn't it? Some kind of second nature."

I almost told him it used to be the other way around, but I held my tongue.

"Just add a dot to the middle and then push it up to the top like this, see?" I said.

Drew leaned in to watch, knocking into the open bottle, pink spilling on my sleeve.

"I'm sorry!" He tried to yank the bottle back, but the damage was already done.

"It's okay—"

The leading staff lady dived in. I didn't realize she was still helicoptering over us.

"Take this into the bathroom. Don't rub it in. Soak it!" She handed me a bottle of polish remover and pushed me toward the hall like I was headed to the ICU. "Bathrooms down the hall. I'll get a shirt from the kitchen crew!"

"It's really fine," I said, but she'd marched away, grumbling about the superiority of footbaths.

I tried to give Drew a reassuring look, but he was engrossed in scrubbing the table with a handful of cotton swabs.

I walked down the hall, passing rooms with design schemes that teetered between hotel and hospital, complete with hand sanitizer and tissue dispensers on every wall. I came to the stark bathroom with glistening sliver handrails, and I started going in, but I saw a flash of color behind me, like a camera going off. I turned. The door there was closed, but I thought I could see a glow coming from the edges of the frame.

A glow of orange.

I tossed the nail polish remover on the bathroom counter and sprang at the orange lined door. The color that called me louder than a name.

Death was wearing a thousand faces again, sitting in a wingback chair as he held the hand of a bedridden elderly man with an oxygen tube taped to his face. The old man's age-spotted eyes were closed. Sunken.

"Hello, Loralay."

I ran in, putting my hands on the man's flabby neck to find a pulse.

"Not yet," Death said. "Only sleeping. He's waiting for a visit from his son. How are you?" I hit the emergency call button on the headboard, starring Death down. "Won't work. We're not inside time," he said, nodding to his gloves that rested on the foot of the bed. "Have a seat?" He nodded to another chair.

"Not if you're going to kill him."

"He's ninety-four years old. How much more time do you want him to have?"

I sat down, unsure. I knew people had to die. It was natural, wasn't it? We couldn't all live forever, but life shouldn't fall between the cracks either. Dying in a clinically detached room, white walls, surfaces made for disinfecting. It was cold, indifferent.

"Will it hurt?" I asked. It was childish, but I needed to know, watching the man's chest stay ominously still in this timeless place.

"Life hurts, Loralay. Death can too."

For once, I didn't mind his quiet voice. It was soothing. I wanted to be soothed.

I picked at the pink polish on my ruined shirt sleeve.

"Will his son make it in time? Before he, you know, dies?"

Death shrugged. A man in army fatigues, and a woman in a sari, faces changing so fast that I dropped my eyes to the floor, so I wouldn't have to see.

"That's not your concern. This soul has been and will be given what is necessary."

"Right, like I was?" I asked, accidentally looking at those faces again. "Please, stop. I don't want to see . . . all those people."

"Is this better?" Death asked. He had my old face again, the two versions of me sitting side by side in the room of a dying man.

"Not really, but it'll do."

"Is that how this life is? You're Nevermore? Not better, but it'll do?"

"No!" I sat straighter. "Sal's living with her grandma, so she's safe. I'm playing music at Drew's house, and for once, I'm not some blubbering idiot who has to rely on everyone else. Can you stop that?" I added.

"What?"

"Holding his hand. Can't you at least let him go if it's not his time yet?"

Death looked at the man, my old eyes studying his face. "You're still confused about what I'm here for. Tell me about Julius."

"Julius? What about him? He went to live with his dad, I guess? It's not like my mom's the only person who has other people parent for her." I paused, but Death was quiet. "You'd better not be blaming me. I didn't know he was messing with Sal. If that's how he really is, then this life's direction fits better."

Death was staring at me, waiting in his expressionless way.

"What? I didn't do anything wrong. You think I pushed him over the edge? Like because we were closer last life, he wouldn't have done something like that?"

"I'm not here to say what I think. That's what you think."

"What is this?" I stood up, but at least now I knew nothing would make me feel bigger than him. I didn't need to feel powerful. I felt right. That was enough. "What's the point of your little visit? Say whatever you want so I can go."

"I didn't come here to tell you anything."

"Then why are you here? You called me, didn't you? With that flash?"

"I came to hold your hand," he said.

Why were my insides so raw, so easy to turn sour? I hated him, making me cry.

"I don't need you." If only someone, anyone else, would care. "I have everything I wanted."

"You think you're the only one who sees this life's value."

Wasn't I? I tried to understand how he could even pretend it was meaningful when it all had to end.

"It was good you asked about this man's son, even though it's not your story. It shows you care, and that's a beautiful thing."

I frowned at my old face, but somehow a little of my loneliness was ebbing away in Death's validation.

"All of this, it matters," he said. "That's why it's so sad when people die."

Chapter Twenty-Three

JAY, THE DOLPHIN

I 'd just put peanut butter on my morning toast when Dad came in and asked if I needed a bike.

"What?" I asked, confused.

"You're going to that boy's house today?"

I nodded.

"You're going there a lot."

"His name's Drew. We play music together?"

Dad waited as I swallowed a bite of toast. I wasn't sure how much more information I wanted to give. I took another bite and tried to figure out how we got into this conversation.

"Soo," He said, pulling the word out of his mouth like taffy. "You'll need a bike to get around. You'll have one next week."

"I'll be driving soon, plus Mom said we couldn't afford it."

Dad laughed, his smile spreading faster than the peanut butter.

"Let's say money's not a problem. I'm your ol' man, right? I'll handle that."

"You selling houses again?"

"Something even better."

I brushed the crumbs off my fingers. He was waiting for me to beg for information, but when I didn't give in, he left the kitchen, hands in his pockets.

I went over it as I walked to Drew's house, but I couldn't figure out his angle. It couldn't be good. This was the man that wanted to lull me into abandonment with ice cream. He had been jumpy. Was it an indicator of drugs? By the time I made it through the forest path, the best answer I had was maybe he'd stolen a bike and wanted to hide the evidence with me. *And drugs*, I thought. They had to be involved. He'd been losing weight, still disappearing, busting into smiling fits. Maybe he stole the bike to pay for drugs? You know you've got a winner of a dad when you'd believe organized crime over philanthropy.

I forgot Dad as soon as I walked past the Smalls' house.

It was getting worse over the years. Mickey Mouse blankets back up over the windows, now faded enough to be passable as curtains. Heath Hennery's toys littered the front lawn.

Sal was safe. She called me sometimes, talking on the phone about her new life.

But Vikki came back, bringing Irene and Heath Hennery with her.

Maybe none of it would happen now. Sal gone meant less stress for Mr. Small, one less mouth to feed. But I kept one hand ready to call DHS, waiting for anything I could report. They only had one year left in the Nevermore.

I stood at Drew's front door, pinching the bridge of my nose. *I need to find a way to balance all of this. Stop worrying about other people and just spend time with Drew.* I opened the door without knocking. Since I was there so often, Mr. Neer kept calling me Replacement Julius, a joke neither Drew nor I liked.

"Honey, I'm home!" I called, keeping my voice comical, even though I only wanted an excuse to call Drew *honey* again. Everything was working a little slower than I wanted. We'd probably be dating soon. I just would not have minded if we started that aspect of our lives early.

Drew came downstairs, white socks sinking into the orange runner. He said something, but I didn't catch it, too busy thinking how that color bothered me now.

"What?" I asked.

"Mountain Dew or coffee?"

"Anything with caffeine," I said.

"You're my kind of person," he said, heading toward the kitchen.

I smiled, tossing my coat on the treadmill that stood in their living room, a monument to the Neer lifestyle. No lounging, just workout. The rest of the house screamed 1970s—thin and tan bricks, ash plank ceiling, macramé wall hangings, and orange shag carpet. But it was nice. The vaulted ceiling was so far from the ground that the Neers had poles for changing the light bulbs. It didn't look like a bus driver's house, but it did look like a tax manager's house, and that was what Drew's mom did. Paying bills by keeping track of other people's money.

I followed Drew into the kitchen, where the famed exercise reward chart shone with workout stars. The chart was pointless though—Drew's muscles spoke for themselves. I rested my hand on the brick wall that joined the wooden ones together, watching out the massive windows that overlooked the strawberry fields. Some of the windows directly faced the Smalls', a picturesque view of poverty.

"The Dew is my mom's. She says everyone's allowed one vice. I'm still not sure what mine gets to be. You like your coffee extra sweet, right?" Drew had an assortment of cartons and powders on the table, spooning them in my cup one at a time.

"Uh-huh. Hey, what do you think of Mr. Small?"

Drew frowned out the window as if he expected Mr. Small to be there, but they wouldn't be back from the store until after seven.

"Nice guy? Quiet. Why?"

"I don't like him."

Drew frowned at me. "Well, uh." He gave me the same smile we'd given to Sal on the bus. I'd pushed too far. "Hopefully, you'll like this coffee. It's how I make it for my mom. It's sweet, so that's vice number two if you're counting."

I hid a sigh. Drew and my mother liked everyone. Mom thought everyone was above her. Drew thought the world was full of his equals. I found both ideas annoying.

Drew, innocent to my negativity, stepped back to show off his creation. Two cups, large enough to be bowls, were on the table.

One was caramel brown with white speckled glaze, the other its match except instead of brown it was caramel and orange. Drew tapped the spoon off before handing me the orange cup. I didn't like it, but if one of us needed to drink out of Death's color, I decided it should be me.

I took a sip as Drew shelved his mess of ingredients. "I think this'll be up your alley." He said.

My cheeks were full of creamy hints of coconut, salt, and cinnamon. He used to make the same thing for me in the Nevermore, with only one slight change.

"Mmm! You make coffee like you make music." I grinned over the side of my cup. I took another sip. "You know what you should add next time? A dash of maple syrup. Just a spoon full."

"More sugar?"

"It's maple, so it doesn't count."

"Well, if *you* make coffee like you make music, then I'll have to try that." He walked past me, brown cup brimming with black. Drew always drank his coffee dark as it came from the pot. His dad had him off sweeteners. It always made me sad, him missing the sweet things in life. But he wasn't a rebellious soul. That was me. I used to carry honey in my purse, sneaking it into his drink. I'd probably still do that when we were dating.

Coffee in hand, I followed Drew upstairs to the open hall that housed Mr. Neer's instruments. You could see most of the house from up here. It was like a castle's battlement, giving the view of the bailey below—a line of windows from every side. Lighting Drew up like a TV screen every night. Perfect for taking photos without a flash. But in the daylight, it felt safe, looking down on everything, proving we were alone.

Drew picked up his dad's guitar, screeching fret noise as he put his finger into position.

"Ready?"

We didn't talk much yet. I needed to get us past that. I sat down to the beat-up keyboard that was officially Mr. Neer's, but everyone in the Neer house called it mine because I was the only one who used it. Mr. Neer didn't play guitar anymore, but no one pretended it was Drew's. And it was going to stay that way.

"Why don't we drink our coffee first?" I asked, coyly leaning in my seat, posing for him.

"Already finished mine." Drew nodded to his empty cup.

Darn, boy. If only he was taking me on that quick.

"I got a new song I learned. Wanna hear it?"

I held back a second sigh, lifting the cup in cheers.

"You start without me. I'll catch up when I get some more of this in me."

Drew played "Stairway to Heaven," head down so hair covered his eyes.

I fixed my smile in place. It wasn't a bad song, but everyone who played guitar played it at some point, a rite of passage. I was tired of Drew being one step behind me. He whispered the words in a graveled melody, singing mixed-up lyrics. I looked down at my orange coffee cup. There was way too much orange in the room. Orange cup, orange shag, a coil of orange extension cord by Mr. Neer's amp. Sunburst guitar slitting orange at the center. I grabbed my knees to steady myself.

"You okay?" Drew asked.

"Headache," I said, and it was true. The pounding was real, but it was happening all around me like the room was collapsing.

There was the buzz of amp feedback, then Drew's hand was on my knee.

"I could make you more coffee. That might help."

Sweet boy, all headaches were caffeine related in his world.

I considered kissing him, right then and there, his pink lips so close.

A car pulled up, clear from our vantage—Drew's mom's car.

Drew let go of my knee a little too fast, making me wonder if he felt the intimacy of the moment too.

"There's still more," Drew said. "In your cup."

I nodded, draining my coffee. Drew stood up and took the cup from me, socks back on the stairs. I got up to follow just as Mrs. Neer opened her front door.

"I'm h-O-me!" she sang with vibrato. She was a short woman. Olive, Italian skin; dark hair in a pixy cut; her signature brow-line glasses. But she made up for her mousy stature by pure volume. "Get ready to go, Drew! We're going out to din—oh! Loralay, I didn't know you were here." She paused to kiss Drew's cheek, or more accurately, paused to squash her lips together, waiting for Drew to come down to her level. "There's my boy. So, you two are spending a lot of time together, *aren't you*?" she sang the last words with a finger waggle, teasing us.

"It's not like that," Drew said, and I hoped my face showed the proper amount of agreement without giving away how annoying I found that fact. "Loralay knows I'm with Anita, Mom. It's not weird."

But I didn't know that. I touched my forehead lightly, suddenly aware of this very real headache.

"Loralay, you're pale," Mrs. Neer said.

"She's got a headache," Drew told her.

It felt like my lungs were being crushed in a vacuum seal, but I nodded, body on autopilot.

Mrs. Neer instantly forgot my headache, clapping her hands together to cheerily demand our attention. "Well, sorry to cut into your jam time, but I just got off the phone with your dad, and we're having our annual dinner tonight!"

"Seriously?" Drew threw his arms up, doing his touchdown dance.

"And it's a fancy place this time, so get ready to go."

Drew bounded back up the stairs. He was still holding my orange cup.

I looked blankly at my feet surrounded by orange carpet. They never got back together. That wasn't a thing. It didn't exist. It shouldn't exist.

"Look at him, so excited," Mrs. Neer said. "It's our little after-tax season restaurant trip. A little something for the boys to make up for all the time I missed when I was crunching numbers."

Oh, I know, I thought. I'd been a part of it. From the year we'd started dating to the year Drew and I lugged Makenzie in, strapped to her car seat. Her first newborn outing, wearing a onesie that was way too big. That was when Mr. Neer held his granddaughter for the first time, worrying about the birthmark on her forehead that would eventually go away. Drew making new dad jokes, all of us laughing together. The tradition died when Mr. Neer killed himself.

But now I wouldn't be a part of it. "But isn't tax season in April?" my autopilot asked. "It's almost June."

"Yes. Well, I got a new client this year. Had me working straight through April and most of May. An eccentric landowner with places in and out of state. So not only was I working with multiple state laws," Mrs. Neer shook her head, laughing. "Her original filing system was a Victoria's Secret box!"

A silence hung in the air. The mask of a smile felt eerie on my face.

"Here you go." Mrs. Neer grabbed my coat off the treadmill, handing it to me.

"Thanks." A long pause drifted between us. I didn't try to talk anymore, but Mrs. Neer filled the conversation void on her own.

"Oh! Yes, and you might even know the house!" she said. "It's right across from yours. The one with the red roof?"

Drew came back down. He'd forgotten the orange cup somewhere upstairs.

"How's this?" He wore dark wash jeans, a button-down shirt, and a blue blazer. His hair was still comb wet, strands slipping down to his forehead.

I held my waist, wondering what would've happened if I'd kissed him upstairs.

"Can Loralay come?" he asked.

I held my breath.

"Oh hon, she's not dressed for it."

"She looks good," he said. I pulled my tangled curls back, hoping I didn't look half as bad as I felt. "Or she could change! We'll swing by her house and—"

245

Mrs. Neer held the door open, gently shooing me out. She closed the door behind us, briskly leading the way to her car.

"Formal clothes are different for girls, babe. We don't really have time. I'm sure she understands. Right, Loralay?"

Drew got in the front seat with his mom, leaving me to the back seat, alone.

"Remember last year when your father tucked the napkin in his shirt?"

"Oh, that was funny. Loralay, listen to this one," Drew said, hands tapping his knees in anticipation.

"So, the year before last, we had lobster, and there were those plastic bibs at the table. But the next year we went somewhere much nicer, and they had cloth napkins on the table, so Mike thought . . . "

I listened to the story, but it was like I heard it on the radio, mind empty. Maybe I was getting sick. I certainly felt ill.

"Well," Mrs. Neer chirped. "We're here!"

"Thanks for the ride, Mrs—"

"Looks like I'll have to stop at the curb. Mind your step. I parked a little too close. Were you saying something, dear?"

"Just thanks."

"Oh, no prob—you okay?"

I'd tripped on the curb even though she'd warned me.

"Yeah. I'm fine. It's good." I waved, but they didn't see me, busy backing up and talking. As Mrs. Neer turned, I could hear them clearly.

"Now, let's pick up Anita!"

"You called her?"

"Of course . . . "

And they were gone.

I trudged up to my house, scowling at the blooming fruit trees, hating the summer sky. I almost kicked the tire of Mom's van— then I saw the reason Mrs. Neer parked at the curb. There was another car in the driveway, a new little BMW.

"Loralay!" Dad said when I walked in. Apparently, everyone got the wear formal clothes memo. Dad was dressed like he was going to a wedding. He looked nice except for a stupid necklace. Leather strips attached to a crudely carved chunk of rock. "You weren't supposed to be home yet!"

I turned to toss my jacket on the couch, hard, hiding my face from Dad, when I discovered our living room was rearranged. Ottoman and chairs in a semicircle. The kitchen table brought in and covered by a blue velvet cloth I'd never seen—a rainbow of glassy crystals on displays.

"What's going . . . " I started.

Doctor Julia walked out of the kitchen. "Oh! We have company!" she said with a smug little bow.

My mind raced. Counseling. Doctor Julia. The only person batty enough to help Mom enable Dad. Why hadn't I figured that out the first time Mom had mentioned it? I felt hot all over.

"Loralay was supposed to be at a boy's house," Dad said, gesturing at me like a scolded dog.

But instead of his usual red, Dad was pale. He anxiously tugged at his sleeves.

"I can be here," I said, stating the obvious for the morons among me. "Because this is my house. Where's Mom?"

247

"What's that?" Mom walked in. She wore a crystal necklace too. "Loralay!" She looked relieved to see me. At least one person wanted me around.

"What is this? A cult?" I pointed to everyone's matching jewelry. Doctor Julia made a disgruntled little huff.

Mom proudly held up her necklace. "It's my spirit animal! The beaver!" She scrunched up her neck, trying to see the pendant as she showed it to me. "At first, I thought the tail was a platypus bill. Isn't that funny? Can you imagine a platypus spirit? Your dad got the dolphin." She looked up, smile bigger than usual. "But I thought you were at *Drew's* house. Are you going back out?'

"The rest of us already talked about this, Mom, but to recap, I can be here because I *live* here. So, you can stop telling me to leave."

"No, I'm glad you're back." Mom giggled.

"It's not funny, Sandy," Dad said. "Today's special, remember? This session is the big one we've been working up to!"

Mom's giggles didn't strike me as normal. She was nervous.

Something was very wrong.

But I was done solving her problems, too sick to think. I sat down on our couch.

"You can't sit there," Doctor Julia said. "That spot is reserved for Jay."

"Not anymore." I rolled my head back.

"No," Dad said. "You're leaving."

"That's okay, Jay," Doctor Julia chimed in. "I came prepared." She picked through the crystals on the table. "I brought gifts," she said in a singsong voice. "Angelite for Sandy, to aid communication and calm. For Loralay . . . " She picked one up, a fairy bottle pendant, hung on wire and filled with chunky sand. She held it out to me. "A vile mixed with red and orange zincite grains. Perfect for a girl your age, budding into new *horizons*. Like that young man your mom tells me you're seeing?" She winked at me, I didn't know *why* she'd done that, but I didn't like it. "You could say I've got you both covered from *A* to *Z*." She laughed, a real ha-ha-ha-ha-ha, in crazy-lady soprano, then reached for me, trying to get the wire loop around my neck.

"Nope." I dipped my head out of the way, making the room spin. *Do not have the flu,* I commanded myself. Unless I could be a carrier and give it to Doctor Julia, then I'd go for it.

"Nonsense," Doctor Julia said, still trying to noose me. She got the necklace around the crown of my head before I yanked it out of her hands, tossing it back on the table. Doctor Julia's hands were fists. "You could've broken it," she fumed. "Maybe I should've given *you* the angelite. Never mind," she told my parents through her teeth. "It doesn't help that I have azurite in my pocket. Loralay doesn't need a boost of inner vision, poor thing. It overwhelms her." She leaned in, looming over my face.

She was almost the perfect distance for punching.

"Ooh," Mom said. "Better keep that azurite away from Jay. The two of them are so much alike."

Stabbing me wouldn't have hurt that much. I got up, feeling queasier as I moved. "Are you going?" Mom asked, eyes pleading with me to stay.

"Sandy," Dad said. "Doctor Julia came all the way here for our *special session*. We don't want Loralay here when we're talking about *grown-up things*."

I grimaced, not just because I was pretty sure Dad was hinting about discussing sex, but because my stomach did a 180 without my permission.

I got up, heading toward the bathroom.

"Where are you going!" Dad yelled. He leaped in front of me, blocking the hall. I had to grab the couch's arm so I wouldn't fall over.

"To the bathroom?" I asked. My stomach raged again. "I thought you wanted me to go?"

"Your room's that way! Or outside, you can go outside!" His voice was loud, ringing in my ears.

"I think I'm going to be sick." I felt too weak to yell back.

"Azurite!" Doctor Julia said. "She's had too strong a dose. Loralay, why don't you go lie down in your room? You'll feel better."

"No," I said, holding my head. "What's wrong with you? Let me go to the bathroom."

"Fine!" Dad growled. "Sandy, you stay here," he commanded, hurrying ahead to stand in front of his bedroom door where he could watch me. "You have five minutes."

If I puked, I'd aim for his shoes. I threw the bathroom door open with a bang and sat on the edge of the tub to catch my breath, waiting to see if I'd need to lunge for the toilet. It felt like I couldn't close my mouth, body forcing me to keep it open, sucking in gulps of air. I glanced at the door, wishing I'd closed it but feeling too unbalanced to get up.

Dad was counting down, aloud. "Five, four . . . "

"Is it time?" a woman's voice whispered. "You want me now?"

I looked around, confused.

"No," Dad muttered back.

It's just Doctor Julia, I thought. But the voice didn't sound like her. I got up, painstakingly slowly, holding on to the towel rack so I wouldn't jar my innards.

"You done in there?" Dad called to me, then muttered, "No, not you! I said stay in there!"

I realized there was a woman on the other side of Dad's body barricade. A woman Dad wanted to hide.

I made it back to the open door, leaning out of the bathroom.

"Hurry," Dad said.

"Make up your mind!" the woman's voice growled.

Dad's eyes met mine.

"Move now, or I'll make you move," he said to me. I didn't.

The door opened.

"Make me wait in a dirty room, and now you're treating me like this?" the woman said.

"No, not you—" Dad scooted in front of the door crack. I saw her—someone around Mom's age, barefoot, wearing an olive green dress that rested high on her hips. For one split second, my confused, potentially flu-ridden brain thought of the squatter I'd dreamed up all those years ago.

"You said it was time," the woman huffed. Dad was still trying to keep her hidden, so she slapped at his shoulders.

Ruse over, Dad got out of her way, and I saw how opposite from a squatter this woman was. The bare feet had thrown me, but her blond hair was perfectly crimped; her thick, dusty rose lips were

251

wet with gloss. She looked like money. Maybe even pretty if her cheeks weren't so wide. They had that unpleasant plastic surgery bulge, dwarfing her eyes with excessively raised brows. But her wispy bangs were perfect—I knew her. I just didn't know why.

"I wasn't talking to you," Dad said to her. Even in his frustration, there was a softness to his voice, a tone I wished he'd use for me. "Sorry, wait a little longer and—"

"What's going on?" Mom called.

"Nothing!" Doctor Julia reassured her. That made everything weirder. How would she know nothing was happening when she was in the other room? I could've been puking my head off.

And that was all my stomach could take. Vomit projected from my nose and mouth onto the carpet. The woman screamed. Dad yelled at me, but all I could do was steady my hands on the wall as I heaved up more.

"Loralay?" Mom yelled, running in the hall.

"Sandy, no, don't," Dad said.

Mom was by me, pulling a towel off the rung and tossing it over the pile I'd made.

"Loralay! You missed the toilet!" she said. At least she rubbed my back.

I knelt lower, picking up a corner of the towel to wipe the spit from my mouth.

A pair of Birkenstock shoes lay next to the toweled vomit.

"Azurite was that powerful to you? Did you experience a vision?" Doctor Julia asked.

Great, I thought. We were all here to enjoy this moment.

Mom stopped mid rub. She froze, hand hovering over her heart, looking sicker than I felt.

"I can explain," Dad said, hands in the air. "It wasn't going to be like this. We were going to talk, Sandy."

I was dry heaving again. I tried to stop, but there wasn't anything I could do about it. I tried to ease my way back in the bathroom where I could be alone, but Mom was in the way, supplying me with the last hand towel. I held on to it like life support.

The mummers and movements around me were lost over my animal sounds. When I recovered, I was surprised to see Mom already had the mop bucket from the kitchen, sprinkling baking soda all over the carpet as Doctor Julia knelt next to her. And then I saw Mom was crying. Streaks dripping from her nose and chin as she scrubbed.

"Sandy, we hoped Jay would get to share his most intimate self with you before we made the reveal," Doctor Julia said. "You can't truly love a dolphin if you don't accept its nature. They're not monogamous creatures like beavers."

"Oh, I love dolphins," the woman said. I might have assumed the plastic surgery kept her from looking concerned, but not one smidgen of her seemed to care that my mother was sobbing. "Do you get to pick your spirit animal? I want to be a bear. They're my favorite."

"Not right now, Rosie," Dad muttered.

I repeated her name in my mind over and over. Why did I feel like I knew this woman?

"You should help her with that, Jay," the woman said. She added in a loud whisper, "She's never been much of a housekeeper."

And then I knew.

Rosie. Shoe hater, bear decorator, and owner of the lakeside cabin.

"You're Rosie?" I asked. "But I thought you were old."

"Excuse me?"

I'd hit a nerve. "At the cabin, all those sticky notes, that was you?" I'd never seen the woman. I'd only assumed she was some gray-haired curmudgeon. But even if that was Rosie, why did I think I knew her when I'd only seen her face?

No, I had seen her, on Dad's cold calls.

Rosie sneered at me instead of answering, defiantly wrapping her hand around my Dad, their hips touching.

My jaw dropped. Dad seemed embarrassed, but he didn't do anything about it. They stood there on the threshold to my parents' room, attached. Rosie held up a manicured finger and turned Dad's head toward her. "You told me it'd be different this time," she crooned. "But look at her whining down there. It's all the same. After all I've put up with, she still acts like she owns you."

Mom kept scrubbing away my mess, tears dropping onto her working hands.

"Let go of my dad." I stood up on shaky legs. Rosie scrunched up her face, overly puffed cheeks looking even more alien. "What is this?" I asked Dad. "You're having an affair, and you were going to break it to Mom over a counseling session? That's why you wanted me gone?"

Rosie snorted. "Like Sandy doesn't know about me. She knew from the beginning, little homewrecker. I'm the civil one." Rosie paused for a beat, and the only sound was Mom's endless puke scrubbing. That seemed to annoy Rosie even more, making her raise her voice. "I could've blacklisted her from cleaning my cabin, but did I? No, never did anything to her. Maybe I should've back when she was making eyes at my Jay. We were engaged, little slut. I was too much a lady, and we both knew you were a road stop, Sandy Agnes. Only you were trickier than that, getting pregnant, making my Jay think he needed to do right by you. No, she always knew about me."

I rocked backward, words hitting me, sending me to the floor next to Mom. My mind was digging through the Nevermore, searching for anything that could've told me this gross alternate history, but it was a blank. I watched Dad, this person I didn't know anymore.

"Sandy, listen," Doctor Julia said, carefully grabbing Mom's hands by the wrist so she wouldn't touch my vomit. "Jay isn't leaving you." Mom looked up, eyes wide. "We're here as an intervention." Doctor Julia patted my mother affectionately. "The dolphin is one of the few animals that mate for pleasure. A female dolphin isn't supported by her mate in the long run but by the community of her sisterhood. Jay is inviting you into a new understanding of his needs, welcoming you to be a part of his fulfillment. He's offering you that sisterhood."

Dad was nodding wildly, coming down on the floor to meet Mom's eyes.

"Sandy, you know how Rosie's got all those places she rents out? Well, she got the place across the street. At first, I was all worried about telling you about it. Any time I say her name, you turn into a mess."

I was so stupid. When he'd called the cabin all those years ago, I'd assumed Mom was depressed over Grandma. But she was losing it over my dad?

"Well, I'm sick of sneaking around. I'm a good man, Sandy, I know you're no good without me, so I won't leave you. I tried,

255

but I couldn't. We're going to make this work with all of us. That's why I told Rosie to come here. She's not going to rent out that house. She's going to stay in it, living right here in town. And maybe over time, when you're ready, she can move in with us. All of us."

Doctor Julia nodded. "Listen to your heart, Sandy. You know he's a good man."

"You monster," I said.

Dad shook his head at me.

"You don't mean that, Lady-girl."

"Never call me that again. No, you know what, call me whatever you want, but I'm done calling you my dad. I wish I could scrub your DNA off my skin."

Jay leaned in, looking me over with red rimmed eyes. "You don't mean that."

"Try me, Jay."

"Stop it!"

He was mad at me? As if I was the one ruining us.

"You told me it wouldn't be this way!"

"What are you talking about, you . . . "

Jay was up, one knee on the vomit towel, veins popping up as he grabbed my shirt. He squeezed my collar like he was trying to strangle it.

"You told me I could," he said. "The night I almost left? Remember?"

I didn't remember, but maybe that was because his dirty hands were too close to me, or maybe it was because he so openly admitted he was leaving us all those years ago.

"I told you to cheat on Mom when I was seven?"

"Don't call it that! I'm being honest about it, coming clean! You said I could have whatever I wanted, and you'd still be by my side. You brought us here, even after I warned you about pushing me too far. It was like you knew. That aura of yours telling me I could! My little messenger. But now you won't stand by me anymore? It's not about the cards you're dealt, Loralay. It's how you play them. I can't change that I'm a man."

I punched him—a jab to his cheek before he could block me. I managed one more on his nose before he had me pressed into the wall.

"Calming energy!" Doctor Julia shouted. Jay let go, dropping me to the floor.

I drug myself up, clenching Mom's hand.

"Come on, Mom," I said, but Mom didn't move. "What are you doing? Let's go!" And then I realized she wasn't leaving.

She was staying with him.

"What's wrong with you?" I asked, letting go of her. "You're going to lie here and take it?" But it was a question I should've asked years ago. No, a Nevermore ago. I'd had a second chance. I could've supported my mother, but I'd chased after the man that abandoned us, just like she had. "He's scum, Mom! Absolute scu—"

Jay had me by the shirt again, dragging me backward through the hall. I stumbled along, gasping for air as my feet knocked over furniture. I scratched at his wrists, yanked on his dolphin necklace, trying anything to breathe.

"Get out of my house!" he yelled, tossing me toward the front door.

I looked back at the hall. Mom hadn't followed. She didn't beg him to stop. Not even Doctor Julia intervened.

"Mom?" I asked, voice cracking after what my throat had been through. She didn't answer.

"Go," Jay said. "And don't come back."

I left.

Chapter Twenty-Four

DRUNK FLU

I was nestled in the frame of Drew's front door. I didn't remember the whole path there, but I remembered dry heaving a few more times along the way, and I knew I'd fallen asleep. The sun was about to set. The sky was hot pink and orange.

I reached up, rechecking their lock, even though I didn't know how many times I'd already tried it. The Neers weren't back from dinner yet. My hand fell back on my chest, wet with sweat.

Please don't throw up again, I begged my body as my eyes fluttered closed.

A car pulled up, but it was in the wrong driveway.

The Smalls were back home from the general store. Vikki was getting out of the passenger side, still dressed in a work apron, hair in a half ponytail. She leaned forward, squinting to see me.

"Loralay?" she called, then turned to Mr. Small. "Honey, I think Loralay's at the Neers' house."

"So?" Mr. Small asked, getting out of the car.

"She doesn't seem okay."

I considered running, but I didn't know where to go, and my body didn't want to get up. All I did was force my eyes to stay open.

The Neers' car pulled up in the driveway, blocking The Smalls from view.

"Thank you," I murmured, closing my eyes.

"Loralay?" Drew said.

I didn't look up, but I might have smiled.

"Is she drunk?" Mr. Small said, disgust on his tongue. If I had enough energy to care, I'd have laughed, a murderer morally objecting to underage drinking.

"Please," I said. "I'm sick. I can't go home."

A car door shut again. Mr. Neer staggered toward us. "Wha-s she doin'?" he asked, cheeks a telltale red. Drew eyed his dad, face turning the same color.

For a moment, they forgot me, Mrs. Neer and the Smalls communicating with their eyes.

I was dry heaving again.

"Is she sick?" Vikki asked. "I should call her mother."

"No," I choked out between gasps.

Mrs. Neer rubbed my back, sweet enough that she didn't care about my puke-encrusted clothes.

"That's right, babe. Let it out. So, what do we do?" she asked the gathering crowd.

Mr. Neer echoed her dramatically, shaking his drunken head. Drew tried to lead his dad away, but Mr. Neer wouldn't go.

"Take her to our house," Vikki said. "We'll put her in the girls' room until we figure this all out. I can help bring her in. Heath Hennery's still napping in his car seat.

"No," Mr. Small said. It relieved me, thinking he didn't want me. "I can carry her in myself. You get the boy and call her parents."

He lifted me. I fought it first, but his touch made me rigid, Mr. Small's hands encircling my body, keeping me close to his chest.

I watched his face, the odd angle casting shadows on his neck, a glow of sunset around his features. He didn't look at me, like he was hauling an oversized bag of rice . . . or cat litter. My stomach lurched again as I feverishly watched Drew help his dad inside the house. There wasn't going to be a way the Neers would let me stay with them, not when they had their own problems to deal with.

New problems. He didn't start drinking again until Nevermore next year.

Mr. Small dropped me on Sal's bed. "We'll get this settled." He tossed a blanket over me and walked out. He left the bedroom door open so he could see me, like a spider keeping its many eyes on its twitching dinner.

Sal's side of the room was mostly empty. Her wall of pictures now an uneven row of sun-bleached squares and thumbtack holes. Her closet hung open, displaying a bare rod, the upper shelf full of taped-up boxes. I found myself staring at a box of Life cereal, wondering what was inside.

"Any luck?" Mr. Small asked. I strained my ears to hear the answer.

"No one's picking up. I don't feel right about this."

"Call the station."

"The police?" Vikki asked. "It can't be that serious, can it?"

"Don't like it. Shouldn't be our responsibility."

I lied my head back on Sal's pillow. At least a police officer sounded better than a murderer.

"I still say she was drinking. I could smell it."

"That was Mike. Didn't you see him?"

"Could be. I'd rather know than wonder."

I rubbed my hand across the blanket around me, wondering if it was one of the ones he'd pack in his car, planning to dispose of his children's bodies.

When the officer came in, Mrs. Small was helping me drink ginger ale through a bendy straw. It was the same man who had been at the store when Sal's pictures were discovered.

"You ready to go home?" he asked me, without so much as a hello.

"My . . . " I paused, wanting to call him Jay but knowing they wouldn't understand. "Dad kicked me out," I said.

Mrs. Small put her hand to her mouth, hearing this for the first time.

"Oh, now," The officer said. "Everyone says things they don't mean. All families have their own little problems. Right, Small?"

Mr. Small leaned into the bedroom door, arms folded. He shrugged in response.

"Well, I'm sure they're worried about you now. You're Sandy's girl, right? Man, I remember her mom when I was a kid. There's an uncomfortable family." He laughed, but no one joined him. "No, your mama's going to be worried about you, you'll see."

I had to sit in the back of the car like a criminal, watching the back of the officer's sunburned neck through the partition. I lay my head back, trying to rest before I had to see Jay again, but when we pulled up, his car was gone.

The officer knocked as I curled up on the porch swing, trying not to rock for my stomach's sake.

"I'm pretty sure I hear someone in there, and I don't think it's locked," he said after trying multiple times. "Why don't you head on inside. I'll be right here."

I clung to the siding, edging my way inside.

Someone was home.

I could hear a rhythmic scrubbing.

I went into the hall, where Mom was still kneeling on the floor, re-cleaning what was now only a wet spot.

"Mom?" She didn't answer. "Mom?"

I'd only ever known two people who were dead inside. One was Death himself, and the other was my Nevermore mom.

I took the scrub from her. She stared at her hands as if she'd never seen them so empty. "He's gone," I said.

"I told him to go," Mom said, and then she cried into those hands.

Chapter Twenty-Five

SHORT CALL

It rang twelve times before Drew picked up the phone.

"Hello?" He sounded so much older now, a man when his father couldn't be.

"Hey," I said, sitting down in the living room, watching Mom sleep on the couch. She wouldn't go back in Grandma's bedroom now. I'd brought her things out. They littered the living room like a bad houseguest. "I know we were supposed to play music today, but I can't."

"That's okay. I can't either."

I listened, not to his words, but the hitch in his breath. I could hear Drew padding through his house, closing the bathroom door before he answered. I smiled a little, both of us on our cordless phones again, like the Nevermore.

"Sucks because I really like hanging out with you."

"Me too," I said. "I'm pretty fun to hang out with."

Drew laughed, harder than the joke was worth, tension cracking him open. "You feeling better?" he asked. "Your cold, I mean."

"Yeah. It was that flu going around. Still coughing, but nothing bad."

"Get some rest. Mrs. Esmer's mom caught that same flu from one of the staff. She didn't make it."

"That's too bad," I said. I wondered if Death held her hand too. "How's your Dad?"

"I don't know. He told Mom all his drinks were virgin. We figured it out after the third, but he wouldn't stop. My mom thinks he assumed he was strong enough to handle it again, but he wasn't. He keeps cleaning everything now. Says he's sorry."

Mom was stirring. I got up, putting another blanket over her.

"I heard about your dad," Drew said. "I don't know what to say, but I'm sorry."

When I hung up, Mom hadn't woken up yet.

I went into the kitchen to make us oatmeal.

I'd found a new respect for jugglers, keeping everything in the air.

I went to school, cried a lot, played piano—right in front of Mom. But she'd only curl up tighter when I did, like I was convincing her she was worthless. When I got my license, she sat in the DMV with me, not a word leaving her lips. I took over the van, her debit card, her responsibilities.

I knew this woman. The Nevermore mother who took a vow of silence, only talking when it'd do the most damage. I worked after school and on the weekends. Days at the nursing home, nights nursing Mom. I'd bring her dinner, tell her to eat. Start her bath and lead her to the water.

I'd call Sal to hear about her new life and, when I was lucky, I saw Drew at work or talked with him on the phone, Anita in the background of our conversations.

"Tell her to get here!" she cooed at Drew.

"Anita says you need to come to Potbelly's." There was static on the line, Drew and Anita giggling over something I couldn't see. It was Sunday night, getting late. Mom was on the couch after a rigorous day of sleeping and watching TV, and I was doing homework on the porch swing, watching our new neighbors in the red-roofed house play basketball. I wondered how Rosie and Jay spent the rent money in their new life.

"You still there?" Drew asked. "Can you make it?"

"Yeah," I said. "I'll be there." Back to juggling. Fighting gravity.

Chapter Twenty-Six

GLOW KIT

I came inside the house, tossing three more letters on the pile of mail Mom wouldn't open.

"I'm going out," I said. Mom didn't acknowledge me, curled on the couch watching poker. I stood in front of the screen. "Gonna meet up with some friends. I'm taking the van." She scratched her neck. I thought about how excited she was when she first met Sal. "I'll be safe."

She didn't say goodbye. I put a blanket on her.

Oak Ridge didn't have trendy coffee shops or cool skate parks like we saw on MTV. We had Potbelly's. Dinner, bowling, arcade. Leagues for the elderly, kids' parties on the weekends. I didn't know many teens who bowled regularly, but it was a popular spot for dates and general loitering. Not tonight though; November wasn't high traffic, and there was school tomorrow.

I parked Mom's van, flicked the headlights off and started picking at my fingernails.

I wanted to see Drew, just not with her. But I felt like Death was watching. I needed to do my part.

Do this for Makenzie, I thought.

I got out of the van, surrounded by crickets and a low wind in the brush. Something about the chill reminded me of Stephen saving me from the storm. We hadn't had many classes together this year now that we were all seniors. I wanted to catch up, but I didn't have time.

I pushed on the big metal door and went inside, blinking at the contrasting colors on every wall, the intense smell of fried food, and an onslaught of neon across the main desk. Only a few die-hard bowlers were out, keeping the thundering sound effects to a minimum.

"You want shoes?" a baggy-eyed old woman asked. Gail. Potbelly's residential curmudgeon. Even if she didn't have a name tag, I knew her.

"That depends. Do you clean the shoes now?" I asked, remembering how she got me in trouble for spraying Lysol in those fungus-encrusted oxfords. Nevermore Loralay considered herself the last defense against an athlete's foot outbreak.

"What did you say?"

Oh, that's right. She liked to pretend she was deaf. What was it with the elderly community and everyone being crabby? "I think I'll pass, thanks."

"Well, can't bowl if you don't, and bowling will give you better hand-eye coordination. It's an easy-to-learn sport, and it's great fun for all age—"

"Loralay! Over here!" Drew called, saving me. I weaved my way through tables to get to the back booth near the arcades.

Drew was wearing a pink polo with the collar popped. The checkboard table held red baskets full of cheesy fries, onion rings, and tacos—food Drew wouldn't be touching. He and Anita smashed together in the booth, leaving the other seat open for me, right next to—

"Stephen?" It was then I realized I was on a double date.

"Hungry?" Stephen offered me a tray. I wasn't anywhere near as healthy as Drew, and at the moment, I needed carbs. I took three rings, stuffing them in my mouth as I sat down. Sweat trickled down my back. Had anyone told Stephen this was a date? When had Drew signed on to helping Anita play matchmaker? More food seemed like the right answer. I attacked the cheesy fries.

Anita didn't say hello, head down, looking at her lap.

"She okay?" I asked, wiping my mouth with my sleeve and swallowing.

"Yeah, she's just checking out her new phone," Drew said. Anita held a phone up out of her lap to show it off without taking her eyes off the screen. "She's trying to beat my record in *Snake*," Drew added.

"Your phone plays games?" Stephen asked. Judging by his question, he was apparently also new to the table.

Had they called both of us at the same time? Were more people coming? Please say they were. Maybe it wasn't a date.

"Earth to Anita," Drew said, waving a hand at her. "Stephen asked you a question."

Anita jumped back, eyes still on the screen. "First, like, don't touch me when I'm playing. Second, yes, it has games but, like, nothing more amazing than a TI-83." She bit her lip, twisting her entire body like it'd help her turn sharper. "Third, I'm not trying. I *am* beating it. Twenty-one points," she said with a sigh, dropping her phone in her lap.

"Don't give up!" Drew laughed. "See how far you can get!"

"Where's the fun in that? If I beat you that bad, you won't play me anymore." She turned to me. "Drew thinks I'm better because he doesn't have time to play, but really he has zero skill."

"Oh, she owned you, Dawg!" Stephen said.

"Why would I be a *player* when I've got you," Drew asked with a smirk.

I started using both hands to eat.

"Have as much as you want." Stephen pushed more trays my way. I did not turn him down. "Me, I'm sick of the food. Ghetto bein' in here even on my day off."

"How do you like working with Gail?" I asked him, seeing that Drew and Anita were in their own little world.

"Gail? Not so much. I'm a trauma victim." Stephen held out an arm. "Wrap me up 'cause she makin' me dead."

I mimed wrapping bandages on Stephen's arm.

271

"Aw!" Anita said, like we were cute. I guess we were? "Yeah know, I always wanted to be a nurse. Hey, Loralay, what's your Myspace name?"

"My what name?"

"No way! You're not on Myspace? Stephen, you have a Myspace, right?"

Stephen nodded.

"Loralay, I'm making you an account tomorrow. You two should be in each other's top eight. Like me and Drew!"

"Technically," Drew said, holding up a hand. "I've never been on Myspace. Anita runs both accounts."

mr. Neer but the school"Something you'll thank me for when we have, like, three kids, and you can show them what you were like as teenagers!"

Drew and Anita with three kids? The food was a bad idea. It was hitting my stomach now.

"Think of it as a memory book." Anita tossed her phone on the table. It bounced, skidding next to the edge.

"You're gonna bust it!" Stephen said.

"Don't care." Anita flipped her dark ponytail back. "My dad will get me a new one."

"We're closing up!" Gail called from the front desk.

"I just got here, motherf—" Stephen muttered.

"Watch your mouth!" Gail hollered, her hearing miraculously healed.

"I was going to say fudge, woman!" Stephen yelled back, putting me in a headlock when I laughed.

We were in the parking lot, sky of a thousand stars above, standing next to our cars. I leaned into Mom's van, flipping the keys around my finger.

"For real?" Stephen asked, bending low to see the red glow kit lining the floorboards of Anita's Mazda Miata.

"Yeah, I helped install it," Drew said. He clicked something on the dashboard, switching the red under glow on and off.

"Are those even legal?" I asked. Both boys looked at me like I'd caught them with their hands in the cookie jar.

"Everything's legal," Stephen said. "If you don't get caught."

Well, at least it's not orange, I thought.

"I hope you daaa-ance!" Anita sang along to her radio. "Oh, I love this one!" She turned the country music up. Stephen doubled over like the sound was physically hurting him.

"That's brutal!" He tossed open her backdoor to dig through Anita's CD case for a replacement. "Is everything you got by Shania Twang?"

"Twain," Anita corrected. "And this isn't by—"

"No, that's twang." He mimed a scream, flipping through faster. "It's all twang!"

"Hey." Drew reached across Anita to turn down the music. "We've got to go. I have practice in the morning."

Anita turned the music back up.

"I'm serious."

"You said we could go for a night drive, all of us!"

"I didn't mean tonight. Our last game is this Friday. My dad's going to kill me if I'm not ready."

273

"It's my game too," Anita said, rolling her eyes. "Stop talking like it's all about you."

My lips twitched as I tried to hide a smile. I shouldn't have been happy they were fighting. No part of this was good, I reminded myself.

"Can we not do this? Please?" Drew pinched the bridge of his nose.

"Please? Are you, like, serious right now?" Anita's voice was nails across a chalkboard. "Look at you, Mr. Attitude. What was the point of calling everyone here for half an hour?"

"Dope, Linkin Park," Stephen said. "It's not rap but—"

"Stay out of this!" Anita barked.

She stopped there, realizing she'd crossed Drew's don't-be-rude-to-anyone line.

"I can walk home," Drew said, voice way too quiet.

Yes, Drew, walk home! Then I can give you a ride. Just me and . . . someone else's boyfriend. I pocketed my keys, chastising myself.

Stephen scooted forward, hitting the eject button like no one could see him. We all watched the Lee Ann Womack CD slide out, reflecting the red glow of her car. He grabbed the CD with two fingers, stealthily sliding Linkin Park in the empty slot.

"Sup?" Stephen asked as if nothing happened.

Anita turned back to Drew.

"See? We're, like, having fun! Stop whining about being tired."

"Why don't we all go?" I said. Drew wasn't bluffing, and I didn't trust myself not to channel Jay's inner dolphin. "We take Drew home and get a fun ride on the way."

"What about your van?" Drew asked.

"Anita can drop me off back here to get my car."

"You're going to put Loralay through that so we can hang out fifteen minutes longer?" Drew asked Anita.

I didn't wait for an answer. I hopped in the back seat with Stephen.

Drew didn't talk on the way home, still upset—his red-tinted head against the window, condensation budding against the glass. We dropped him off first, and he hardly said goodnight. I knew he was having trouble keeping his eyes open. Anita, it seemed, did not.

"Goodnight, loser!" Anita called playfully.

It wasn't playful. Drew looked back, a quick glare, the closest he ever got to flipping anyone off. We all watched his front door close.

Stephen climbed up front, showing Anita what roads to take to get to his house, simultaneously taking over her CD player. If this was a date, at least he seemed uninterested.

"You got an iPod?" He pulled a black rectangle out of her cup holder.

"You want it?" Anita said, still annoyed. "I don't."

"You wiggin' out?"

"I'm, like, not even going to pretend I know what you said, but if you want it, it's yours, m'kay?"

Stephen looked back at me. "You see good back there? I didn't gank it?" I nodded. Stephen shrugged, pocketing her iPod. "Whew, this shady. Well, it's cashed. You want the headphones back, though?"

"Like seriously, take it all. My dad said he'd get me the white one, but he didn't. Figures."

Stephen shook his head.

"How many dead presidents does your dad have if—naw. I don't want to know. I'm good with this. I'm liable to feel sorry for you, shooter."

"What are you even saying?" Anita said.

"Dead presidents? It's bones. Yeah know, money."

"No, like why don't you talk normal, like, I don't know."

"You mean you want him to, like, talk, like, you, Anita?" I said, thinking maybe Drew cheating on her with me wouldn't be so bad.

"I'm out," Stephen said.

"What are you mad at me too now?"

"No. I'm out. Right here. We have arrived. This my place. Stop!" Stephen yelled.

Anita screeched to a halt. Sending us all shooting forward.

"I'm so sorry! Did you have your seatbelt on?" Anita asked me. *You don't die from a car accident with a driver trying to get insurance fraud and not wear your seatbelt.*

"I'm okay," I said. "Your CDs took a nosedive, though." I broke into a cough. It didn't take much to get me coughing, a souvenir from the flu I'd had on the day Dad left.

"Look, chica," Stephen said. "I can talk *normal*." He made a big show of clearing his throat. "You think I talk this way around the dinner table at home? I don't talk *normal* because it doesn't suit me. I emulate a culture that I *identify* with. Plus, you try being the little Asian kid in a school of bamas, excuse me, I mean in a

276

school where there are more racist rednecks than guys like me. If I'm homie G, People leave me alone. No more, 'Hey, Mr. Slant Eyes math tutor, why don't you show us karate.' Educate yourself." He opened the car door, putting on a nasally voice. "Now, thank you ever so much for the lovely evening out, Miss Anita." He dropped the voice. "I'm gonna bounce."

We watched Stephen walk up to his house just like Drew. I winced when his door slammed.

We sat there in silence for a while, my throat itching. Anita breathed hard through her nose.

"Are you, like, going to move to shotgun?" she asked.

"Oh? Uh, sure," I said, getting out. I hadn't thought about sitting next to her.

The neon light was more intense up front, the flaws of our skin perfected in its filter. I buckled up, waiting to go. We didn't. Anita was picking at a fray in her distressed jeans.

"You're right about me," she said. "I don't like it."

I had no idea what that was about, but I was sure I didn't want to know.

"The red looks cool," I said, mentally begging her to drive.

"My dad paid for it. He's never around, so he like, tries to buy me crap."

Stop it. I wanted to scream. I wanted to hate her. I needed this. Somehow sitting in closer proximity made her more of a person and not just an obstacle to Drew.

"I'm sick of it. New phones, this car, tricking it out. Like, that's all he is to me after the divorce." She threw her shoulders back, keeping her arms steady on the steering wheel. Maybe other people would miss it, but I knew all about suppressing emotions.

277

"Remember when you told me to be better to Stephen?" I didn't think I'd said that, but I didn't interrupt. "You're like, so right. I want to sound like I'm better than him, then anyone, but I'm not. I told my mom I wanted to be a nurse, and she was all like, 'But you'd need to have empathy for people.' I told her I did, but she didn't believe me. Why should she? I'm such a bitch. I don't know what Drew sees in me."

"Drew's a great guy," I said, dismissing her with a wave of my hand. "He sees the best in everyone."

"Yeah," Anita said. She backed up. Her jaw was tense. I crossed my arms.

"I keep being stupid around him," Anita added, not taking my hints. "Like, what's wrong with me? I know I'm high maintenance, or whatever, but I'm just a girl who knows what she wants." She brushed her hair back. I saw she was really wiping her eyes. I sighed. It wasn't fair.

"Caring's a good start," I said. "Knowing what you want doesn't make people jerks. Not caring about what other people want does. Drew is exhausted, Stephen wants respect, and I want—" *Your boyfriend.* "It doesn't matter what I want. You don't pay attention to other people. You should. Life's too short not to." Great, I'd become an inspirational poster.

"Do you think Drew and I are good together?"

There it was. I should've stayed home. But my own words were ringing in my ears. *You should care about what other people want.*

"I think he's lighter around you. You make him happy." If only that was a lie. Anita smiled a smug little smirk. But why shouldn't she? I was the creep here.

"I know you're right. It's just that everyone has a crush on him. Like last night Sal was all up in our business. Drew didn't even tell her off. Like—"

"Sal? Sally Sue Small? What do you mean last night? She doesn't live here."

"Duh, she like, came home?"

I didn't have room in my head to take that information in, so Anita's words stayed in the air, knocking into my skull until I absorbed them.

"When?"

"I don't know. Two days ago? Oh, that's right, she's like your friend or whatever. Sorry, I just think she's weird."

I couldn't speak. I squeezed my thighs together. No one told me. It couldn't be true. She didn't call. Anita was an idiot. She was talking about Irene, right?

"So, what do you want?" Anita asked me.

"I told you, it doesn't matter."

"You said I should pay attention to people. I'm, like, starting with you or whatever."

"I want a story with a happy ending."

Anita dropped me off at the van, and I went home. Mom didn't say hello, but she'd opened the mail.

A notice of foreclosure sat on top where I could see it.

Chapter Twenty-Seven

SMALL VICTORIES

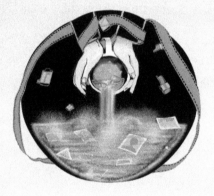

Sal wasn't in school Monday. I'd pestered Drew all day, and he assured me she was back, but he knew nothing else. So, when I got home, I threw on a hooded sweatshirt, filled the center pocket with some carefully chosen contraband, and called in to work.

It was four thirty when I drove Mom's van to the Smalls'. The store wasn't closed yet, but Vikki's car was in the driveway, so she must have been home for Heath Hennery's nap.

I crossed their yard at a run, soaking my pantlegs in the November puddles, passing a toy beach bucket leftover from the summer.

It was stupid, but that bucket made me feel bad—a symbol of neglect. I should've been watching closer, even after Sal left. Maybe tried to strike up a friendship with Irene Isabelle.

They could die. Right here, under my watch.

I hit the door with my palm, pounding for an answer.

Vikki opened it but didn't undo the chain, only a crack between us. Her eyes, on the other hand, were wide.

"Loralay? Is that you? Is everything okay?"

"Is Sal here?" I was craning to see inside, using Jay's door-to-door etiquette. But their living room was dim as always, leaving me nothing.

"Oh, Sally Sue? Uh, yes."

Vikki shut the door in my face. What was I doing? I shouldn't have banged so hard. But she was only undoing the chain to open it the rest of the way.

"Somebody hurt?" she asked.

"I heard Sal was here. I wanted to see her?"

"Oh," Vikki said. "She's in her room." Something in her voice told me I wasn't welcome. I didn't know why, but I took it as a sign I needed to stay.

I went straight to the girls' room. Vikki muttered what I assumed were objections. I nodded along as if she was being polite.

Sal was sitting on her bed. The room was still deconstructed, but now there were more boxes in her closet and clothes on the hangers. She was writing in a notebook that was propped on her lap. She nearly dropped her pen when she saw me.

"I heard you were back," I said.

"I am," Sal said.

Of all the word combinations we could choose from, the best we managed was to state the obvious. Maybe we had more in common than I thought. I sat down next to her, noticing Irene Isabelle was in the room too, folding clothes on her bed.

"Why didn't you call?" I asked.

Sal glanced at Irene Isabelle.

"She's not supposed to," Irene said. "Because you're a drunk."

"Is that what your dad said?" I asked, but I knew. At least now I understood Vikki's reception. "It's not true. It was the flu." Not like that would convince Mr. Small. "How's Heath Hennery?" I added, watching Irene fold his clothing.

"He's figured out how to climb everything now," she said, sounding like a proud young mother. "Even got on the counter twice." Some of the shirts she was folding were worn nearly see-through. If anything screamed poor, it was roughed up children's clothes, considering they grew out of everything so quickly. There wasn't anything wrong with it; Drew and I had our share of end-of-the-line hand-me-downs for Makenzie, but our kind of poor didn't mean our kid ended up dead.

Irene finished her basket load, taking the hamper out with her.

I bent, leaning into Sal. "It's not your fault what happened with Julius," I blurted in a whisper, desperate to get as many words in as I could before Irene came back.

Sal jerked back when I mentioned his name. We'd never talked about it on the phone, but that was because it felt better pretending nothing was wrong when she was far away.

I couldn't pretend anymore. "It's okay. Look, I just need you to know I'm on your side. You can tell me anything. I'm your friend, Sal."

"I don't take pictures of Drew anymore," she said, as if obsession was my primary fear. If only it was. "I know that was weird now. My dad told me if I ever did that again, he'd—" She picked at the frayed edges of her comforter. "My dad took my camera."

"Oh, Sal!" I said, probably too loud.

"He didn't know I was taking so many. Said it cost a fortune. Grandma thinks I should be a journalist. That's why I write now." She pointed to the notebook in her hand. "You can get them on sale for ten cents each. Grandma sent me a whole paper bag full."

I didn't want to talk about notebooks. I wanted to be sure she'd live, but Sal was digging under her bed to show me. A disposable coffee cup rolled out too. I recognized the Black Day's Coffee logo. The same place Drew sometimes ran in the morning.

It wouldn't have mattered, but the way Sal shoved the cup back under the bed spoke volumes.

"That's the cup Drew had on the bus, isn't it?"

"No." Sal flinched.

I put my hands on her arm, trying to calm her. "It's okay, Sal, you can tell me. I'm not—" It smelled like Drew under her bed. There was an empty bottle of Calvin Klein One, and a few of Drew's origami frogs. "What is this?" I asked, holding up a pink wad, pressed between what appeared to be two pieces of picture frame glass.

Sal blinked at it, deciding what to say. "My gum. I was . . . saving it for later." I put the pilfered gum back under her bed and massaged my forehead. Had she really kept Drew's gum? Did she chew it too? I couldn't make it about this; we didn't have time.

"Sal," I said. "I want to help. You're still finding signs, aren't you?" Sal nodded. I glanced at the door, checking that no one was listening. "I understand it. All of it. Drew's your escape story." Sal's eyes brightened for a second. "You use him to get by, and I don't blame you. Your dad, he hurts you, doesn't he?" I said it so low it surprised me Sal heard.

"No," She said, all too fast, the light inside her going out. "Well, not bad. Mom doesn't let him get too—"

A door slammed.

"Vikki!" Mr. Small called. "Is that the Grayson van out front?"

I locked eyes with Sal, digging in my side pocket.

"I brought you something," I whispered. Sal scooted back like I was pulling a gun. I held out Jay's Motorola phone. "This can be your new escape story. It's not hooked up to call anyone, but you can make emergency calls. Use it if things ever get bad. No one will know you have it. Okay? Just keep it better hidden than the rest of your stuff. Bury it if you have to."

Sal didn't take the phone, and I could hear her dad's footsteps coming, so I stuffed it into her pillowcase, along with the charger.

"One last thing." I pulled Sal in so I could whisper in her ear. "If he brings cat litter home, you need to get out. All of you. That's your sign."

"We don't have a cat," Sal said.

I tried to answer, but Mr. Small came in, arms folded like he'd caught me stealing from his store. Apparently, our feelings toward each other were mutual.

"Grayson girl. You'll excuse me, but we'll be cutting this short."

"Why?" I asked.

Mr. Small chuckled. "Impertinence for one. I've been thinking about how friendly you were with the Ray boy, about how you threw yourself at the Neers' front step, drunk."

"For the last time, I had the flu."

Mr. Small shook his head. "I didn't need to make mention before, but I saw Mr. Grayson on the way out of town. Stopped by the store to pick some things up before he traveled."

In all the things I'd imagined Jay had been up to after he'd left us, stopping for road trip snacks wasn't something I'd pictured. But more than that, I didn't know what it had to do with me.

"He and I gotta talking," Mr. Small said. "Told me you busted up his nose." I'd actually hurt Jay? I didn't think my punch did much—one point for me.

"He was cheating on my mom."

Mr. Small sucked his teeth. "It's harder than people know, running a family. Men gotta do what they can." Mr. Small was chewing his cheek like cud. "Feel pretty good, punching him?"

What kind of question was that? Mr. Small kept chewing at his cheek.

"He deserved it," I said. I crossed my legs, then uncrossed them, feeling vulnerable no matter how I sat.

Mr. Small, arms still folded, put a leg up on Sal's bed. I couldn't think why he'd done that, but if he was trying to make himself intimidating, it was working a heck of a lot better than me standing on a table.

"My Sally Sue's an impressionable girl. I don't need her befriending a wild child. Your daddy strikes me as a good man. Maybe if you'd been less of a handful, he wouldn't've left. You sleep on that. It'll make a good girl out of you. I will not ask you to leave again."

There wasn't room for me to fight, but I gave Sal a long hard look, saying things I couldn't speak.

Chapter Twenty-Eight

WOOL THERAPY

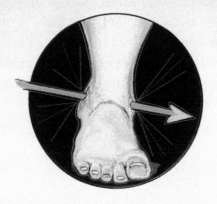

I leaned my elbow on the kitchen table, thinking about Sal instead of the phone call I was on.

"I can't look up the case unless you're the homeowner," the man on the phone said for the sixth time. "But yes, according to the dates you provided, you're pretty late in the process. That'll add a sticky amount of fees."

All that time, I'd thought Death tipped the scales, moving us out here, but in reality, Dad ran out of cash, taking a mortgage out on the house.

Mom shuffled in. It wasn't often she left the couch.

The man kept talking in my ear. "Although, if you don't resolve the delinquency, you'll lose the home. I'm sorry. I know that's harsh."

"Thank you," I said even though he hadn't told me anything new. He was nice enough to call me back on the weekend, so that was special. "Happy Easter," I added before I hung up.

Mom took the trouble to get herself a glass of water but abandoned it on the counter after a sip. I reorganized the pile of papers in front of me as if I was rearranging a jigsaw puzzle, only this game wouldn't end.

"Are you going to help?" I asked Mom, gesturing to my jigsaw. She shook her head, still eyeing her glass of water. Another person with nothing new to tell me. "Why? Let's at least go to the bank and see how much we have left. Jay could clean us out! And don't tell me he wouldn't do that." I shook the papers at her. "He left us without a house."

"I didn't want the house," Mom mumbled. "And I don't want it now."

"Ugh! Mom!" I pulled at my cheeks, yanking my eyelids down in desperation. "We live here! Jay's off probably on some cruise, and the only reason he hasn't drained us is he doesn't need to yet. But he will."

Mom put her hand out like she'd take another sip, then gave up, slumping into the counter.

"You keep talking like you know the future," she said to the glass.

"Then let's pretend I do and listen to me for once."

Mom did nothing. She didn't even sigh, just existed across the room. I went back to moving a letter from the bank from one side of the table to the other.

Someone knocked on the door.

I waited, obviously working, but Mom didn't make a move.

"Could you get that?" I asked her. "I'm kinda busy trying to fix your life."

She shuffled back toward the sink window, trying to peek at who it was. When I realized she was checking for any sign it was Jay, I slammed my hands on the table and got up.

"Does knowing the future make you angry?" Mom asked, quiet like she wasn't sure she wanted an answer. I gaped at her. It was like we were back in the car leaving counseling, the missing pieces between us.

The knock came again.

"Maybe it does," I said. Then I turned, heading for the door, ready to tell whoever it was to go away. It'd been a last-straw week. On top of managing our finances, I'd spent all yesterday at Drew's house, hanging out with him and Anita so I could watch over Sal. That was the closest I could get anymore outside of seeing her at school. It wasn't so bad until Drew had to exercise, and Anita spent her time editing my new Myspace page, informing me that Drew, Stephen, and I were, like, *so* going together to prom, and shouldn't we go dress shopping because that would be *fun*.

I tossed the door open.

"Mrs. Esmer?"

She had a purse over her shoulder, three plastic shopping bags around her wrist, and a solemn expression. Mrs. Esmer handed me two bags before saying hello. They were overflowing with yarn.

"Heard about it all," she said. "I know, I'm late."

"Uh . . . " I frowned at the yarn.

"It's not a bad thing I didn't know. Never been one to gossip, but someone mentioned it to me at church this morning, so there's no going back." She unloaded the third bag on me, coming inside.

"What am I missing here?" I asked.

"Something missing? Don't know. It's not my house."

"I wasn't talking about the house. What are you do—"

She was at the couch, tossing the blankets off one by one, clearing Mom's clutter. "It's better in here than I thought it'd be. Well, not spotless by a long shot, but hygienic. I'm ashamed to say, but I didn't do a dish for two months after my husband died. Took my mother coming to live with me to fix that."

"Does my mom know you're here?" A yarn ball escaped the bag in my arms, sending a line of woolly scarlet across the floor.

"She must know. Saw her looking out the kitchen window, poor thing. Better pick that yarn up." Mrs. Esmer folded a throw blanket. "I got the good stuff. No acrylics for a broken heart." She slapped my arm with the back of her hand. "You don't want to know how much that cost. It's an outrage. Unless, you knit?"

I shook my head.

"Crochet? Weave? Make pom-poms?" I watched her *tsk tsk* my lack of skill. "Ah well, then it's better I find your mother."

She was marching through the house, looking around.

I gathered the red yarn, rewinding the ball as I chased her.

"Mrs. Es—" She was already in the kitchen, holding Mom by the arm and bringing her to the living room couch. The glass in mom's hand threatened to spill.

"There we are, have a seat," she said. Mom seemed just as confused as I was, but she let Mrs. Esmer cow her onto the now-clear couch.

"I guess Mrs. Esmer is here?" I said.

"We'll make a blanket," she nodded. "Did the same thing when my husband died. Well, not right away—had to mope about first. Good thing I learned my lesson by the time my mother passed. Keep the hands busy. Sooner the better."

Mom looked at me, mouth clamped closed.

"Jay didn't die," I said. Another yarn ball escaped my arms. Mrs. Esmer took the bags from me, setting them all down on the coffee table.

"Didn't need to. Grief isn't picky." She dug in her purse, setting out hooks, needles, and stitch markers. So many implements she could've been prepping for surgery. "Look at you, still standing there," she said, sizing me up. "I know I'm barging in, Missy. I wasn't about to wait for an invitation. It's easier to push everyone away when you hurt, but that's not healthy. I don't have much, but it's all I've got to give, and I'm darn well going to give it until I'm in a pine overcoat. That's a coffin to you, youngster."

Sometimes you know people, way deep down, but they still manage to surprise you.

Mrs. Esmer was back to digging in her purse. "Better drink that water up," she said to Mom. "You're going to need both hands free. I've got pattern books, but I find it's easier to start with something plain. Maybe a granny square or two. Hop to it. For

291

you, though," she said to me, pulling out *Monty's Second Piano Manual*. "You're probably ready for this one."

"Thank you," I said, but I wasn't talking about the manual. Mom had her hands on the wool, running it through her fingers. She picked up a hook, starting a chain.

"Still haven't given me back the first one," Mrs. Esmer said because she was definitely talking about the stupid manual.

I left them there, heading to my room.

Mrs. Esmer did more than she'd known, showing me my next step.

It took me two hours to get everything together, but I was back at the Smalls' door, holding a manila envelope, knocking softly this time.

No answer. The beach bucket was still in the yard, now full of stagnant water.

Mr. Neer pulled up. The look he gave me when he got out of his car told me he knew I wasn't welcome at the Smalls' anymore.

I knocked again.

"Strawberry's," Mr. Neer called.

I frowned, confused.

"They're in the fields."

I waved thanks, hopping off the porch to run to the back.

The strawberry fields were made up of knee-high dirt mounds in rows, plants peaking up top, bringing the smell of fresh soil and lawn trimmings. Sal was a few rows away, wearing gloves, digging out dead leaves and stems.

She looked up at me, but I went past her, walking three more rows up to Mr. Small.

He was kneeling, patching a rusty wheelbarrow with duct tape—his scalp sunburn red.

"What's this?" he asked me, glasses reflecting light.

"I was hoping to talk to you alone." I clenched my jaw so it wouldn't shake. *I don't have much, but it's all I've got to give, and I'm darn well going to give it.*

Mr. Small nodded, jerking his head to tell Vikki to come with us.

I didn't make eye contact with Sal, worried that wouldn't help her.

The sunlight was strong enough that the room was green when we went inside. I blinked fast, forcing all my senses to function around Mr. Small.

"Please have a seat," Vikki said.

I sat, then shrieked. The couch had swallowed me, my arms in the air for balance.

"Oh!" Vikki pulled me up. "So sorry. Heath Hennery must've jumped on that side again!" She dug her hands under the cushions, hooking a spring back in place. I was shaking when she patted it for me to sit down again.

"That's embarrassing," Mr. Small chastised his wife.

"No, no. It's fine." I sat carefully. "I'm just overly jumpy, that's all."

"Yes. You are," Mr. Small said.

We watched as Vikki checked other sections of the couch, muttering apologies. I kept telling her it was fine, but she didn't seem to hear me.

"Why are you here?" Mr. Small asked. He didn't sit, standing rigidly above me.

There wasn't much window dressing to do—everything was already awkward—so I held out the envelope I'd been carrying.

"I know times are hard," I said. "I wanted to help."

"There's money in here."

"And a check." I nodded. I knew handouts could hurt, but when we'd been homeless, that was how we got by. Making things matter of fact tended to be easier on both parties. I'd promised Death he could have it all if it saved a life. Now I was proving it with my college savings. "It's not a bribe. You don't need to let me be friends with Sal." According to his face, that statement didn't help. I squirmed. *Keep it simple, Loralay.* "Last time I was here, I saw Heath Hennery might want some new clothes. That's all. You don't have to like me, Mr. Small, but that doesn't mean you can't—"

"Yes, it does," he said, tossing the envelope back in my lap.

"I'll buy jam then."

Mr. Small was breathing hard.

"Leave," he said.

"But—"

"I don't want charity, and not from some hissy." He threw the envelope at me, its corner jabbing into my stomach, causing a bright dot of pain. Vikki backed away, bumping into a lamp and nearly knocking it over. "How dare you come here to suggest I can't care for my own?"

I exhaled, slow, refusing to acknowledge the sting in my abdomen.

He was pacing, arms on his head, roughing up his hair, little wisps catching static. It was clear, the way he was looking at it, he wanted that money, eating away at him that it was mine to give.

"It's not like that," I said. "No one thinks less of you over a little help."

Mr. Small's head jerked up, eyes bulging. "Help, is it? You think I'm worried about being less than a little girl? Get out."

I didn't move.

"I said get out!"

I looked at Vikki, not sure if I should leave.

"Get out!" he screamed, spit flying off his tongue.

I fell backward, couch sucking me down.

"Get out, get out, get out!" He was coming, neck disappearing in the bulk of his shoulders.

I dug my nails in the armrest to pull myself free, ducking out of reach.

"No!" He yanked the envelope off the floor where it'd fallen. "You take this. You get it off my land, or I'll make you eat every dollar. Right down your throat." He pushed it into my chest. Knocking me back two steps. "Go!" he pointed at the back door we'd come through. It was still open, a slice of sunshine cutting the dark.

My legs were moving before I made a choice, passing the kitchen and the . . .

A shiver ran through me. The laundry room was disorganized. Baskets of clothes filled the doorway, and floor space was taken up with large bags, twenty or more, stacked.

I didn't leave. "What's the cat litter for?" I asked quietly.

Mr. Small's head twisted from the laundry room to me, face tight as his fists.

I was too slow.

He was beside me in two strides, hand in a fistful of my hair, pulling at the nape of my neck. My head jerked backward, looking up at him.

I should've fought back, but I didn't know how to. I'd forgotten how to breathe.

"Should've known you couldn't understand simple sentences." His lips were pulled back, showing teeth. "When I say go. You go. When I say jump, you say how high." He let go of my hair, shoving me into the wall, my body slamming into Vikki's collage of flowers. I shot up, trying to make it to the door. "Now, jump!"

He kicked me, one swift jab from his steel toe boot to my Achilles' heel. I stumbled out, limping, running to the Neers'.

Chapter Twenty-Nine

DOUBT

"Call the police!" I said for the fourth time. Mr. Neer told me to calm down.

I was sitting on the living room weight bench, legs crossed, cradling my ankle. Anita knelt beside me, glaring at Mr. Neer. She'd been hanging out with Drew when I'd barged in and now was the only person taking me seriously. Drew sat on the foot of the treadmill, sweating, eyes darting between us all.

"Let me see it again," Mr. Neer said. I pulled my pant leg up. My heel was red, a welt on the surface, but the throbbing was worse than it looked.

"It's not even bleeding." Mr. Neer sighed.

"He hurt me." I was already sick of explaining. We all watched the window. Mr. Small stood in the strawberry field, glancing back at us.

"This is ridiculous. Let me go talk to him." Mr. Neer headed outside. "I'm sure we can sort it out."

We watched him through the window, joining Mr. Small.

Anita groaned, getting up. She grabbed the Neers' cordless phone.

"Where are you doing?" Drew asked.

"She said call the police, so I'm doing it."

"But my dad—"

"Is slow," Anita said. She dialed. "Hello? Yes, it's an emergency. This old guy kicked my friend."

I hadn't heard her call me her friend before.

Drew and I looked at each other as Anita told the dispatcher our location. I knew how hard this was on him. Any confrontation was bad enough, but Mr. Neer was going to be a handful after this.

"We could play some music as we wait?" he suggested. Anita and I glared at him. "Sorry. I didn't think you were that hurt."

"How—" I was going to ask how he could possibly be so immature, but Anita cut me off.

"That's not the point." She popped her hip. Then she turned back to the phone. "Yes, I'm still on the line."

We could see them out there: Mr. Neer talking, Mr. Small folding his arms, shaking his head. At one point, I saw Mr. Neer laugh. Old neighbors, talking about the crazy troublemaking girl.

The officer took his time, but Mr. Neer was still out there talking when he pulled up.

Mr. Neer darted back inside.

"I leave you kids for once second . . . "

The officer walked up the drive, adjusting his belt. The same guy every time, but I'd never learned his name.

"Afternoon." He turned down his radio. "We havin' a disturbance out here?"

"Nothing we can't—" Mr. Neer started.

"Mr. Small kicked me."

The officer raised his eyebrows, pulling out a notebook.

"You two again." He said it as if Mr. Small calling when I was sick constituted a history. "Let me see where."

I twisted my leg to show him the welt. "Looks like a blister. Your shoes too tight?"

"No. He kicked me. *And* pushed me into a wall."

"Didn't happen," Mr. Small said. I hadn't seen him walk up. "Excuse me," he added, coming in the room to stand in front of me. "Why you going around sayin' things about me?"

"That's not—"

"Let me handle this one, Small," the officer said.

"Sorry," Mr. Small said, bowing his head in mock humility. "Gets me pissed off, lies going around. You have a Breathalyzer? She might've been drinking again."

"I never was! I—"

"All right, let's back up," the officer said. Mr. Small's lips were tight, but I could see he was holding a smile in. "Do you have anything else to show me? Cuts or bruises from the attack?"

"He . . . pulled my hair."

I knew it sounded stupid the second it came out of my mouth. Like Mr. Small and I were teenage girls in a catfight.

Drew blew air between his lips, eyes on the floor. Only Anita nodded encouragingly.

"Dipped her hair in the inkwell too," Mr. Small said. "Knocked her schoolbooks in the mud. Regular bully I am."

"Vikki saw it," I said.

"You mean Mrs. Small?" the officer asked. I hadn't thought about it, but I never called her that in my mind, separating her from her killer's name.

"The door was open, so Sal probably saw it too. And Irene, but they wouldn't say anything." I was breathing too hard, getting worked up. "They won't tell anyone that their dad hurts them. No one notices what's going on in that house!"

That changed the climate in the room. The officer looking up. Mr. Small jerked back and Mr. Neer's face paled.

I wondered about Mr. Neer's drinking then, the way it went full blast after the murders. Drew didn't know what was going on in that house, but that didn't mean Mr. Neer didn't. Was there some sort of honor code? Mr. Small looking the other way when Mr.

Neer snuck out with a bottle? Mr. Neer forgetting to mention sobs coming from the Smalls' house?

What was it that Mr. Small had said? *It's harder than people know, running a family. Men gotta do what they can.*

"The girl was at my house offering charity," Mr. Small said, pointing at the envelope in my lap. "I'll admit, it cut my pride. But this storytelling . . . " The adults looked at me.

"She is making quite the list of accusations," the officer said.

"She's a hellion," Mr. Small cut in too fast. "Troubled family life. Her father told me she'd been going to counseling more years than a hand's got fingers. Assaulted her father . . . hangs out with that Ray boy."

"Hey!" Anita said. "Stephen's nice!"

It was sweet, her coming to his defense now, but it wasn't like he was the moral example we needed at the moment.

"I know about Miss Grayson," The officer said. I didn't like him calling me that. It made him sound like he was on Mr. Small's side. "We go way back, don't we?"

"Uh, we do?"

"Got a call for a runaway about five years ago. Found her at the Halloween bazaar. Kid didn't even live here. Broke into her deceased grandmother's house, trashed the place. I told her mother she needed to get some outside help."

He *was* the same cop—every time.

All eyes were on me. Drew's were too, but he looked away when I met his glace.

"He kicked me," I said.

"Well," The officer said. "I have to say, you look okay to me."

301

"What's the cat litter for," I asked.

There was Mr. Small's rage, just for a second.

"What's she talking about?" the officer asked.

"It's nothing," Mr. Small said. "I bought too big an order for the store, and my supplier doesn't take returns. Kid's making a deal about it to rub in how much it cost me. Probably thinks it'll make me take her money."

"That's not—"

"I think it's time for you to go home," the officer said. "Why don't I give you a ride?"

"We'll walk her home, thanks," Anita said, nose in the air.

Mr. Neer snorted. "Not Drew." Then to soften the blow, he added. "Kid has a lap to finish."

I got up, my heel still screwy, but Anita had my arm. We left.

Together.

Chapter Thirty

OBSESSION

"And then there's this one," Anita said, setting yet another printout of prom dress possibilities on the table. "It sucks that I only get to wear two." She sighed, circling a big heart around one with her pen.

"Two?" Stephen asked. He paused his efforts on the origami lucky star I'd been teaching him how to fold, leaning in to see. Anita flopped on top of her paper stack.

"You can't look!" she whined. "Not before the big night!"

"You're thinking of wedding dresses," Drew said, chewing the end of his pencil.

Mrs. Corrin had the choir practicing in the music room before graduation, so we'd gathered in the library during lunch. Drew was using the opportunity to catch up on math homework, but I had an awful feeling he was avoiding me.

"How many times you fine ladies gonna be changing dresses?" Stephen asked.

"She's not," I said. "Anita gets *her* prom too. She's not graduating yet, remember?"

"No, that's it!" Anita was jumping in her seat. "I could wear two! It's like, here's Anita! Oh, she's leaving? Gotta, like, powder my nose or whatever. Then, psych! Here comes the new dress!"

Stephen laughed. "I see you, shooter."

"Why do you keep calling me that?" Anita asked.

"Because you got the coin, and you show it. Me? I'll be going in a tank and some JNCOs."

Anita leaned back into her seat, jaw slack. "You wouldn't do that to Loralay!"

"It's fine," I said. "I'm not wearing much better. I think there's a cocktail dress in my grandma's closet?"

Anita gasped like I'd run over her dog. "You wouldn't! Isn't she dead? That's, like, so gross!"

"Why? She didn't die in them. Plus, she was close to my size. I'll just add a belt."

Nevermore me already did the fluffy prom dress. It was electric blue to match my eyeshadow. I looked over at Drew,

304

remembering the white rose corsage he'd brought me. I missed the simplicity of it all. Now I had a mortgage to think about.

When I looked back, Anita's eyes were clamped on me harder than a shark bite.

"We're going shopping. I'll drive. As soon as school gets out. M'kay?"

"*We're* going out," Drew said to Anita. "Remember? My mom wanted to do dinner."

"Okay," she said. "Tomorrow then."

"Sorry, Anita," I laughed, releasing nerves that she and Drew were still so close. "I am *not* buying a dress for one night out."

Stephen clapped. "Pound it!" he said.

Anita pushed his fist down to the table. "You are totally *not* going to 'pound it' for that. This is the biggest day of your life!"

Stephen and I laughed. Even Drew chuckled.

"I mean, so far!" Anita corrected, but we were laughing too hard now. "Come on, you guys!"

The bell rang. I helped Anita gather her dress printouts, stuffing them in her binder. When I looked up, I saw Sal in the hall.

"I gotta go," I said.

"Why?" Anita asked, but then she saw Sal. "Loralay, don't. It'll just be trouble."

But they didn't know.

"It already is," I said, walking away. Anita called after me, but I just waved as I left the library.

Sal's hair was down. I didn't realize it was so long—lank, blond strands, crisscrossing over her backpack.

"Hey, Sal," I said.

She jumped, noticing me for the first time. "My dad said I'm not allowed to—"

The hall was crowding. I grabbed her arm, leading her to the girl's bathroom where we'd be alone.

"Sal, I've been so worried." I checked all the stalls. It was just us. When I turned back Sal's arms were crossed.

"About what?" Acid was in her voice—the seething cyclone back again. I hadn't seen it since sophomore year. "You didn't have a problem getting my dad mad."

"Oh no! Sal, did he hurt you?" My eyes swept her for bruising. Nothing. She looked away, grinding her teeth. "Sal, I told you. The cat litter, remember? That's your sign. Why didn't you—"

"Stop it! You never liked me. I knew it from the beginning when you didn't wanna come to dinner."

I paused, thinking I must've missed something. "What're you talking about? I came to dinner."

"Not like you wanted to."

My stomach dropped. Had I been that transparent?

"But you realized I lived next to Drew," Sal said. "Then you came."

"That's not true! I've always known you lived next to him."

"So that's why you wanted to be friends? You wanted to be near Drew?"

"No." I laughed, still on a high from laughing in the library.

Sal's nostrils flared.

"No, no. I'm not laughing at you. It's like you said his name backward. Near, Drew, Drew Neer. *Neer, near.* Never mind, it's stupid." How could I explain it? My mind was slipping, so stressed out. I needed to focus.

The bell rang again. We were late to class.

"Everyone thinks I'm stupid," Sal said.

"No! That's totally *not* what I'm saying, Sal."

"Yes, you do. But Drew? He doesn't." Her eyes darted around at nothing. "He knows I'm smart enough to pick up messages. That's why we don't talk in person. We don't need to. I understand him." She took her backpack off, pulling out a notebook. I held in a grimace, expecting more pictures. But it was all words. Full of words. Sal's handwriting was so tiny she fit two rows between the blue lines, writing top to bottom with no missed space.

I tried to swallow, but my mouth was dry. Sal didn't notice. She flipped through the pages, all of them with that tiny narrow cursive, pointing to things like they made sense.

"I'm supposed to deal with Dad until the right time." Her hands flicked through the pages. "It's all right because Drew loves me. See? Right here." She pointed to a clump of words then flipped through again. "You know how strong he is? That's for *me*. Getting tougher so he can fight back." She was rocking on her heels, hugging the notebook, a strange smile draped over her teeth. "One day he'll save me. We'll run away together, get married. He wants to make sure he's ready to prove he cares. Julius tricked me. Now you're doing the same. You scared me. I almost did run away when there was cat litter. But nothing happened. When Dad got mad, that was you! But Drew knew how bad it was. He ran three extra laps after you came over to show his dedication. *That's* our story."

I wasn't laughing anymore. I'd done it all wrong, downplaying her stalking Drew, so she'd trust me. All that time, she'd been padding herself in stories.

Sal's lips were a snarl, mind gone primal. "I can't leave. He wouldn't get to save me. I'm his princess. Waiting in the tower proves I love him back. He tests me sometimes, kissing Anita, hanging out with you, but that's because he knows I'm weak. I need testing."

"No one would do that, Sal." I wanted to break into the dark world she lived in. So many things I still didn't know about this girl. But her eyes were blank, and I didn't know how to fix it. I put my hands on her shoulders, ready to hug her to me, show her I cared, keep her safe. "Love isn't about being alone. If someone wanted to keep you to themselves, it wouldn't be loving. That's sick."

"You're going to be my counselor, then? Just like you do with everyone else?"

"No! I'm trying to be your friend! And you're making it freaking hard!" I shook her like I could knock the wall in her mind down with physical force. But it was the worst thing I could've done. Sal's eyes widened.

She was afraid of me.

Sal pushed me off, trying to stuff her notebook back in the bag. It fell on the ground, and she scrambled to gather it again.

I stepped on the strap.

"Hey!" Sal said, trying to yank it back. "That's mine. *He's mine!*"

"I'm sorry," I said. "You can't do this anymore." I took her bag, grabbing the handle before she could put it on. I left the bathroom with steady strides. I sped up when she chased me down the empty hall. Sal was screaming fear and rage, but I didn't stop, sliding flat into the closed door of the counselor's office. When I tossed the door open, the counselor had already left her seat. There was a study hall in progress, four kids in desks reading books.

Sal's screams came around the corner behind me.

"What on earth?" The counselor said, slapping her hands over her ears. I dumped the open bag on her desk, notebooks skidding out.

"Help her," I said as steady as I could. "Please."

We spent two hours waiting in the principal's office. Sal wouldn't look at me. When they sent me out, they told me they'd handle things, but I couldn't shake the feeling they didn't understand.

"He hurts them! I don't know how, but he's not going to stop. She could die!"

"Okay. Thank you. We'll deal with it," the principal said.

Sal wasn't on the bus home.

None of my friends were. I'd forgotten Anita took Drew home early so she could drive him to dinner, leaving me no one to talk to. I sat there, hugging my knees as Mr. Neer kept his eyes on me like I was going to combust. I pressed my head to the window. It felt cool across my burning face, but it couldn't calm the coals in my stomach. Sal was right. She shouldn't trust me. I was the only person who knew what was coming. Stalking, abuse, murder. Why did I think I could fix it alone?

We turned at the cul-de-sac, and I saw the new neighbors in the red-roofed house. They were out, playing basketball, laughing— more strangers with perfect boulevards.

And then I knew what I had to do.

I got off the bus, running to the red-roofed house.

"Hey!" I called. "Hey! Sorry. Do you know the phone number for the people you're renting from?"

One hour later, after three false leads, I heard his voice.

"Lady-girl?" Jay asked.

I swallowed my pride. "Dad?"

"Who's on the phone?" I heard Rosie ask.

"Loralay," Jay said.

"Who?"

"My daughter. Lady-girl? How you doing? Things good at home?"

Home. He still called it home. "You hurt us. But I shouldn't have hit you." He was quiet. I went on. "I'm sorry."

"No, don't do that." For the first time in my life, I thought he sounded choked up. "That's not. I don't know, kid. That was hard on all of us. I did a lot of things that were . . . I expected you'd call."

I grit my teeth. I certainly didn't expect it.

"You probably know now, about the house. I let it slide for a while. Rosie said she'd pay for it if your mom . . . well, you know. But Sandy didn't want the place, anyway."

He thought I'd called about the foreclosure. But it had taken something way bigger for me to call him.

I could hear Rosie grumbling next to him. "I'm not paying one dime to that house! Does she know what time it is? There's a time zone difference, and I still have jetlag!"

I closed my eyes—the First World problems of a homewrecker. "Dad, this isn't about the foreclosure. It's about the Smalls' store. They're out of funds. They can't sell the place. It's getting so bad—"

"What is it, baby girl?" he asked. "Are you crying?"

I cleared my throat, coughing. "No. It's just. They need help. I don't know what to do."

"I'll take care of it. Don't you worry. Your old man has it covered."

"Not on your life!" Rosie said. She must've picked up a different phone in her house, her voice as clear as Jay's. "I see what this is. Sandy works there, doesn't she? It's like a trap to help that little—"

"Naw," Jay said. "Sandy doesn't work. You know that. It's Loralay's little friend. Suzie Q or something. Local poor kid. Makes the world's worst jam. Real *Oliver Twist* stuff." I was 97 percent sure Jay never read *Oliver Twist*. "Lady-girl, Don't worry about it. I'll take care of you."

Rosie laughed.

"With my money? I already checked out the place a while back. It's a black hole. Molding was literally falling off the wall from moisture damage. And I swear I heard beetles tapping, so the hardwood floor is ruined."

"Can't we just help her out?" Jay asked. I squirmed, realizing he was using this as an absolution for all he'd done.

"Listen, sweetheart," Rosie said to me. "We'll call you back."

They hung up. I put my head on the kitchen table. It felt good, something solid. I imagined the table that Drew and Anita were sitting at, having dinner with Drew's mom. I didn't remember her taking *us* for special dinners, just the big family ones. But then again, by this time in the Nevermore Drew was already telling them he was going to take a year off before college, waiting for me. Everyone was in an uproar.

The phone rang.

"Look, sweets," Rosie said. "I don't have nothing against you. It's cute, you helping your friend. We can make this work. Maybe you can come visit us. We'll make it fun."

I still had no idea where they lived. I tapped the table my fingers drumming faster and faster.

"As long as this doesn't come back around to your trampy mother, then it's a deal." My fingers stopped mid drum. I tried to come up with an answer, but she wasn't waiting for one. "Jay wants to talk to you."

"Loralay? You hear that? I gotcha covered, didn't I?"

"Thank you," I said, finding my voice.

"See, things are good. I'm doing good. You should see out here! Palm trees, like you wouldn't believe. Rosie and I, we've got plans. I'm going to expand her real estate gig. Just you wait and see. Big things. I got your troubles taken care of."

When I hung up, there was a victory smile on my face. I didn't care where the money came from. I didn't care how I got it.

The world wasn't always right. But it was better.

Chapter Thirty-One

PROM AND PURGATORY

"So, DHS was there? And they didn't take them out of the house?" I asked Anita, taking the stairs to her bedroom. She'd invited me over to get ready for prom. I'd never been to her house. Mrs. Corrin seemed to have a habit of starting projects then giving up—her home was filled with unused things, monuments to each failed attempt. Gardening tools in the sunroom, kitchen cupboards full of cake pans even though Anita said her mom didn't bake, and an oversupply of bug books from when Mrs. Corrin took to entomology. She'd only finished one board, hanging a framed collection of dead butterflies in the stairwell. I looked at it as we passed, a pin through each thorax.

"I told you, I don't know," Anita said. "Maybe DHS is going back. Maybe everything's fine."

"It's not fine. They're getting abused."

"Can we, like, not, right now? The hairdresser took way too long. We only have, like, four hours left!" Her hair was pretty, though, all of it curled, pulled back in a loose bun with butterfly clips. Only her long bangs were straight, hugging the sides of her face to show off new chunky highlights. "Oh! And I picked your dress."

I looked down at the black cocktail dress I'd brought.

"Yeah, um. Like, not that thing. It's a dress I wore freshmen year, but like, with a cropped jacket and jeans underneath because that was a thing. Anyway, no one'll notice."

Anita took me up to her room. It was hilariously like my grandmother's pink and lace bedroom, only with a teenager spin. She dug through her closet.

"Won't notice? It's not like people keep tabs on what dresses—"

She held up a red sheath dress, spaghetti straps, and a pattern of champagne sequins at the waist. When I picked it up, Anita yanked Grandma's dress out of my arm, tossing it toward her hamper. It landed on the floor, covering a pair of platform flip-flops.

The dress didn't fit right, but Anita went to battle with safety pins until it yielded.

"Aren't you going to get changed?" I asked as she did my eyeshadow, both of us sitting on her bed.

"I'm going to change when we get there. I don't want my dress to get wrinkled on the drive. It goes down to my ankles." She paused, thinking. "I figure you should know. Drew and I, we're not really a thing anymore. He's still taking me and all, but it's like, not going so hot."

My heart skipped. "Why?"

"I know, right?" Anita said, missing how selfish my response was. "It's like, so weird. I knew something was up for a long time, and then, like, when we were in the library, and he was all doing his math homework to avoid me."

"You?" I said. Anita nodded, still missing my meaning.

"Yeah. Lame, right? And then dinner was awesome, and then we drove back in my car just me and him, and Drew was all, we need to talk, so serious. I don't know," Anita wiped her eye. She was starting to cry, and here I was, ready to celebrate.

"I'm sorry," I said.

Anita shrugged. "He told me he'd still take me to prom because, like, he already got the corsage. It was such a Drew thing to say, you know? I was so mad, but like, I didn't want to be a downer with you and Stephen. I mean, it'd be like ditching everyone. I can't go to prom if he's not my date. So, I said screw it."

I wondered if Anita was right. Maybe it was the most important night of our lives. Or at least, for Drew and me.

We picked Drew and Stephen up in Anita's car. Drew wore a black tuxedo with a pink dress shirt underneath that matched his lips. Stephen didn't wear his JNCO jeans, but he was proud to point out he had a sleeveless tank under his suit's jacket. He even had his Element sweater ready for slipping back into at the end of the night.

315

When we were all in Anita's car, we were perfect, smoothed by the red lights of Anita's Mazda, so young with so much time ahead of us.

"You look good," Drew said to me. "I like that you wore your hair normal. I thought you'd straighten it or something. That's what happens, anyway. Big day comes, and people want to be totally different than themselves." Anita's hands tightened on the steering wheel. "Oh, sheesh, Anita. I wasn't talking about you. It's nice." He lifted his arm like he would pat her shoulder but seemed to think better of it, rubbing his palms together instead.

Stephen looked at me, eyebrows asking what was up with the lovebirds. I silently linked my pointer fingers together, making a chain, then pulled them apart to represent a breakup. Stephen whistled.

"What is it?" Drew asked.

"Nothin'," Stephen said.

I helped Anita with her dress in the girl's bathroom. The same spot that Sal showed me her notebook. *Rosie's buying the place,* I told myself. *It's okay. I can enjoy this.*

"How do I look?" Anita asked. Her dress was white silk with a black sash around her chest, the lack of color bringing attention to her lips, painted as red as a solo cup.

"Perfect," I said, thinking how fitting a color solo was now that she didn't have Drew. But I winced at the thought, toes curling in my pumps.

I'm the world's worst friend.

"What is it?" Anita asked, eyeing me through the mirror. "You went all pail." She pinched my cheeks to bring out some color. "Is that a scar?" Anita pointed at my elbow, exposed in the spaghetti strap dress.

I twisted my arm toward the mirror, looking at how I'd scared myself with changes.

"Never mind that," Anita said, putting my hand down. "Stephen's not going to know what hit him when he dances with you." Anita was a better person than me. How impossible that I once thought it was the other way around.

But I couldn't stop. A thousand friends weren't worth my daughter.

I danced with Drew. Not at first, but somewhere after taking group pictures and drinking punch, he had his arms around my hips.

"I can't believe it's over," he said. "All this talk about finishing up school, going to college, now it's here."

"You okay?" I asked.

"Yeah."

But he wasn't okay. I took his arm, leading him across the red carpet made of construction paper, to our table. It was still wrong. Too much sound, a strobe light flashing. I grabbed Stephen's hoodie, tossing it on over my dress, taking Drew out of the building.

"Where are we going?" Drew asked.

"Music department," I said, taking us past the bust of ol' Franz.

The main building was locked, but we sat down in the vestibule, just the two of us, our backs to the same brick wall, knees touching.

"Thanks for getting me out of there," he said. "I didn't know I needed it, but man, I feel better now. So much is happening so fast. My mom was already talking about how she's going to turn my bedroom into an office. And I'm sure Anita told you, about, well—"

"You broke up. She told me."

Drew put his head in his hands. "Of course, she did. I don't know what's wrong with me. I just can't see us together past high school. I should've told her after prom, but I didn't want to lead her on. Keep things honest, yeah know? But she's mad at me. I feel like I just blinked, and now I'm here, and my whole life is over."

I wanted to hold him and tell him no—we had so much time left.

"I'm making everybody mad. I told my dad I don't want to go to college. I hate football. The only thing that's mine is music. I'm thinking about taking a year off—just figure myself out."

I'd heard it all before. I considered telling him about the factory job he'd get stuck in, but I didn't need to. Drew didn't have the backbone to turn down the scholarship. I was the idiot that pushed him to stay. So, I just nodded at his venting, eyes on my shoes.

"I wish I could do something in music," Drew said. "I'm not nearly as good as you are, so it's not like I have a shot, but I don't care how good I am. I just want to chase that feeling. You know what I'm saying?"

"Your dad makes all your choices, but now you're going to do things on your own, and you don't even know what you want."

"Exactly!" Drew said, slapping his palm and fist together. "You get me, Loralay. You always have."

"Because I love you." I was shaking, not sure if I should have said it out loud.

Drew froze. "Did you just . . . " He cleared his throat. "I don't think I heard you right."

"I love you," I said, louder now, but my hands were still shaking.

"I don't . . . " Drew cocked his head, smiling, unsure.

"I couldn't say anything because you were with Anita. I've liked you since we first met." *A lifetime ago.* "And now that you're not . . . well, now that that's over, I needed to tell you. Just like you said, keeping things honest."

Drew pulled at his shirt collar, tugging it away from his reddening neck.

No.

"That's really nice of you, Loralay," He said. "but . . . "

No. "Drew. We'd be good together. You need time after Anita, but I'm just telling you I'm here."

"I've always thought of you as a sister. Or, more like, I don't know, a mom."

"A what?"

"Yeah. I mean, you're always one step ahead, organizing things. It's nice. You make me a better person. Like when we practice music together, and Anita starts talking, you're the one that pushes us back on track. Or when we worked together at the old folks' home? You always know what to do, and I'm just bumbling along. Spilling polish on your nice shirt. You're worried about Sal all the time, taking care of her like she was your kid or something. It's sweet, I just. I can't see me . . . us . . . it doesn't seem right."

"But we're so much more than that, Drew! We make music together."

"Yeah?" Drew frowned. "It sounds weird when you say it like that."

"No, it doesn't. We're perfect. We ride in the back of the bus. You, me, and Julius, like a team. I slip honey in your coffee because you always drink it black. We ride our bikes to the concrete pad to get away from everyone."

"You don't even have a bike."

I didn't, did I? It was all running together in my mind.

"But we talk about your dad! Dry drunk, remember?"

"Yeah, you help me with stuff. Like a mom?" He was getting up. I put my hand out, wanting him to stay, but he was out of reach. "Listen, this got weird. It's probably my fault. I've been messed up lately. Can we just forget about it?"

"But—"

"I'm gonna head back in. I'll see you in there, okay?"

Drew left. I couldn't understand. We were unraveling like that blanket Death made, leaving me snatching at strings that were missing. I left the vestibule, staring into the eyes of Franz Schubert. "I'm going to have Makenzie," I told him. "Death promised." Drew was part of that package deal. No, he was the deal. Sure, he was young now, but my Drew grew up into a man who was sweet and steady, a rock.

I wandered back into the dance. The speakers were too loud, and the bass line was distorted in the blaring. Drew was talking with Stephen. They both looked at me, then looked away too fast.

But we were supposed to be in love. We'd get married next year, running away together. Our story didn't end like . . . *our story.*

I put a hand to my mouth. Seeing it for the first time.

320

I was just like Sal. Making up stories in my head about the handsome boy with pink lips and olive skin. I was the person trying to keep Drew to myself. My Drew, my obsession.

I'd ruined us.

The music stopped. I didn't really notice, just accepting it because my head was blasting just as loud as that distorted bass. I wanted to run, but the person I wanted to run to didn't exist anymore, lost in the Nevermore since Death wore his face.

Teachers scurried to shut the gym doors. Someone ran up on the stage, the microphone screeching as they turned it on.

It was the principal. "Hello? Is this on?" *Tap, tap, tap,* more screeching. "Okay, hey. We need everyone to stay calm."

Cell phones lit up, ringtones playing in pockets and purses. People answered their phones with a finger in their ear so they could hear.

"What's going on?" someone in the crowd shouted.

"Mom?" said someone else. "I can't hear what you're saying. The reception sucks."

"What do you mean, where am I? It's prom, remember?"

"We're on lockdown," the principal said. "There's been a—" He put his hand over the mic as Mrs. Corrin came up to whisper something in his ear. He nodded, speaking into the microphone again. "There's been an incident. The police requested that we . . . " Some teens tried to push past the chaperones. "No one's allowed to leave. I repeat—"

Douglas Milenhill, Sal's lunchtime bully, walked up to Drew, a cell phone in hand.

"Hey, Drew, don't you live next to that old guy with the strawberries? The police are looking for him."

Someone screamed on the other side of the gym, a tussle over the door.

"You mean Sal?" a voice next to me asked in whispered gossip.

"The police are on the lookout for a man—" The principal said, but all of it was so hard to hear with the blaring in my head. " . . . request we stay indoors. No one may leave until . . . "

Mrs. Corrin wasn't back at her post yet, one exit unattended.

I ran.

"Loralay!" Stephen called as I ripped off my heels, tossing them behind me. I made it to the parking lot, dress riding up my thighs as I tore down the road.

Come on, I told my legs. *Faster.* I had to get to Sal.

In the Nevermore, Drew complained that our houses were so close to school. Now it was my only hope, lungs burning, a stitch in my side. It was dark, but I knew the roads. All of Oak Ridge was home—my thumbprint on a map.

She'd be okay if I got to her. Sal didn't die until summer. It wasn't time yet. She'd be okay. But if I believed that, why was I running?

Sal was in front of me. I'd only made it halfway, but she was standing in the road.

Relief rushed over my body like warm air on frostbitten limbs, so good it hurt.

"I was so worried," I said. "You can't even imagine. It was crazy. Something about your dad and the police. I—" Sal hadn't moved. Her eyes were bottomless. "Sal?"

Coming closer, I saw odd little details, like her hair, messy with dirt, bits of leaves tangled in the back. "Come on. You're scaring me, Sal."

Her face, sunken and expressionless. The tint to her lips, nose, and cheeks—the color was all wrong.

Because the night surrounding us wasn't black, it was orange.

"So stubborn," Death said.

"No!" I shrieked. "Take her off!"

I came at him, an animal. A slap wouldn't be enough. I'd claw her face right off him. I grabbed his shoulder, fist pulled back, ready to punch him just like Jay. Death didn't disappear, waiting as my body heaved with every breath.

But my hand wouldn't do it, because it was her face too.

"Murderer!" the word wrenched at my throat. But I didn't know how to take away this new reality. "Go back, I'll make the deal again!"

Death was still.

I crumpled at his, her feet, knees grinding into the asphalt. "I can't. It's not real. I don't want it to be real!" I pulled him closer. "I called DHS too soon. I worried about Drew when I should've been watching Sal. I pushed too hard! Just let me try again!"

"It doesn't work like that."

"Why? I did it before! You stacked it against me. You made it not work! Sal didn't die until summer! I had time!"

"You weren't sent back to manipulate the world into your ideal."

"Then what for? You told me I could change the variables!"

"You did."

"Not in any way that mattered!" I let go of him to see her face. "I'm so sorry, Sal," I said, even though she wasn't there to hear.

"She was afraid you wouldn't forgive her," Death said. I sucked in air, hard, suffocating at those words. "In her last death, she wondered if she'd failed Drew, now she wondered if she'd failed you. You gifted her a moment of sanity."

"That's not better." I didn't have the strength to scream anymore, words like gravel falling off my tongue. "She shouldn't have died."

"They never should."

"Then stop."

"I will."

I didn't dare breathe.

"You claim mortality, but every soul is eternal. I am the only mortal among us. Man's choice created me, and sin is my mother. You call me Angel, but I am only the entry. When I carry a soul, I look down at their body and see a fate that only I will truly have. Once the death bond is gone, the gloves unravel. I end."

I reached for Sal again, but Death was gone. He'd left me barefoot in the dark. I put my hands to my chest, covering the cavern inside me—the place where I'd unraveled.

I didn't take the main roads home. Step by step, bare feet aching, listening to police cars nearby. I ended up at the old concrete pad, the same place the bus dropped me when I ran away. Strange that I hadn't been back in all those years. It was different now, faded graffiti across the entire slab. Stephen had been here sometime in the past, claiming the spot Drew and I never used this life. A melting clock. It must have been one of his earlier attempts. His tag *Swayer* still had a dorky chain letter *S*. I sat down on the clock's twelve, pulling Stephen's hoodie over my legs, watching the sunrise. It reminded me of the morning my dad never came home. Death was right. One life was enough suffering.

The sky was turning blue when Drew found me.

"Loralay!" He tossed his bike in the ditch, running across the pad. "Shit, I thought you were dead." He sat next to me, breathing hard. He was still in his tuxedo, missing the jacket. Shirt and pants stained. "I've been looking all over for you. Everyone is. I mean, you were there, then gone."

"Not everyone," I said.

"What?" Drew asked, breathing hard, kneeling beside me to refill his lungs.

"Not everyone's looking for me because Sal can't."

Drew pulled me into his chest, smothering me in the smell of Calvin Klein One and sweat. Connected to the rise and fall of his lungs, the movement of alive. I'd thought I couldn't cry anymore, but I shriveled, sobbing into his shirt. Drew didn't pat my arm and say it was all right. We just existed—him in shock, me in sorrow.

"Heath Hennery wasn't even four," I said when I could speak again.

"Yeah," Drew said. "Where is he going to live?"

I pulled away, using Stephen's sleeves to rub my face. "Drew, you don't know. He's dead."

"No, he's not."

I looked up at Drew, sickened by his innocence. "Mr. Small killed them all. Vikki, Irene, Sa—" I couldn't keep naming them.

"Who did you talk to?" Drew asked. I didn't tell him, hiding behind the sweater sleeves again. "Well, they were wrong. I only know because my dad—Shit, this doesn't feel real." Drew sighed, collecting himself. "I don't know everything. Just that Irene had a cell phone. She called nine one one. I guess Mr. Small ran when she did? Dad said he was watching TV when she banged on the window. He got there, and Vikki Small was dead, but Sal, she . . . " Drew was hollow. "He held her."

She didn't die alone.

"Shit Loralay, I gotta get you home," Drew said. "Your mom's freaking out. They didn't find Mr. Small for like five hours. Anita was telling everyone about how he kicked you, all of it. Got people thinking he might have been out for you. She and Stephen are driving around to find you. I was riding for half an hour before I remembered you were talking about a concrete pad before you ran, so I thought you might be here."

They'd caught Mr. Small. He hadn't killed himself. I didn't know how I felt about that. Maybe glad he'd face trial? But that emotion was so far from me I couldn't be sure.

"Everyone's crazy right now," Drew said. "You shouldn't have run like that."

"I know."

"You did know. All of it. You and Anita calling the cops. I was so stupid, just sitting there. I mean, what if I'd believed you? We could've done something. I still don't believe it now. This kind of stuff doesn't happen. This is someone else's life."

"Don't think what if," I said. "It's an ugly question."

Drew helped me up, leading me away from Stephen's clock, arm around my shoulder in a sideways hug.

What a stupid world, Drew holding me when I didn't care anymore.

Chapter Thirty-Two

MOTHER

Yellow tape enclosed the Smalls' house, but it didn't stop the foil balloons and bouquets from being brought to the front porch.

It was evening, and the road was full of people. They weren't all ours—news crews, city gawkers, the society of mourners ready with cards and teddy bears. Fewer came this time, only two murders to spectate. But they still came, grieving at the door of strangers. Not that anyone was left to take them, Irene and Heath

Hennery already living new lives far away. Only one reporter came, no pictures of Drew fuelling a documentary.

And then there were the people I did know—kids from school, adults from town. Mrs. Corrin handing out stick candles with drip protectors, Douglas crying as he talked to the single reporter, a circle of teens kicking a footbag waiting for the service to start.

And I came, through the forest path, carrying Stephen's sweater and an old cigar box that rattled my goodbye.

I didn't deserve to be here. The guilt of Sal's blood was on my hands. Every sleepless night came with a new list of ideas, words, ways to save her. My brain tried to fix it again.

"It's over," I said, but I didn't believe it, so I'd say it again and again.

The Neers' yard looked awful. Trampled plants, a chicken wire fence thrown up to keep their personal space, a tasteless divide that made them stick out. I'd wondered before, but now I was certain Mr. Neer had dirty hands, overlooking signs something was wrong. He wasn't even outside, harbored behind a metal moat, hidden in his glasshouse.

Drew was in the grass, hands in his pockets, talking with Stephen. They were looking at the Smalls' house, now a place that haunted everyone and not just me. Being here again reminded me why Drew and I got married young. When the world falls apart, sometimes all you want is to make a quiet bit of happiness to hide in.

I stepped over the chicken wire, holding out Stephen's sweater. Instead of taking it, Stephen hugged me, the cigar box trapped between us. I felt Drew's hand on my shoulder, a sentinel of protection.

"Light your candles, please," Mrs. Corrin said over a megaphone she'd taken from the cheer squad. "Buckets of water are at the barricade for extinguishing." I didn't want a candle, I'd already burned myself out, but Anita came with one for me anyway, lighting mine with hers.

There were speeches, but I didn't pay attention, noticing those who didn't show. Not just Mr. Neer, but the school counsellor who admitted she hadn't read the journals. Sal's handwriting had been too small to bother. Or the nameless officer who had been there every time before. I wondered how they would move on, how they would heal. Because I didn't know how I would.

When it was over, Anita took Stephen home. The people cleared away, too late to stay and clean up.

I tossed my candle in the bucket with the others, putting out the light. I still had my box, unsure when I was ready to put it down and make things final.

Drew was in his garage. He turned on the headlights to his dad's car—the light reflecting off the cellophane of abandoned flowers.

"Better?" Drew asked, walking toward me. "The light, I mean," he said.

I nodded even though it wasn't. I wanted the dark.

"Glad you stayed," Drew said. "It's creepy here alone." There were still a few stragglers, but I knew what he meant.

"Isn't your dad here?" I asked. "I thought he was inside."

Drew shook his head. "Stayed at the hotel. I'm just grabbing a few more things before I go. I'm not staying for the graduation ceremony."

Drew at college. That was right. We'd go together this time, He wouldn't miss scholarships, and I'd follow him there, the only thing right this time around.

"You leaving tonight?" I asked. "Driving in the dark?"

"Yeah," Drew said. "Dad wanted me to go yesterday."

We walked toward the Neers' garage, headlights beckoning like a guidepost. "He was all gung ho about leaving the hotel so we could pack. We were here all morning. He didn't want to see the service, though. It'll feel good driving up there on my own. I need some time to clear my head."

"Wait," I said. "You're taking his car without him? How's he getting it back?"

"He gave it to me," Drew said. "Graduation present. It's a relief. Thought I'd have to bike everywhere."

We were in the garage. Mr. Neer's car was packed full. Mr. Neer's guitar case was tethered to the top.

The world didn't turn orange, but time stopped all the same.

That guitar on our doorstep, the three missed phone calls before the end. It wasn't due for years, but time wasn't in order anymore.

"He's been generous to a lot of people lately," Drew was saying. "Gave some sports memorabilia to some of the guys at school, donated stuff. This whole thing set something off in him."

"Like it set him off drinking?"

Drew fiddled with the side mirror instead of looking at me. "You can't blame him. He saw some serious stuff."

"I'm not blaming him. He's blaming himself."

Drew didn't get it. He was too young. I'd done it again, imagined a world where this boy was mine. I'd decided Drew should go to college with me, keeping him for myself when other people needed him. I was watching the last thing I wanted to shatter.

Drew tugged at the tether, checking it was on tight. I put my hand on his.

"That's a common sign of suicide."

He frowned like I'd just rattled of a random fact.

"That's not . . . why would you . . . "

"Mood swings? Is he talking about death?"

"Yeah, we're all talking about death. Look, I know things are hard right now, but he wouldn't do that. You need to back off. You're freaking me out."

He didn't believe it, but he couldn't question me, not after Sal.

"How's he going to get to work without a car? Did he get a new one? Did he tell your mom he was giving it to you? What's your dad's biggest fear? He's been telling you every time he gives you that awful football speech. A low bid, a lowball, and a low-down loss? You think just maybe ignoring Sal's abuse ticked some of those boxes?" I was raising my voice. "People with histories of substance abuse are more likely to end their lives! You don't take risks with this stuff. You get help. Grow up!"

I threw my goodbye box on the ground. It broke open, the butterfly pog and cassette tape falling out, surrounded by a hundred origami stars, the final wish I'd given up.

"Okay," Drew said, a scared kid listening to his mother.

Dad and Rosie never called, not to buy the store or to see how I was. Drew did. He told me I was right. My reward was a million thanks and a single goodbye. They were moving. Somewhere next to a rehab facility and a music school. I didn't catch the name. That was another chain to the string of Oak Ridge's empty houses. Smalls' house and store, Drew's parents' house, and then Grandma's house, all abandoned.

Mom moved in with Mrs. Esmer. I stayed with them for a little while, watching one good change that should've always been. Mom was healing. Not because of me but because she was a kid again, her own second life, soaking up the love of a surrogate mother. Something I never could've been. Mom emptied the bank account, handed me a check, made me promise I'd do more than she'd done for us. She crocheted me a blanket before I left. It wasn't orange, but it might as well have been.

I went to college with Stephen, Anita planning to follow us next year. Stephen perused art, I did general studies, not sure who I wanted to be. I only knew I'd finished with piano.

My life didn't have music anymore.

Chapter Thirty-Three

MAKENZIE'S BIRTHDAY

I leaned over Stephen's car, an old Pontiac he'd covered in graffiti, pulling my curls over my shoulder.

"Take me with you. Anywhere," I said. "Please. I don't care if it's legal. I just need to get out of here."

"Calm it, spaz. I gotta job." His slang had calmed down since college started. It made me happy when he fell into it again.

"Anywhere," I said.

"You okay?"

"No."

He nodded, and I got in, knocking his backpack out of the way. It was the end of summer, our second year about to start. Anita was supposed to be down soon. She'd come up a few times, and we'd gotten an apartment together, but the move wasn't fast enough, not with my last important Nevermore anniversary about to pass.

"Whoa, whoa, whoa," Stephen said, pulling the bag up. "Careful, I've got tools in there."

"What, spray paint?" I asked.

He let his head hit the back of the seat. "You got so much to learn. Open it."

I unzipped the bag, not sure what I was looking at.

"I got markers, mops, daubers. There's more in the trunk. The dude paying me only gave me like twenty-five bucks, so I'm doing scrap cans."

"They pay you?" I'd never kept up to date on his tagging, just knew it was a thing he did.

"I *said* I was working. I got some places that hire me. They get toys messin' up the place. I make it good. People respect the art. You throw something up that shows you got talent, they leave it alone. Not always, but enough that some people pay me."

We pulled up to a baseball field with a concrete concession stand. Even though it'd been whitewashed, old tags still showed through.

Stephen got out of the car with a sketchbook, pencil swaying as he drew up some ideas.

334

"Homeslice," he called. "Bring me the bag." I did, trying to not count the minutes passing by. His phone beeped, but he was still sketching. I pulled it out of the side pocket.

I sighed. "Anita says she's not coming tonight."

"Why?" Stephen asked.

"Her mom wants her to go through her cooking collection to see if there's anything she wants to take."

"You already got stuff," Stephen said, scowling at his drawing. He erased a line. I tried to look at what he had, but he wouldn't let me, holding up the book.

"I know that, she knows that, but Mrs. Corrin wants to unload more junk. I'm surprised she didn't add her butterfly collection."

"Butterflies? I like that," Stephen said, still drawing. "What else you got? Name some stuff. Random, whatever's on your mind. Free associate some shiznit."

"Cigarettes, yarn, guitars, cassette tapes."

Stephen stopped drawing to lift an eyebrow at me. "When I said random, you took me serious. Psychiatrist shrink thyself. What you got going on in that head?"

I nodded, looking away. I hadn't mentioned the one thing running in my head. A time, 11:23 a.m., the moment Makenzie was born.

"I got it. I was gonna do a throw up with a squid, but I guess I'm gonna do a crazy piece then," Stephen said. "Tell me when you figure it out."

He pulled milk crates full of spray paint cans out of the trunk. I'd always seen the aftereffect of his work, never the creation. There was something peaceful about it, the performance of art.

After rolling down the windows so he could blast music from the car, he spent his time changing caps on the cans, and then he started.

I sat on the hood of his car, watching it take shape. I knew it was a girl. Skin tone, red lips, wide-open eyes, but there was something strange about her hair. He kept changing cans, adding layers, blowing on the wall before it could drip. I didn't realize it was me until he added the gap between my teeth.

"What yeah think?" The wall was full of curls, strange things tangled in my hair. A cassette tape with butterflies crawling on the side, yarn ball coiled next to a pack of cigarettes. A guitar headstock near my forehead. Everything I mentioned was around me, and one thing I didn't. There was a skull on my shoulder.

I swallowed.

"You made me pretty," I said, trying not to mention the skull. "It looks old-fashioned."

"I was goin' for Alphonse Mucha, but it got too Gibson Girl, so I just let it be its own thing," he said, standing back to survey at his work. "Wadda we call it? All the things in Loralay Grayson's head?"

"Nevermore," I said.

Stephen scratched his stomach, frowning.

"Sure, wig out. You gonna try your first tag?" Stephen helped me down, pulling his backpack out. "Here, try the mop on some paper. You don't care about those clothes, right?"

I tried writing words with the oversized pen, ink leaking everywhere, black on the paper and my palm.

"There you go. Squeeze it," Stephen said. "Those drips got me into tagging, looks sick, lines everywhere." He took my hand, helping it along. There was paint on his fingers, sticky between our skin. I could feel his chest pressing into my shoulder.

And I wondered a strange thing, a thought I'd never had. He wasn't Drew, he never could be, but what if Makenzie had eyes like Stephen's, her hair black instead of brown? I missed her so much that I bit my lip, leaning into that possibility, and finally, into Stephen.

When he turned to smile at me, I kissed the boy whose lips were mauve instead of pink.

"Aw, man," Stephen said, backing up. "My girlfriend's not so tight on me making out with other chicks."

I jumped back, paint spilling on my pants.

"Damn, girl, my bad, I didn't mean to make it look like a date. I just got moves too smooth even for me." He was laughing.

I couldn't join him, my shoulders up to my ears. "You have a girlfriend? Since when?" I could feel the heat, bringing in my ears and cheeks but mostly on my lips.

"Since Anita messed with my Myspace. She played around on it way back, found a cute emo chick. After that, we chatted, met up. It just kept getting more fly from there."

I rubbed the ink on my pants as if I could rub the kiss away. "Why didn't you tell me!"

"I'm tellin' you now, chill."

"But I wouldn't have done that if I knew! You can't bring me out here, paint a picture of my freaking face and then get all cozy and not expect me to think something's up!"

"No, you're right. I just didn't . . . " He shrugged. "I was using you as a model because you was here, but that was dumb. I mean, I had it hard for you back in the day, but it never happened, so I guess I figured it wasn't a thing. Clean your hair up, girl, you got too many things in there." I was up, pacing the concrete, eyes avoiding the painting that started it all. Stephen stood, dusting himself off. "You're not mad at me," he said. "You're mad at that." He pointed at the concessions stand.

"Yeah. Because you made me think you liked me."

"No, that!" He pointed at the skull. "You never been right, not after Sal. You think I don't know? You ain't kissin' me, you're escaping." And I was, but not from Sal. It was someone else that died in the Nevermore, my Makenzie. "I'm taking you home," Stephen said, packing up.

Home, the opposite of homeless—I once thought that was what I needed, but what's a house without family? Was this what my mother had done? Somehow driving a van, picking me up from school, and making a bed seemed like huge accomplishments. I'd become her—both of us hurting over men that never loved us, both of us pushing away our daughters with our choices.

That night I rolled over in my bed, holding my pillow close, reliving the strange feeling of kissing Stephen, a thing that didn't belong. I watched as 11:23 became 11:24.

Makenzie should have existed. I knew that. Things happened at different times, but I could feel her missing from the world.

"Okay, Death," I said. "You lied. Try fixing that one."

I sat up. My room was gone. What once was my apartment became white tile floors and a check-in desk. I was on a hospital bed, stranded in a hall—a hospital stained orange.

"Not here. I don't want to go back," I told Death, but he didn't appear. The hall beyond looked the wrong kind of peaceful, like a loved one in the casket, when everyone says they could be sleeping.

I knew where I was intended to go, wordless whispers calling me. A place where the light grew brighter, a place that knew my name.

"Fine," I said. I kicked my feet off the edge, letting them fall, *plip*, *plop*, then all of me. "It's over then? Another worthless try?" The orange flashed and broke away. I was further down the hall, bed behind me.

"Can't you just leave me alone? I don't . . . "

Orange.

I was in a small rectangular room with rolling carts, something wrapped in bleached white blankets, edged in pink and blue. Babies. There were four—two sleeping, one stretching, another frozen in a yawn. I ached to smell the amniotic fluid on their heads, to press petal-soft skin to my lips, but none of these babies were mine.

But—the third baby, the red-faced one with tiny wisps of downy hair. It wasn't just the pink name card taped to the rolling cart. It was the birthmark on her wrist. The same one I'd asked every doctor about, worried it meant something was wrong with my child. They smiled at me and said it was just discoloration. Called it an angel's kiss.

I reached for my Makenzie, but before I could lift her, the Angel of Death put his gloves down on top of her tiny, blanketed chest.

"No! She's mine!" I said.

Death tapped a red fingernail to the name above Makenzie's, the name that should've been mine, but a different mother was there, printed out hastily in ballpoint pen. Death's hands morphed again, a ginger-haired young man, stroking the head of my child.

"You should be happy. You thought she wouldn't exist. People's lives are more important than that. They're knit together before they're even born."

I tried to edge my fingernails under the gloves to lift them off, careful for the sake of Makenzie's paper-soft skin, but time was too heavy to lift. Only Death could take it.

He put a hand over mine. "Makenzie isn't yours, but she's here."

"She's not here! She's in that stupid plastic crib! Here is in my arms. Here is with me!"

"It wouldn't be right."

"Why not?"

"Because you're not the mother she needs anymore."

I stopped struggling to pick her up. "I don't want this."

"I know," Death nodded, an elderly man with a balding halo. "It's not right. It was never meant to be right. But people aren't blank slates. She needs a mother like you were, not like you are. So, I'm here to hold your hand."

"Am I dying now?"

"No," he said. "But grief isn't picky."

I kissed her, over and over, whispering promises like secrets, holding her fingers. They weren't cold this time.

"Another gift is coming," Death said. He smiled a sad, lonely smile that filled the room with orange. I was back in the dark, sitting up in bed, arms still out to hold my girl.

Alone.

Chapter Thirty-Four

ORANGE

I looked at the alarm by my bed, blinking light and blaring sound. It'd been going for over an hour, but I didn't move to stop it, remembering the night last year when my daughter was born.

"I hate you," Anita said, voice morning gravel as she stormed over to slap a hand on the snooze.

"Me too," I said.

"Not you, Loralay. I was talking to your clock. It went off when I was having a good dream."

"In subtitles?" I asked, not caring if I made sense.

"Wait, did you just say you hated yourself? Like, not funny, m'kay?"

I rolled over, not willing to talk. Anita took it as an invitation to poke at my arm. "When was the last time you took a bath?"

"Last week," I lied. It'd probably been two.

"A week? Ew!" Anita was pushing me out of bed.

"It's different for curly hair," I said.

"Fine, don't wash your hair, wash you!" She brought me to the side of the tub, prepping my toothbrush with paste.

"You're too good to me," I told her, a truth to replace the lie.

"You were coughing again." She handed the brush over. "You've had that cough for years and it's *not* because you had some *flue* in high school so don't even start with me. This stuff is serious."

"I'll take a shower," I promised, placating her inner med student. It didn't work.

"I'm setting you up with an appointment."

"And I'll be sure to avoid it," I joked, but she wasn't listening. She was already talking about some guy on campus calling her.

"What?" I asked, mouth full of paste.

"Jeez, Loralay, your mom? I said she called me six times this morning."

I spat. "I thought you were talking about a guy."

Mom never called me. I called her. I took Anita's phone, looking at the number. Six missed calls. It made me think of Mr. Neer.

I splashed water on my face and hit call.

"Loralay!" Mom said, sounding chipper. She'd been acting that way ever since Mrs. Esmer had her selling her crochet at bazaars. Mom making money all her own. "I've been trying to get ahold of you."

"Mrs. Esmer's okay?" I asked. "I thought that's why you were calling." I pulled on the same pants I wore yesterday—the ones stained by Stephen's ink. That happened months ago, but stains were like memories.

"She's fine. But hon, your dad's not. He's in jail. Called asking one of us to post bail."

I stopped pulling, one leg still naked.

"Hello?"

"What did you tell him?" I knocked over Anita's shampoo as I pulled the other leg on.

Mom laughed. "I told him no."

I smiled, maybe the first time in weeks.

"But it wouldn't be right if I didn't tell you, so I thought I'd call."

"Anita!" I yelled, hopping out of the bathroom with my shoes half on. Anita was at the kitchen counter, eating a Pop-Tart. "I gotta go," I said, tossing her phone in her purse. "Can I borrow your car?"

It took me three hours driving, a metal detector pass, a pat down from a female guard, not to mention a day of skipped classes, but I found myself in a concrete room with folding tables and a few guards watching over visitations.

"Lady-girl!" Dad said, sitting down at the table with me. His tan shirt and sweats made me think of my old teacher Mrs. Banks. I was pretty sure crackheads wore clothes like these more often than rainbow toe socks. Dad still tried, his perfect smile in place, though his cheeks were hollow.

"Hi," I said, still not sure why I came. I just knew I needed to be here, deep down in my bones.

"It's been such a time since I saw you. Grown up, haven't yeah? You wouldn't believe. Rosie, oh, bad thing I did there. Let me tell you, woman left me high in dry. Never should've left."

"What'd you do?"

"You wouldn't want to go over that. Legal stuff, over your pretty head." Dad smiled wider like he was trying again after the first one hadn't worked right.

"What did you do?" I asked again.

"That's what this is about? Worried your old man's a criminal?"

"I can go," I said, starting to get up.

"No." Dad slapped his hand on the table, hard enough that the guard hovered behind him. "Uh, no," he repeated softly, chewing on his thumbnail. He leaned in, one hand up to his mouth, a faux secret. "Insurance fraud."

I blinked at him.

He leaned back, trying to gauge my response. "It'll never stand up in court. All of this over a fender bender." *Key-key-key.* "Lady cut in front of me too fast. It's a bad deal. It's not really me. It's just that she'd got a wheelchair and everything. Got a doctor in her pocket. Money does everything in this life, Lady-girl."

"The old truck. It was you," I said, then nothing else, because there was nothing more to say.

"Don't make your old man feel bad. Did you bring bail money?"

344

"No," I said, smiling back at him. "I don't have that kind of money. I'm on my second year in college."

Dad was rubbing his hands. "Well, that's okay. You can get a bondsman."

"No. I'd never do that."

"Is this because of your friend's store? Rosie was the one who—"

"No. It's not about the store, or Grandma's house, or your affair, or the time you put soap in my mouth. It's because I'm not your parent."

Dad's mouth twitched.

"I'm going now. But thank you. I needed this more than you can imagine."

And I left.

I drove to the closest coffee shop and ordered the sweetest coffee they had, enjoying every last sip. I wondered if that was Death's last gift. Because I felt something new.

Ever since my mom called I'd had a wonderful feeling, knowing that I didn't know what was coming next. I'd ruined so much, and yet there was still a tomorrow ready for me to be in, a world of possibilities.

And that was when Drew walked into the coffee shop. "Loralay?"

I stood, looking at a different man than I'd known. It wasn't easy to pinpoint the change. The way he held himself? The confidence in his gestures? Drew, but not Drew. He hugged me, an old friend, something we used to be.

"What are you doing here?" I asked like I belonged.

"I play here. Guitar. It's not much, but it's a paying gig. Guess I'm a professional dreamer now. This is amazing, bumping into you like this. Fate, huh? I've never seen you in town before. Are you transferring?"

And then I realized what was different.

Drew was an adult.

Someone my own age.

Chapter Thirty-Five

DIS

I hug Drew's arm, looking at the little bungalow. It's small, old military developments, a street of houses like a matched set. It's nothing like Grandmother's house, but that place is gone, owned by a retired doctor who I sometimes see when I drive by, raking leaves in a pile for his grandchildren.

"I think I felt DIS on the way up here," Drew says.

"Did you pick up some slang from Stephen?" I ask, frowning at my husband.

"You don't remember? Subtitle dreaming? That feeling when we were on the way home. I wrote a song about it. DIS, it's an acronym. Anyway, this might be the one."

I smile at him, at his reference, but I didn't feel anything like it on the way here. The drive up felt new. Curves I didn't expect, possibilities in unexpected potholes. I love everything about it, the not knowing. Nothing in my life is past tense anymore.

"So, what do you do?" the relator asks, making small talk as she unlocks the front door.

"I'm a musician," Drew says. "And Loralay's a counselor."

"Music?" the woman asks, excitedly tucking her hair behind her ears. "Would I have heard you before?"

Drew shakes his head. "No, not really. Mostly I work in commercials, soundtracks, things like that."

The relator fakes interest, and I smile, squeezing Drew's arm as I think of how many times I used to say the same thing.

We walk inside—empty rooms like bone without marrow.

"Two bedrooms. And a spare room that's just the right size for a nursery," the woman adds with a wink.

"Oh, we don't have kids," Drew says. I turn away, pretending to examine the fireplace.

"You never know," the realtor sings.

"Loralay can't have kids," Drew says. "Complications after chemo."

"Oh," she says, and I can feel her eyes rest on my back, heavy with pity. "I can't imagine."

I force a smile, readjusting my wig before I turn around. "Let's see the kitchen."

It's dated, with orange Formica counters. I put my palms on them, leaning to look out the window over the sink. I can see the fenceless yard shared with neighbors—a child playing outside. She's holding a stick like a sword and tapping on the dryer vent as a lazy Labrador rolls his eyes to watch her.

And just like that, I know what Death's last gift was.

"It needs redoing," The real estate agent says, trying to draw my attention back. Drew starts talking about the cupboards, and I excuse myself to look around the yard.

The girl I'd been watching out my window had crossed further into our yard, stick still in hand, poking at something under our Rhododendron bush.

"Are your parents home?" I ask. "We're your new neighbors." She nods, then goes back to her poking. "What do you have there?" I ask, inching close, trying not to cry.

"It's a robin," she tells me, pointing at a stiff sparrow under the brush. "He's not moving." I look at the little creature, eyes already sunken in. "Can you keep robins? He could live at my house."

"I'm sorry, sweetie. He died." She seems unsure. Death still too new a concept. "Our bodies are like houses, and death is when we move out of the old house, leaving it behind."

She nods sagely, pointing to the old lab that still hasn't gotten up. "That's what Mom says'll happen to Shipper." The old dog wags a tired tail.

And then she leaves, back to her driveway, stepping carefully over nubs of chalk and monochrome rainbows.

Drew comes out, rubbing my shoulder. "It's going to need work," he says. "There's no telling what we'll find when we

349

remodel. We could keep looking. Wait for something with a clearer plan, so we know what we're getting into."

"No. This one," I told Drew. "This is a good house."

Drew follows my eyes, watching the girl throw her stick for the unimpressed Shipper.

"Cute kid," Drew says.

"The neighbor girl," I say. "Her name's Makenzie."

Acknowledgments

I was a terrible reader as a kid, but I adored books. To me, authors were untouchable masters of words. The idea of being in their ranks seemed impossible but worth every hopeless attempt.

YOU are making that happen for me. If you read this book-loved it, or hated it-I want to thank you. A little girl who dreamed of this moment is here because of you— the reader. I am honored you let me tell you a story.

This little girl grew up to be many things, but an island isn't one of them. That's why I am bubbling over the brim to thank Mollie, my editor, for being able to squint at my manuscript and see what it could be. Her work was phenomenal and I take credit for any leftover errors sprinkled throughout. (Like ending that last sentence with a preposition.) There is an outstanding possibility I was cursed by a grammar fairy as a wee child to forever typo, word murder, and poor-spell my way through life.

Before this book is was in Mollie's hands, I was blessed with beta readers, who put up with my (cursed) spelling, painfully inadequate football knowledge, and took the time to tell me what did and didn't work. Each of you—I can't thank you enough for seeing me through.

And before that came my family. My kids, Alex, Tidus, Demitri, Zoey, and Noel. My favorite thing in this life is being your

Mama. Thank you for putting up with me writing—each of you is already a gift—letting me have this dream come true is another bundle on top of the stack. And here's your spot, Mr. Incredible. I married my best friend, and I ended up with a cheerleader, cabana boy, alpha reader and assistant. You need to pick up some bad habits soon because your awesomeness is annoying.

Also, to the friends who gave me time to write— I'm talking to you Stacey Mathews and Carrie Nehring— Time is a gift, and us mamas know its value. Thank you!

I'm missing people. Some because they have already held Death's hand—their names etched on my heart, others who encouraged me early on even though we've lost touch over the years. My lack of acknowledgment here doesn't lessen the impact you all have been. So thank you.

About the Author

Winter Krane is your average underachiever. She writes books, paints, crochets, DIY's everything she can get her hands on, and in her free time she raises her five kids with her husband. She also lives with the mathematics disability, dyscalculia. Which means she has L and R tattooed on her hands so she can remember her right from her left, smiles and nods when people try to talk numbers to her, and constantly counts on her fingers when adding anything above six. She lives on the Oregon coast, and no, she doesn't mind the rain.